JUSTICE
ON
HOLD

To: Monica,

7/26/14

JUSTICE
ON
HOLD

DONALD REICHARDT
JOYCE OSCAR

Best Wishes,

Donald Reichardt

Joyce Oscar

UNLIMITED PUBLISHING LLC

First Edition

ISBN-13:
978-1-58832-221-0

This fine book and many others are available at:
http://www.unlimitedpublishing.com

PROLOGUE: It's Simply Murder

BONNIE VINCENT forced her eyes open and looked into the bathroom mirror, waiting for the fog from the shower to clear. After another restless, anguished night, she was virtually sleepwalking through her preparation for another day. She stood motionless and fixed a pained stare at the glass, seeming to anticipate something detestable when it unclouded.

As her image crept into view, she drew back and winced at how much she had changed from the woman who attracted admiring glances from men in a crowded room. She emitted a resigned sigh and then turned her eyes upward toward the skylight, searching for a clue about the weather as the morning light sifted through and glowed.

"I hate February in Dallas," she said to her reflection. "It's such a guessing game. You never know what to wear."

"Guessing game" was an apt description for North Texas winter. Sometimes, shards of icy air invade overnight and hang there stubbornly, sending unwary residents scurrying for an overcoat stuffed in a guest closet or scrambling for an ice scraper squirreled away in a tool box. At other times, a frosty chill whips through in the earliest hours but just as quickly recedes, yielding to a cool, blue day that permits shirtsleeves by ten and a comfortable tee-off by noon.

In either case, late Texas winter is consistently unsettled, much like Bonnie's volatile, unpredictable marriage to Udo Holthaus.

She returned her attention to the haggard image in the mirror. The redness of her eyes and furrow in her brow signaled the toll that her stormy union with Udo had taken since their move here.

"You have to get ready," she whispered a desperate pep

talk. "They need you at the office for staff meeting."

Bonnie's morning routine rarely varied. She had perfected it quickly after she and Udo had come to Dallas and she had grasped the importance of pattern to her sanity, and of getting out of the house quickly each day.

As a reporter in Austin, her daily activities had been dictated by the speed bumps and gales that define news reporting. Now, she was adjusting to the slower, more predictable corporate world.

She had eagerly embraced the change. Months earlier, the Pearson Accounting Company had offered her an attractive position as public relations director. Her drive to succeed propelled her enthusiastic reaction.

Her husband didn't share her joy.

"It's not a good fit," Udo had protested adamantly when she told him of the offer at dinner. "You've just started improving your journalism skills. Now you want to go off and become a God damned corporate PR hack in a city you don't even know?"

"It's a wonderful opportunity," Bonnie argued, ignoring his profanity. "I would be working for a prestigious company, and the salary is fantastic. Udo, they want me."

"Tell them no."

"I can't let you make my career decisions for the rest of my life," Bonnie asserted stubbornly and then assumed a more caustic tone. "I know you're an important news director and I'm just a newspaper reporter, but it's about time that I made career decisions for myself." She paused nervously, but there was no stopping the words from tumbling out. "You can follow me or not—it's your choice."

Udo narrowed his eyes at the threat.

She softened, appealing. "I love you, Udo. And admire you. You mentored me in the business when I was naïve and unsure. But I can't be satisfied any longer with riding shotgun."

"Tomorrow, call them back and turn it down."

A gaping silence fell between them. Bonnie's response

was to pour a second glass of wine and shake her head hopelessly.

Bonnie accepted the job the next day and was waiting in the kitchen for Udo when he arrived home from work.

"I took the Dallas job," she said curtly.

He grunted, unspeaking, and disappeared into the den.

Bonnie had stood up to him, and they went to Dallas.

She thrived in her new environment, where she had a staff of writers and fellow department heads she quickly grew to respect. She was making excellent money and dressed the part, upgrading her wardrobe to designer outfits. She moved in circles of people who mattered—not movers and shakers, for only the natives of the propitious sperm club inhabited the innermost circle of society in Big D. But entrenched with a group of young go-getters in business, she sat on non-profit boards of directors, served on civic advisory panels and managed the company's contacts with the media. Bonnie Vincent assumed a position of civic importance for the first time in her life.

The more she experienced the stimulating new world of enterprise, the more an ominous rift developed between her and her husband. Udo was growing so much meaner and more sullen that Bonnie finally sought out counseling.

On this late-winter morning, Bonnie prepared to launch into her daily ritual of drying her hair and applying mascara. She had always been pretty—not movie star stunning nor even cute in a cheerleader sense—but her smooth, radiant face, sky-blue eyes and stunning white smile, framed by short, lustrous brown hair, set her apart. As she lined her eyes and her likeness stared back, it was obvious the deteriorating marriage was aging her. Streaks of gray hair and lines deepening the corners of her eyes had arrived far too early at age thirty-two.

Bonnie could hear Udo dressing in the bedroom. She sucked in her breath, as if anticipating something unknown and unpleasant. "Udo," she called out, faking cheerfulness. "Let's go out for dinner tonight."

She saw his image appear behind her in the mirror. He was dressed in a white shirt and navy pants. He laid his jacket on the vanity and began tying his necktie. His gaunt face and hollow gray-blue eyes formed a blank wall of indifference. He had never been a handsome man. When Bonnie first met him, she told her sister Elizabeth that she didn't care about his looks—that she liked his considerate attitude toward her.

Increasingly, as she matured and enjoyed success, the dramatic contrast became more evident between Bonnie's professional appearance and the rumpled impression her husband made. It wasn't that he wore cheap suits or inexpensive shoes—he didn't. But his clothes always seemed to fit poorly. His shoes were never polished, his shave was not quite close enough, and his hair invariably needed combing. As Udo tied his tie, the odds were good that it would be loosened and sloppy by lunchtime.

"What do you think? About dinner?" she repeated.

"Can't," Udo answered curtly. "I'll be home late."

Bonnie's face contorted unpleasantly from the words Udo had uttered countless times in recent months. "Please?" she pleaded. She tried to put her arm around his shoulder, but he pushed it away and continued to attend to the necktie. "Please, Udo. I know where you've been going every night."

He didn't respond.

Desperate, Bonnie grabbed her handbag on the vanity and her hands trembled slightly as she pulled out some credit card bills. "Saucy Lady. Girls Galore," she read from the receipts. "You don't need to go to those places. Come on. I'll take off early and we can have a romantic evening together."

She watched his mirrored reflection and saw the familiar expression. Udo's frown and pursed lips told her he was becoming annoyed. He grasped her arm. Instead of the gentle touch she had told her therapist she craved, it was abrupt and rough.

"You don't tell me where I can go. Okay?" Udo

commanded. "I run my own life."

Bonnie crumpled up the receipts and dropped them on the vanity. "I'm trying to make our marriage work," she sniffed, her eyes edged with tears. "I've eased up on my work schedule. I'm seeing the counselor..."

Interrupting, Udo snapped, "That stupid shrink? She makes things worse."

"She does not," Bonnie shook her head at Udo's reflected image. "I suggested dinner tonight because Dr. Jablonsky thinks we should spend more loving time together. You shot it down." She waited, but he was silent. She began to cry. "Now you're demeaning the value of the counseling," she added, sounding more bitter. "You're wrong, Udo. Dr. Jablonsky is helping me a lot. You have no idea how much."

"What does that mean?"

"When I called yesterday to set up an appointment, she asked how we are doing since you got fired."

Udo jerked his head around in her direction, immediately flustered. His eyebrows went up and he gazed at her for several drawn-out seconds, as if searching for a lie to tell.

"Is it true?" she tossed the question tearfully against a tower of silence. "Do you have any idea how humiliating that was, to hear it from her?"

Udo scowled and didn't answer. Instead, he turned back to the mirror to straighten the knot he had just tied.

"Udo, what happened?" Bonnie persisted.

He scowled again. "Those bastards canned me for no reason." Udo paused, and with no rejoinder from Bonnie, he continued arrogantly. "I'll go to as many bars as I want to. Hell, I might as well—we don't have sex anymore."

Bonnie stared in disbelief. Her tears became a torrent. "That's not my fault," she argued. "Dr. Jablonsky says..."

He interrupted again. "Dr. Jablonsky! I've had enough of that bitch." Udo put on his jacket and turned to walk out.

Bonnie grabbed his shoulder from behind and tried

urgently to pull him back. "Come on, Udo," she begged. "Don't walk out. Let's discuss this before it's too late."

The words stopped him as readily as her tugging at his shoulder.

"What do you mean, too late?" he snapped.

She braced herself. "I'm going to talk to a lawyer today if you don't want to work on our marriage."

"You want a divorce?" he asked, his question ripe with incredulity.

Bonnie could scarcely get the words out. "I know I don't want to live like this," she said, her eyes searching his for some fragment of hope. "We're not getting anywhere."

Bonnie's tears were badly streaking the fresh mascara. There was desperation in her voice. "Why couldn't you tell me they let you go? You've been hanging out at bars and paying dancers with my charge cards. What do you expect from me?"

Udo drew closer, his face inches from hers. She recoiled.

"I expect you to shut the fuck up," Udo's voice rose derisively. "We're not getting any divorce. And if I want to charge my entertainment on your cards, I will."

"If that's your attitude, then I'm going ahead," she knee-jerked the warning.

"Damn it, you're not!" he shouted.

Udo grabbed her arms and shook her. Bonnie lurched back against his grip, her expression filled with disbelief. As she tried to pull away, he slapped her. She recoiled as the sting of the blow shook her entire face.

"Stop!" she screamed, her mounting fear obvious in the frantic cry.

Udo squeezed his wife's arms harder and pushed her brutally. As Bonnie fought back, he slapped her again, and they became locked in a wrestling match.

"Let go of me," she pleaded. "Are you crazy?"

Udo's eyes opened wide, zombie-like, displaying the same dazed fear that had crossed his face that day she proposed the Dallas move.

"I'll show you crazy," Udo roared in a voice so ferocious it was barely human. "You think you're leaving me? Hell no. You're staying right here."

He spun Bonnie around and shoved her violently. She grunted as her body slammed against the wall. She shrieked, pummeling him with her fists. Udo grabbed her throat and choked her, his fingers digging in. Her eyes grew wide with surprise at how far this fight had escalated.

"You're not going anywhere," Udo rasped.

"Stop, Udo," Bonnie managed, sputtering.

A surge of adrenaline and fear shook her body as she fought back in renewed desperation, kicking Udo in the legs and thrashing at him with her hands and arms. He became more wildly enraged and strangled her with greater might, shuddering with resentment. Bonnie's face was flushed crimson as she struggled to escape from the suffocation washing over her. She shuddered, laboring to breathe. She tried to knee Udo in the groin, but he was too strong and vicious.

Udo's face contorted with rage. He pulled Bonnie closer, continuing to choke her. As life drained slowly out of her, in uncontrolled ferocity Udo bit her on the neck, his eyes wide with fury.

His hands trembled as he unclenched them. Bonnie slumped to the floor. He flexed his fingers, trying to control the shaking.

Without looking at his wife's limp body, he spun around and stumbled out of the door, slamming it behind him.

CHAPTER 1: Udo Whatzis?

CALL IT FATE. Call it providence. Call it good luck, dumb luck, no luck. An elevator taken, or not. A phone call returned or ignored. A yellow light run or obeyed. Every element of life has a word, a glimpse, a moment that can change its outcome forever.

When Grace Gleason arrived at work on that bright, crisp February morning, she could not have known an event hurtling toward a violent end in another part of town would introduce into her relatively calm life not one, but many of those moments. They would collide to infuse her days with more twists and turns than she had known in all of her previous thirty-nine years combined. They would conspire to change who she would become and how she would view the world.

Grace couldn't understand all of that on this day. Standing in the parking lot of TXDA television, smelling the fresh air and wishing she could be excited about being there, she wondered if she was on a treadmill to nowhere. She stood silently for a moment, remembering how coming to Dallas had been so exciting a prospect. Her husband Jeff had made an easy transition to his new law firm. His big chance at a larger, more prestigious practice with potential for a partnership was the reason they had moved from Austin months earlier.

Their daughter, Megan, hadn't been too pleased, being a rising senior, but she was a trooper and was adjusting.

"She still misses her friends," Grace had grumbled a month after the move, as she and Jeff dressed for bed.

"A little," Jeff answered. "I think it's Austin itself that she really misses. She's been planning to go to the University of Texas most of her life."

"She can still go there," Grace observed. "She'll be

reunited with some of her best chums. Besides, it's marvelous the way her new classmates have gathered around her and made her feel welcome."

Grace could clearly tell that her daughter and her husband were making the transition.

She was the one paying the price for the move. A new reporter in a huge media market, she was getting the worst assignments.

Ever since a brief glimpse into the news business at a middle school career day, being a reporter had been her only ambition. Making good decisions and lucky turns through a maze of challenges in high school and college, Grace had reached her goal of becoming a newswoman. But the career she had carved out at Austin's number one station now seemed a faded memory. Stories she had starred in as the lead reporter were forgotten. Dallas' TXDA-TV, with its cadre of veteran news people, had relegated her to the bullpen of soft-pitch traffic accidents and groundbreakings.

A car pulling out of the lot jolted Grace's mind back to the present. She locked her car and walked toward the building, but stopped for a moment to watch the sunlight sweep over the treetops. It would be a clear, dazzling day. *At least*, she thought, *that will make whatever pablum the assignment editor serves up a bit more palatable.*

Grace was fifteen minutes early for the morning meeting, as usual. She liked to arrive in time to check voicemails and get a feel for the day. The time went quickly, and she trekked reluctantly to the conference room.

In these meetings, the station's managers, producers and reporters discussed the obvious stories of the day. Then they suggested ideas for enterprise stories that no one else had. Of all she disliked about TXDA, she dreaded the negative dynamics of these gatherings the most.

"All right, let's get started," said Wallace James, the assignment manager who ran the sessions. Wallace was a humorless, middle-aged man whom Grace decided could easily be mistaken for a mid-level government bureaucrat. Wallace led the discussion, but he actually had little power.

"First up, there's that brouhaha at the county jail over failed inspections," he began his recitation of the stories everyone already knew were out there. He droned on down the list and ended with, "What else do you have?"

"There's a fight brewing between the machinists union and Dallas Steel Fabrications over the layoffs they announced," suggested Midge Rodriguez, a young reporter. "Looks like there might be a walkout."

"Is that all you've got?" scowled John Mendell, one of the managers, rolling his eyes with mock boredom.

Grace closed her notebook, disgusted with how quickly the higher-ups turned the gatherings hostile when reporters advocated stories. She thought the managers were like sheep; if the news director, Lloyd Hamilton, liked an idea they would fall enthusiastically in line behind it. But most of the stories Lloyd favored were the predictable accidents, crimes and fires.

Meanwhile, it seemed to Grace that Lloyd thought every idea pitched by his favorite reporter, Mitchell Court, was a great one. *After all*, she rationalized to herself, *Lloyd hired Mitchell.*

She favored the can-do attitude at the Austin outlet where she had started. The station's small-market spirit and close-knit cluster of homegrown personnel presented an opportunity to do highly esteemed work. Here, At TXDA, the decision-makers gave her suggestions little importance, and she was usually assigned a blood drive or meaningless groundbreaking.

As they left the meeting, Grace fell into step with Midge Rodriguez.

"These guys frustrate me," Midge said.

"Same here," Grace sympathized. They paused as they reached the newsroom. "I want some solid assignments."

"We have to keep trying," Midge encouraged.

"I know," Grace sighed. "I remember what a thrill it was

when I reported on a drug-related, accidental killing in Austin. A poor woman was just shopping and got caught in the cross-fire. It was exciting to use a tragedy like that to expose a gang war. I swear, I'm going to campaign until I get some respect around here and they give me more important stories."

She returned Midge's smile as they returned to their cubicles.

Grace began making contacts on the Irving Art Festival story she had been assigned. She had no inkling that another event was about to change her life—an incident so ripe with defining moments it would engulf her existence and push it perilously close to a cliff.

Grace made her last call to set up the art festival story and began revising notes on her laptop, trying to devise a way to nail down a whistle blower inside city hall about some missing funds. She wanted to pitch the potential lead story to Lloyd Hamilton, but getting her source to give up more about what he knew would be the key.

She scanned the news feeds on the screens overhead and smiled to herself at a report from Chicago on the weather channel. Most of her family and friends from high school were still up there. The report of a ten-inch blizzard showed video of sand trucks and parka-clad residents digging their cars out of snow banks, reminding her why she and husband Jeff had stayed in the South after finishing college nearly two decades ago. She e-mailed several of her Chicago friends and teased them unmercifully about needing snow tires and overcoats.

Lloyd Hamilton interrupted Grace's focus on the monitors. The news director rarely paid attention to her, and she was surprised when he stopped at her desk.

He was a news veteran, a balding, square-jawed man who rarely smiled. Once a radio announcer and then part-time television anchor, he possessed a naturally deep broadcasting voice and enunciated every word as if Walter Cronkite's reputation depended on it. He spoke slowly and thoughtfully in a boring monotone, and even jokes seemed strangely serious to him.

"Grace, that was a fine job at the zoo yesterday," Lloyd intoned.

He seemed sincere, but there was a guarded edge in his manner that she interpreted as gender bias. Lloyd had a reputation for giving men in the field a break over women. He had only hired Grace for TXDA because her general manager in Austin, a former university chum of Lloyd's, had recommended her when Jeff's great career opportunity arose in Dallas. Grace had done an outstanding job at the Austin station after graduating from the University of Texas communications school, so Lloyd did his old friend a favor and hired her.

Lloyd's compliment about the zoo story was the first praise he had offered her since she had started at TXDA. She was pleased, but she considered it an opening for an appeal.

"Thanks," she responded. "But there's no public corruption to uncover in the panda cage at the zoo. When are you going to give me a real assignment?"

Grace could see that Lloyd looked a little hurt. She imagined he considered her an ungrateful employee, since he had obviously made a point to come and commend her. Yet she couldn't resist even the tiniest opportunity to step up the pressure.

"You've only been at TXDA a few months," Lloyd cautioned her. "You have to earn the best assignments around here."

"How can I earn them doing zoo stories?" she shot back. "It's not as if I'm a kid right out of college, Lloyd. I have experience. Don't forget, my Austin report about the university employee caught in that gang fight was nominated for a regional Emmy."

She watched his teeth clench, making his square jaw jut out. Lloyd paused, as if conjuring up a clever comment. Looking addled and clearing his throat, he finally said, "Everyone wants to tell the news director how to run the show. Just keep doing your job, Grace, and you'll get your chance."

"Meanwhile," she retorted, undaunted, "keep my

mouth shut, go fetch coffee and run out with my notepad when the pandas come to town?"

Lloyd brightened, obviously missing her sarcasm. "That's the spirit," he responded. He paused for effect and quickly changed the subject. "How's that daughter of yours? Martha, is it?"

"Megan. She's..."

Lloyd turned away as Grace began her response. Richard Stone, the general manager, was coming in from outside, and as he passed by Lloyd scrambled to get his attention. Richard had been brought in by corporate to shore up the news operation, and his pointed questions and clipped demands struck fear in the staff, including the news director. Lloyd looked for any opportunity to collar Richard and score points.

"Richard," Lloyd called. "Could I have a word?"

Richard nodded over his shoulder but continued quick-stepping through the newsroom. Lloyd hurried after him, a pup following the big dog.

Slightly insulted, Grace finished anyway, toward Lloyd's retreating back, "...just wonderful. She got a Nobel nomination yesterday. Not bad for a seventeen-year-old, is it? She gets her doctorate next week. And thanks for asking about my husband Jeff. No, not John—Jeff!"

Grace returned to the notes she had been poring over, but she stole occasional glances at Lloyd and Richard. They were standing outside the news director's office, laughing and bantering. Richard was carrying most of the conversation, poking and jabbing Lloyd's chest good-naturedly and the usually stoic Lloyd belly-laughing uncharacteristically at his boss's chitchat.

Mitchell Court, one of Grace's fellow reporters, rushed into the newsroom and stopped where Lloyd and Richard were talking. Despite Mitchell being one of Lloyd's favorites, Grace liked and admired him. She believed that one day he would be a strong anchorman. He was a bit full of himself, she thought, but he was a smart reporter and looked solidly professional on camera. Grace especially liked the way Mitchell treated her with respect—like a colleague.

She stopped typing but didn't look up. She sat quietly, listening intently as Mitchell talked to his superiors.

"I got the story at Pearson Accounting, Lloyd," Mitchell beamed. "They're denying any responsibility for that financial mess at Transit Oil."

Grace stole a glance at the trio. Lloyd and Richard seemed impressed as they listened with interest to their future star.

"Did you get to interview the CEO?" Lloyd asked. "What's his name? Crawford?"

"Calloway," Mitchell corrected.

Grace was somewhat gratified that Megan's name wasn't the only one Lloyd couldn't remember.

"He didn't show up," Mitchell told them. "He sent his lawyer to talk to me. Apparently their PR woman has turned up missing."

"There's an amusing oxymoron," Lloyd mused in his typical habit of diverging from an important point in a conversation. "Why do we say, 'turned up missing'? If it's missing, it wouldn't have turned up, would it?"

He delivered the quip as dryly as he might give a traffic report, yet Richard and Mitchell laughed. Grace scarcely noticed, her instincts were so energized by Mitchell's information. She jumped up from her desk and joined them, her curiosity peaking.

"Mitchell, did you say Pearson Accounting's PR woman is missing?" Grace asked.

"Yeah," Mitchell replied. "Someone named..." He paused to search his memory, and then pulled a notepad from his pocket, rifling through its pages.

"Bonnie Vincent?" Grace asked before Mitchell could find it.

"That's it," he acknowledged, surprised. "Do you know her?"

"Udo Holthaus," Grace blurted to three puzzled faces.

"Udo Whatzis?" Lloyd laughed. The curiosity in his question seemed to overshadow his mildly annoyed appearance at this intrusion by his newest reporter.

"Udo Holthaus," Grace persisted. "I'll bet he had something to do with this."

Mitchell and Lloyd looked at each other, obviously confused, and Mitchell shrugged. Richard leaned back against a desk with his arms folded, listening intently.

"I knew Bonnie when I worked in Austin," Grace explained, barely containing her excitement. "She was an *Austin Tribune* reporter who married a man who was news director at another station, a man named Udo Holthaus. He was a sneaky, sleazy person. I never trusted the guy."

Lloyd frowned and leaned toward Richard Stone. "Here we go. Mrs. Intuition working overtime."

"Seriously, I never understood why she stayed with that creep," Grace said. "He had absolutely zero respect in the business. To top it off, he had a sinister look about him, and this weird Teutonic accent."

"He was German?" Mitchell asked.

"Germans settled a community in Texas in the 1800s. That's where he grew up."

Grace paused, surprised at the attention these three were giving her.

"Bonnie got an offer to work for Pearson," she continued, feeling her heart beating faster at being the center of interest. "We all bet she'd leave him behind. I heard they had a huge argument about it right in front of her fellow reporters at a big media dinner. But Udo finally gave in. He took a job at one of the state agencies here and moved with her."

Mitchell flicked his hand into the air. "She'll turn up, probably with another guy in Las Vegas or Reno," he said.

"Bonnie would never do something like that," Grace shook her head. "I saw her several months ago. That's how I learned where she was working. She hadn't changed much. She wears more expensive clothes now—designer handbags and shoes—things like that. But she's still the same loyal Bonnie."

Richard had been concentrating quietly on the exchange, obviously trying to decide what to make of it. "Did she talk about her husband?" he prompted Grace.

"I asked if she was still married to Udo," she answered. "She gave me a moon-eyed look and said, 'Of course.' He has something to do with her missing. They're going to find that poor woman dead."

Richard, Lloyd and Mitchell looked at each other again and six eyebrows rose skeptically at Grace's rash prediction.

Lloyd shook his head in dismissal. "Mitchell's right," he said. "If this Udo guy is that bad, she probably left him."

"She wouldn't do that," Grace insisted, feeling as if she was futilely running through deep sand. "Not Bonnie. Lloyd, let me pursue this story."

She surprised even herself at her audacity. But her instincts were in overdrive. There was not a crumb of doubt in her mind that the Udo Holthaus who had repulsed her in their brief meetings in Austin was capable of something more deeply sinister than nauseate a young television newscaster. Grace was convinced that Bonnie had been clinging to an illusion—that the man Bonnie hoped Udo to be and the man who married her and trailed her to Dallas were two different people. She was also sure Bonnie's naiveté was bound to be dashed at some point by the shady Mr. Holthaus. *There's a story here,* Grace thought, *and I'm going to cover it.*

Lloyd frowned again. "We're not going to chase a ghost who isn't there. It's not a story," he said with finality.

Grace felt the words crush her enthusiasm. Mitchell smiled at her sympathetically and retreated to his cubicle. Lloyd slapped Richard on the shoulder and they disappeared into the news director's office. Grace was left standing alone, frowning and dejected.

She returned to her desk and stared at her phone. Grace had never been one to shrink from a challenge, and she knew immediately this was one she couldn't pass up. The question was how to begin. She thought for a moment, opened her smart phone and pulled up Bonnie's home number. She squinted at it for a long time, considering, and then in a moment of sudden decision, dialed.

"Hello?"

Grace's stomach did a flip as she recognized the voice she could never forget. "Udo Holthaus?" she ventured. She waited for what seemed like minutes. She knew it was Udo, and she guessed from the charged pause that he remembered her voice, too.

"Yes," she heard finally.

Her stomach churned again, taking her emotions back to the first time she had met Udo, when she was a neophyte in the media business.

Grace had been a product of the Chicago public schools, where her iron-worker dad and alcoholic mother had no expectations except for her to graduate high school, get a job, find a husband and make babies. But she had other ideas. One day, as part of an eighth-grade career unit, a woman anchoring the news for WWON television came to speak.

"I get a chance to keep up with what's happening, here in Chicago and all over the world," the woman told Grace's class. "I'm lucky enough to learn about it first and see it from behind the scenes, and I get to share what I've learned with my neighbors and my community. It gives me a strong sense that I'm helping raise the public's awareness and making a difference in their lives. And all the while, I'm advancing the reputation of women in what was once the good-old-boy club."

Grace listened, transfixed. The message resonated. She knew from that moment that she wanted to follow that woman's lead and become a reporter, maybe even an anchor.

She worked on her high school newspaper and joined the radio club. When she graduated, a local AM radio station hired her as a gofer, based on a compelling application letter she had written and a recommendation from her school counselor, who doubled as the radio club's sponsor.

"I'll hire you," the station manager said when he interviewed her, "on the condition that you enroll in community college at night and take all the English and history classes requisite for getting into journalism school."

"It's a lot to take on," she told him, "but I'll try."

"You're talented, Grace, and I think you can make it. Otherwise, I wouldn't be wasting a job on you."

Grace lived at home during her two-year stint at the station, saved her money and learned as much as possible about the business. She earned nothing less than an "A" at the community college, which landed her a scholarship at her station manager's alma mater, the University of Texas. Her grades, work resume and his recommendation put her over the top. This bright young woman whose speech patterns were as different in the Lone Star state as Udo's were, saw a little of the world outside Illinois for the first time.

A paying job on the university FM station gave her added experience, and she worked hard to perfect a neutral broadcasting accent. "No more 'baad dawg,' It's 'bad dog' from now on," she told one of her classmates as they worked together on a news program, giving the phrase her best St. Paul imitation.

Her work in television news classes began to attract attention. When Grace graduated, she was a natural hire for the top Austin television station, first as a weather forecaster and six months later as a reporter.

When she was still fresh out of school, Grace crossed paths with Udo for the first time.

"Grace, this is Udo Holthaus," her news director Jinx Daley introduced them at the bar of the Dallas Press Club during a reception to introduce a new Associated Press writer. "Udo's the news director at that other station—the one that tries harder."

She laughed at the joke and extended her hand. "Nice

to meet you, Mr. Holthaus."

Udo conjured up a dry smile at Jinx's good-natured prodding and grasped Grace's hand. An eerie sensation ran through her that she couldn't remember ever having felt in a previous meeting. It screamed to her instincts that this man was not to be trusted.

She only encountered Udo a few times at business gatherings and never exchanged more than a few words with him. On one of those occasions, a Press Club pre-party for the Emmy awards, Grace also met Udo's newspaper reporter wife Bonnie Vincent.

"She's pretty," Grace told fellow reporter Carolyn Mason as they sipped cocktails at the bar.

"I know. And petite," Carolyn agreed. "And nicely dressed and classy. All the things we should hate about her." They laughed. "But that husband of hers..." Carolyn didn't finish.

"What's his story?" Grace asked, intrigued. "Those shifty eyes and hunched posture make him look like a weasel."

"His story," Carolyn responded, her voice thick from liquor, "is that he has no respect in the business. On top of that, he has a horrible reputation as a bar crawler—a frequenter of the ugly side of Austin's nightlife."

"Seems a perfect match for that disheveled appearance and crooked smile," Grace said. "He and Bonnie do make a peculiar couple."

"You know he announced that she was hired by Pearson Accounting in Dallas and he was resigning," Carolyn seemed to enjoy the gossip. "They say you could hear a collective sigh of relief in his newsroom."

Now, hearing the weird man's voice made Grace realize how ironic it was that they found themselves once again in the same city, thrown together by a strange quirk of fate. His raspy response conjured up the memory of the eerie sensation she had experienced the first time she met him.

She swallowed hard and tried to sound normal on the

telephone. "Udo, it's Grace Gleason. I knew you in Austin. Do you remember?"

There was another long silence. "Yes," he replied.

"I heard Bonnie is missing," she said tentatively. "I'm really sorry. What happened?"

"I don't know what happened," he snapped at Grace, sounding exasperated at this encroachment. "She...just disappeared, that's all."

Grace thought Udo sounded nervous and tense, not at all like a worried husband. She was certain she could detect suspicion in his response. "But you and I know that's not like Bonnie," Grace tried to prolong the conversation, searching for a word, an exclamation, a clue that her instincts were right. "Don't you think she must be in some terrible danger?"

Udo didn't respond. Sitting on a sofa in his condo, his uncomfortable squirming was evidence that he was highly irritated. Just months earlier, he had told Bonnie he had a vague recollection of this girl from his news director days in Austin. The occasion was the afternoon when Grace and Bonnie bumped into each other on a downtown Dallas street. Later, at dinner, Bonnie had described the reunion to Udo.

"Don't you remember her?" Bonnie asked. "Paul Heggendorf hired her right out of UT. We met her several times at media functions."

"Sort of," Udo appeared more interested in his cocktail than this bland conversation. "I have a fuzzy recollection of a young reporter over there who broke so many crime stories my people had trouble catching up."

"She told me," Bonnie related, "that a friend of hers once heard you cursing her name in a local bar. So you must have known her."

"She hasn't been on my radar for a long time. A lot has happened since you insisted that we move here."

Grace took a deep breath, inexplicably nervous. "I'm working for TXDA here now, Udo," she pressed. "Will you talk to me on camera and ask for the public's help in finding her?"

"I'm not ready to do that." He sounded incensed at Grace's persistent questioning. "I'll call you if I change my mind. Right now, the police are on it. I don't know where Bonnie is. I have to go."

"Wait..." Grace started. Just before the phone on the other end slammed down, Grace heard the words she was certain weren't meant for her ears.

"God damned nosy bitch."

In that moment, Grace's gut told her Udo knew where Bonnie was.

CHAPTER 2: *No Help at All*

GRACE WAS AN ONLY CHILD, and growing up in a house dominated by a tough, uncompromising father and a weak mother failed to prepare her for being assertive. Yet she surprised herself, not to mention Lloyd Hamilton, when she decided for the first time since coming to WTXS that she would stand her ground on a story.

Lloyd had been there a long time. Grace knew he was no stranger to career struggles and had a reputation for sometimes erring on the cautious side when making news decisions—whether or not to carry a controversial story, for example, if it might draw public criticism of the station.

The day after her nerve-wracking phone call with Udo, Grace went to lunch with Mitchell Court.

"Let's drive somewhere," he said. "I want to find out more about this Holthaus character, and if we go to one of the usual spots the other staffers won't give us any privacy."

When they had settled into a booth at the coffee shop of a local hotel, Grace said, "I'll regale you with my Udo stories if you'll do me a huge favor."

"Shoot," Mitchel said.

"I'm thinking about having it out with Hamilton this afternoon. It might help if I know his story."

"Lloyd was the son of an IRS agent," Mitchell told her after their food was served. "They say he inherited his father's serious demeanor and conservative lifestyle. Lloyd grew up wanting to be a banker, of all things, but that didn't happen, since his worst school grades were in math."

"Do you know where he went to school?"

"He majored in business at North Texas State in Denton. In his sophomore year, he volunteered to be business manager of the student newspaper to gain experience. He was apparently not very good at selling ads or keeping the books, but being around the newsroom whetted his interest for the news business. Lloyd took some journalism classes, changed his major and volunteered to be wire editor for the paper. The second semester he was named associate editor."

Mitchell paused. "When is it your turn? Holthaus, remember?"

Grace waved a hand in the air. "Oh, we'll get to him. But more about Hamilton. You remember all these details from what people have told you?"

Mitchell shrugged. "I believe in knowing everything about my boss. You never know when it'll come in handy. Want me to go on?"

"Please do. I'm fascinated."

"When Lloyd was a senior at NT State, he was selected for the paid position of managing editor of the paper. He was famous for making conservative decisions. I got that right from Hamilton himself."

"What do you mean?"

"One night several months ago we worked late and had a couple drinks together afterward. He got a little tipsy and started to reminisce about college. He said his editorial page writers wanted to crusade against the school's bookstore pricing policies, but he convinced them they would hurt the university at a time when the legislature was making budget decisions. When he talked about it, he seemed to be wearing it as a badge of honor."

"That sounds about right," Grace commented.

"Anther time," Mitchell went on, "when his news editor planned a full page on fraternity hazing, he vetoed it. He reasoned that it would hurt the school's reputation and recruiting activities. You have to conclude from all of this that our boy plays it safe whenever he can."

Mitchell drew a large breath and sat back. "Now, about Udo Holthaus..."

The knowledge about Lloyd Hamilton gave Grace cause for confidence later that afternoon as she confronted the news director over the Bonnie Vincent missing person story. Standing outside Lloyd's office door, holding a "Have You Seen This Person?" flyer, Grace pled her case.

"I know something horrible has happened to Bonnie," she argued to a blank face. "Lloyd, I know her. She's not the type to disappear with no word. She has a good job, and she's a very loyal person. Bonnie wouldn't simply walk away. We have to do this story from that perspective."

The unemotional face morphed into a deep frown. "Grace, I have a feeling that you could run with this story and captivate our viewers," he boomed on. "You're enthusiastic, and you seem to smell a good story. But something is telling me not to pull the trigger on this one. I don't want to discuss it again."

He took a step into his office, but turned back again. "Most missing people turn up okay. They run away with their lovers or for one reason or another check out of their lives. We did the initial report, but it's not news any more."

She gathered her courage one more time. "Please, Lloyd. I understand your reluctance to chase the story down," she persisted. "But my gut tells me this case is different."

Grace waved the flyer at him, unintentionally making him flinch. "Her company was distributing these flyers a few hours after they learned she was missing," she said. "They must suspect she's in some kind of trouble. Bonnie's too responsible to run away."

She could tell from his sour reaction that her doggedness had pushed Lloyd miles beyond his comfort zone. She had a mental picture of a drawbridge going up. The moat was full, and the battlements were reinforced to protect the kingdom from sneak attack. The protector of the realm had donned his armor, and his expression had turned to granite. Grace would have been amused by the imagery if she hadn't felt passionate about the story, and if Lloyd Hamilton weren't so impervious to argument on the matter of missing person Bonnie Vincent.

"I don't want to talk about it anymore," Lloyd declared in his customary stentorian tone. "If we do this one, every Tom, Dick and Clarence whose wife or uncle is missing will be all over us wanting coverage."

Lloyd paused, looking into Grace's angry face. "Don't you have a ground-breaking to cover at the new auto plant?" he asked with a dismissive air.

Lloyd disappeared into his office. Grace watched him go, feeling dejected. She stood staring at Bonnie's picture, shaking her head, as disappointed as she had been at any time since coming to work for TXDA.

She returned to her cubicle and sat staring into the screen saver of her computer. As she seemed to be doing often these days in the wake of so many disappointments, she drifted for a moment to the animated, negative disagreements she had with her father after the career day lecture whetted her ambition to be a journalist. Money for college was tight. Grace's mother had drunk herself out of her job, and although Hal Narlesky made a decent living, he hadn't saved up enough for Grace to attend journalism school after the mortgage and bills and rehab costs had been paid.

One night, after her mother had collapsed into bed and her father watched television sleepily on the couch, she broached the subject of college.

"I'll work to help out," she promised as her father frowned at her through droopy eyelids.

"None of our family have ever gone to college, and they've all managed just fine," he grumbled.

"These are the 1980s," Grace complained. "Daddy, everyone's getting degrees now. If I don't keep up, my classmates will get all the good jobs, and I'll have to work at a cosmetics counter or the phone company."

"There's no disgrace in working at the telephone company," her father groused, his tone becoming harsh and dictatorial. "You can do what your aunts and uncles did—graduate high school, get a job and start a family."

Grace stormed away, slammed her bedroom door and turned a Cyndi Lauper song up full volume. She knew her father would still be sitting on the couch, seething, as the tune and lyrics of "Girls Just Want to Have Fun" pounded away at him from her room.

Remembering the spat and reflecting on her subsequent, self-made success, even in the face of Hamilton's negativity, gave Grace hope. She would continue to nag Lloyd, and maybe even Richard Stone. She wasn't going to settle for feel-good feature stories much longer.

Grace pulled up her files on her computer. She knew the afternoon would become a disaster if she didn't focus. She promised herself to do a commendable job on a story that meant little to her, even though Udo Holthaus and Bonnie Vincent were eating away at her mind.

An hour later, as she rode with cameraman Matt Robertson to the site of the new Honshu Auto facility, she forced herself to plan out the assignment she considered nothing but fluff.

The plant site was a massive, wide-open field just off the main highway. The area had already been cleared, and footings for the foundation had been poured with tons of concrete and thousands of steel reinforcement bars emerging toward the sky. As they pulled off the highway, Grace marveled at what a breath-taking sight it was—a testament to the size and power of the Japanese "invasion" and to Dallas for inviting it there. She felt lucky to be living in a city whose core of politicians and business powers were aggressive and ambitious and full of Texas can-do spirit.

"Austin was all about academics and state politics and country music," she expressed her reaction to Matt.

"That sounds good to me," he responded.

"It was exciting, but it was also provincial," she said.

"Dallas is about money and world-class commerce. When I think about that, and about the bloated political scene and thorny labor atmosphere of my hometown Chicago, I get energized being here."

She decided she would give this story her full attention.

Matt pulled the van onto the site in a flurry of dust. Cars, trucks and two other television vans were already parked there. A small crowd was emerging from the vehicles and walking toward a make-shift platform with wooden folding chairs where assorted dignitaries were seated, waiting for the ground-breaking event to begin. Nervous public relations and marketing managers paced around the area, counting chairs in the press section, greeting media representatives with enthusiastic handshakes, and handing out seating arrangements to arriving dignitaries.

A podium sat at the center of the platform, and a huge billboard with an architect's rendering of the new plant served as a backdrop for the makeshift stage.

Grace and Matt climbed out of the TXDA van and walked toward the platform. She liked Matt. He had an easy-going way about him, and his aw-shucks manner could just as easily have marked him a ranch foreman as a photographer. He wore blue jeans and boots, and a two-day reddish-blond beard hid a remarkably smooth, young face. Grace had worked with Matt on several stories, but they had never talked about much except the story at hand. Still, by now she felt comfortable with him.

"You're a bachelor?" she asked as they approached the platform.

He nodded, wincing self-consciously at the obviously unexpected question.

"So what about it? Big party tonight?" she asked, grinning. "Lots of girls?"

He smiled back, wider, and she thought she saw a hint of a blush. "No big party," he said. "That's not my style." They continued toward the platform, and he grew serious. "I heard you got into it with Hamilton today."

Grace hadn't expected their banter to turn businesslike, but she liked the prospect of having someone at the station she could confide in. "Word gets around fast. Where'd you hear it?" she remarked.

"It's the gossip around the station. What's the deal?" Matt seemed genuinely interested.

"The deal is," she explained, "that this person I knew in Austin—a PR woman named Bonnie Vincent—is missing. I think she's in trouble, and Lloyd won't let me pursue the story."

"Lloyd's not one to stick his neck out," Matt said. "Not unless Stone pushes him."

"I know," Grace acknowledged. "Maybe I'll do the story anyway. Want to shoot it for me?"

Matt laughed as they reached the platform. A technician hooking up the microphone at the podium leaned in to try it out as Matt started setting up his camera.

"Testing, one, two, three..." the technician's voice echoed across the open air. He turned to one of the Dallas County commissioners seated on the stage and nodded, then hopped down off the platform. The commissioner stood, pulled some notes from his coat pocket and looked out at the crowd, waiting for the chatter to quiet down.

"No, Grace, I think I'll pass on this one," Matt whispered before the speech began. "I like my job too much."

"Coward," she kidded.

He flashed her his joshing grin and turned his attention to his camera as Grace scrambled for one of the chairs in the section marked *"Press."*

The commissioner cleared his throat. "Good afternoon, and thank you for coming..." he began. Grace absently pulled the missing person flyer on Bonnie Vincent off her clipboard and stared at it, engrossed in thought, barely hearing the commissioner's words.

The next morning, Grace and Jeff were in the master bathroom dressing when the tensions that seemed to be increasing between them re-emerged. The argument began so benignly that Grace didn't see it coming.

Although their married life was far less demonstrative than in those first passionate years, she liked how they had settled in. Early in their marriage they found time for a "roll in the hay," as Jeff liked to call it, if not daily, at least several times a week. Grace had no idea how couples could continue that pace and then show up fresh and energetic for work the next day. Now she was happy if they found time for sex once a month, as long as occasional kisses, arms on the shoulder, pats on the butt or playful winks in a crowd didn't disappear. She sensed that arrangement suited Jeff as well.

Bedtime every night became a ritual. Grace would fall asleep to the sound of her husband leafing through legal briefs. There was no way she could have known that their transition from nightly affection to a constantly present work regimen was a warning of troubling ripples in the air, blowing in like the blue-grayish clouds that gather unexpectedly on the Texas horizon and foretell a "nor'easter" about to storm through.

Grace was happy with their busy life and new home. They had moved to Brookwood Acres, a quiet, upper-middle-class Dallas suburb only blocks from Megan's high school. The two-story brick Georgian style house resembled most of the others in the neighborhood—four bedrooms and baths, a three-car garage, and a large deck in the back for entertaining, grilling and sitting out on nice evenings with a beer or glass of wine to watch the big Texas sky light up with a million stars.

All the neighborhood lawns were neat and elaborately landscaped with Saint Augustine grass, junipers, spirea, crape myrtle, Asiatic jasmine, vinca and mondo grass. Most were maintained by a crew that came through once a week and left the area looking like the White House rose garden.

Inside, the Gleason home was white and spacious and tastefully appointed with double-crown molding, chair rails and sparkling hardwood floors. The kitchen was granite and stainless steel and appliances with all of the latest gadgets. Grace especially liked the huge master bedroom, carpeted with deep pile, set off overhead with a triple crown-molded tray ceiling and double ceiling fans. With their extensive business wardrobes, plus casual wear, they packed the his-and-hers walk-in closets. One of the most striking features of their master suite, and Grace's favorite, was a bathroom spacious enough for them to co-exist in their daily routines and lounge together in a huge whirlpool tub when time and their moods permitted.

The million-dollar price tag was a stretch, even for their new higher salaries.

"We can swing it, but it's way higher than our place in Austin," Jeff complained to John Statemon, one of the partners in his firm as they relaxed over a cocktail after work.

"You should bite off more than you can digest for the moment," John advised. "Hell, a partnership can't be too far on the horizon if you live up to your billing. Maybe you should be looking at two million dollar houses."

Jeff stopped in mid-sip and searched John's eyes for a glint of teasing. There was none.

Grace and Jeff shared a long vanity in the master bath with a large mirror. As Grace blow-dried her hair, she liked to watch in the mirror while Jeff shaved. She had always been attracted to his smooth, tanned face, his solidness and his short-cropped, corporate haircut already flecked liberally with gray. Too many of their male friends still sported the long, untidy hair of their college days, seeming to hope somehow to salvage their rapidly fading youth. Jeff had always seemed to rise above that need to find himself in some good-old-days fantasy. He lived with enthusiasm and eagerness for the moment, and he made a success of it.

Grace had met Jeff when she was working on the campus station and he was a third-year student at UT law school. They got off to a stormy beginning when they were learning to deal with each other's stubborn personalities. Their first few dates were peppered with barbs and trivial challenges, and Grace was actually surprised that the relationship continued at all. But for all the initial unease, she realized there remained something between them—a mutual admiration that carried through the rough patch and seemed to settle into a comfortable partnership. They established a weekly dating routine that surfaced a friendship through their mutual interests—current events, politics and good conversation.

They agreed to date exclusively that summer, but the relationship was tested that September as they met in a coffee shop for a study date.

"What are they?" she asked Jeff as he waved a handful of tickets in the air.

"My season tickets for Longhorn football," he crowed.

"I have to tell you, Jeff, I don't care for that stupid sport. I'd rather stay home and read a good book."

"I get that," he answered. "But you know I have to be at every home game. Can't miss my 'horns. And I don't want to go alone. Say you'll go with me."

She hesitated, shaking her head in mock disgust at his hangdog expression.

"Please?" he begged.

"All right," she agreed, a heavy dose of obvious resignation buried in the reply.

"Say it," he teased, throwing his arms around her in a gentle bear hug.

"I promise I'll go with you to the Texas football games," she giggled into his chest.

Grace never grew to appreciate the sport or even to understand much of it. But she learned to enjoy the communal atmosphere and fervor of the hometown crowd, and she and Jeff developed a stronger mutual affection at after-game parties in the Longhorn Pub near the stadium. They simply learned how to take pleasure in each other's company.

They were married in a simple ceremony, with just family and close friends looking on. As they began their family life, Grace was increasingly proud of Jeff. He had graduated from UT law school with honors and was immediately snapped up by an Austin firm. He went through the usual clerking step while studying for the bar, which he passed the first time through.

After baby Megan was born, their routines changed dramatically, as most new parents' do. Their social life essentially ended, except for occasional get-togethers with others who had similarly aged children. They converged at home after work, shed their office clothes and centered their activities on their daughter. They watched television, occasionally played cards or chess and less frequently made love. They argued more often over minutia and settled in like older married couples they had known and laughed about. And Grace saw less of her husband because they were both ascending up the ramp of promising careers that featured odd hours.

For all of Jeff's success and promise, the thing about him Grace liked most was that he was still basically a down-home good old boy from Abilene. She tolerated the requisite social climbing at charity dinners and endured the corporate events where the young lawyers had to impress the partners with which Scotch they drank and what cigars they carried. But when the suit came off and they hung out with friends at Spike's Sports Bar watching their Alma Mater play the hated Oklahoma Sooners, Grace liked him best.

Only one topic seemed to bring tension to their life—having a second child. Driving home from their ritual Sunday movie one soft October evening, Jeff initiated the familiar discussion.

"Tonight would be a good time to try for that little quarterback," he said as he drove. He glanced over in time to see her frown.

"You're keeping track of my cycles again?" she asked, annoyed.

He laughed.

"I don't want to give up my career," Grace harped. "And I know with two, you would be on me incessantly to stop working."

"Maybe you're right. I don't like seeing just one kid shuffled from home to daycare and back, much less several." Jeff sighed loudly. "Maybe some day we'll get a dog."

"Oh?" Grace registered surprise at how quickly he had surrendered, for this discussion usually escalated into an argument. "And who, Mr. Gleason, is going to bathe, feed and walk a dog?"

"Forget it," Jeff snapped and fell into silence.

The idea of another child or a pet died. Jeff didn't bring the topic up again.

His career took off, and he scored many big wins for his firm. When a larger Dallas firm came calling out of left field with a lucrative offer, fifteen years after their final discussion about expanding their family, Jeff phoned Grace at the newsroom as she was about to leave on a story.

"It's a bigger practice with a hell of a rich client base," Jeff told her.

She was excited. "It sounds like such a great opportunity."

"You think I should take it? What about your work at the station?"

"I can probably catch on at a Dallas station," she assured him. "I think my general manager has some connections over there. We could advance both of their careers."

With different work situations and higher ambitions in the new city, their mornings were especially frenetic. Both were preoccupied with their plans for the workday. Megan had learned to get her own cereal for breakfast and dress for school.

On this particular morning, still in her bra and panties, Grace leaned over the vanity going through her hair and make-up routine. She finished just as Jeff toweled off the remnants of shaving cream, and they simultaneously hurried into their large master bedroom. Grace pulled on her blouse and skirt while Jeff climbed into his "monkey suit," as he referred to it. He looked handsome in his classic pinstripe, she thought, feeling lucky to have landed such a smartly tailored man with exquisite taste that still didn't destroy his homespun manner.

But the reality of this morning woke her from the fantasy. Time was tight, and the Gleason household seemed disorganized as they scurried around to get ready.

"Jeff, honey, would you make sure Megan's up while I finish getting dressed for work?"

"I have to finish dressing, too," he answered, his voice flat and businesslike.

This was not the first time they had had this conversation. Over the years, Jeff had to Grace's dismay increasingly left the household work and parenting to her. Not only the increased workload, but the mere discussion about it, exhausted her. "You never help with her," Grace parroted the frequent complaint. "If you'll make sure she's up and getting ready, I'll drop her at school. I have to be at my meeting at eight-thirty. God knows, I'll be happy when we get her that car."

Jeff went to the dresser, pulled out his cuff links and began putting them on. His body language told her he couldn't be bothered. "You're the one who wanted a career," he said. "I have an important client meeting this morning. Can't be late." He pulled on his jacket, picked up his wallet and cell phone from the dresser and stuffed them into his pocket.

"Why do we always have to go through this?" she agonized. "You know my career's important to me. I'm doing what I've wanted since I was thirteen years old. How about some support?"

Jeff strode across the room to her as he buttoned his jacket, as if to say "enough," startling her. Even though he was grinning, he didn't seem amused. "You've wanted to do zoo stories since you were a teenager?" his tone was caustic. "And for the crap salary they pay you? I earn twice what you do, and I'll be a full partner soon, so you don't need to work."

Jeff had never made a secret of his wish that Grace were a stay-at-home mom. But never before could she recall him belittling her career. Years earlier, she had told him the story of being inspired by the Chicago newswoman. Jeff had listened with empathy at Grace's recitation of the woman's words and the positive effect they had had on a young eighth grader's ambitions.

As she revealed that innermost experience to law-student Jeff Gleason and told him how that message had crystallized from that moment what she wanted to do with her life, he had seemed genuinely moved. Grace was certain she saw liquid in those deep brown eyes of his, and she felt the reassuring touch of his strong hands on hers as he reached across the table in their student hangout.

Now, for the first time, she felt he had belied that important memory. Her husband seemed to be disrespecting everything she had worked for all of those years. She was shocked and hurt.

"Go on to your important meeting," she erupted. "I'll take care of our daughter, since you don't give a damn. And I'll still get to work on time. Go build your important career, Jeff, and when I'm anchoring the news and you're still writing wills and suing people for dog bites, maybe you'll give me some respect."

Angry and uncharacteristically bitter, Grace had seized the momentum. She stormed out of the room, leaving her husband standing there boiling. Even though she was working hard on measly assignments, she was not ready to throw in the towel. She would show Jeff and Lloyd Hamilton how tough a Chicago girl could be.

CHAPTER 3: Ned Moore

GRACE HAD LEARNED how to multi-function at an early age. She worked part-time in high school and still made excellent grades. In college, her tasks at the campus television station kept her hopping, but she balanced it with dating law student Jeff Gleason and keeping her course work on track for a grade point average that never dipped below three. And so on this day, although steamed at Jeff and with a full workday in the offing, she managed to drop Megan at school and still arrive at work on time for the morning meeting.

Not that she was eager to get started. She was souring on TXDA. The news decision process was wearing her down and her work there seemed meaningless. Lloyd Hamilton's reluctance to let her cover important stories was beginning to depress her. But she was still a professional, she reminded herself. There was a story to cover before noon at the Mary Kay Cosmetics plant about how lipstick is manufactured. She was sitting at her computer, researching the topic on the Internet, when Lloyd approached her. Matt was at his side, lugging a camera.

"Grace, this is the last thing I want to do," Lloyd said, "but I need for you to cover a press conference. The Dallas PD is going to update the Bonnie Vincent situation."

"You want me to cover it?" she asked, simultaneously confused and energized.

"No, I don't," Lloyd barked, perplexing her further. "Holthaus is all over us for that harassing phone call you made. I don't want you anywhere near this story. But we're short-handed. The press conference is scheduled for twenty minutes and everyone else is out on assignment."

"What about the Mary Kay feature?" Grace asked with

her tongue planted firmly in her cheek. "I've really been looking forward to it."

Lloyd looked perturbed, squinting at her and jutting out his famous stone jaw. She knew he would think she was being facetious but couldn't openly accuse her of it and risk being wrong. Taking the bait of barbs wasn't in Lloyd's makeup.

"Call their PR guy," he grunted. "He won't have any problem postponing it."

Grace glanced at Matt and grinned. She had managed to ignore the reprimand about Udo and stick her elbow in Hamilton's ribs over a lame assignment at the same time. Matt grinned back, and she knew he understood the "gotcha."

"Okay then, no problem," she said as she jumped up and grabbed a clipboard. I'm there already. Let's go, Matt."

She rushed for the door with the photographer chasing after her, but Lloyd called out and stopped them. "Just one thing, Grace," Lloyd ordered. "I don't want any of your hypothetical nonsense. I don't want to see any 'I know she's dead,' implications or 'I know that guy Holthaus did it' kind of hints, okay? Straight reporting of what they tell you. The facts, nothing more. You got it?"

Lloyd's admonition didn't faze Grace. This was the story she had fixated on for two days, and now she was going to cover it. She could feel her heart pumping like a geyser. She nodded and was out the door, with Matt scrambling to keep pace.

The Dallas Police Department was housed in a building completed less than a decade earlier on South Lamar Street to replace the old headquarters. The newer building was modern and sleek, its brick and glass and concrete structure of sharply delineated lines and angles screaming out "efficiency." Yet whenever she came here, Grace felt a strange and indefinable sense of disappointment, remembering the awesome feeling of having seen the stately old columned structure that had served the city on those fateful days when the country lost its leader and the world seemed to stand still.

She had visited the older building several times when she lived in Austin, first as a journalism student and later after her marriage to Jeff. That was when it was still the center of Dallas' police activity and a worldwide curiosity. It was a grand but aging limestone and brick edifice not far off the Thornton Freeway. Grace would never forget her last visit to the old building before it was replaced.

When their daughter was ten, she and Jeff had taken Megan there to see what the entire world had focused on for a November weekend nearly four decades earlier. They had waited until Megan was old enough to understand the enormity of what had once occurred in Dealey Plaza and later at this police headquarters building. Standing in front of it, their eyes had traced the storefronts across the street—a gaggle of restaurants and bail bond offices from which shocked patrons had strained to watch the mass of journalists and police swarm into the area.

"Right there, Megan," she said pointing at the parking garage entrance adjacent to the headquarters, "is where Jack Ruby ambushed Lee Oswald. Remember seeing the film in school?"

Megan nodded, her eyes wide.

"And see those huge limestone columns at the entrance?" Another nod. "They had bundles of television cables snaking up the side of the building into the police chief's office window—right up there."

"That's amazing," Jeff exclaimed.

"And enterprising," Grace added. "There was no precedent. Television newscasting was barely hitting its stride during that horrible time."

Most remarkable to Grace, as she held Megan's hand and silently surveyed the site, was that despite its moment in infamy, the building was still nothing more than a municipal police building.

On that day when the Gleasons climbed the front steps,

there was confusion and commotion that surrounds any major police facility. Law enforcement officials rushed in or out as they handled their business of investigations, arrests, releases and reports. A diverse sea of people streamed to and from the building—lawyers in vested suits, suspects answering summonses, citizens arriving to get or give information, file a complaint or solicit help.

The routine here was daily chaos, yet Grace knew it couldn't compare with the pandemonium of that day when Police Chief Curry announced he was holding the man who had assassinated the president and gunned down Dallas' own Patrolman J.D. Tippett.

Now, as Grace and Matt approached the newer, state-of-the-art center, she was struck by the reality that most Americans, like herself and Jeff and Megan and Matt, had not even been born on that day some historians referred to as the end of the nation's innocence.

Since that terrible time, the country had been through several wars. The highest and lowest financial times since the Great Depression. Exploding technology that was tweeting and texting. A raging debate over a sea change of government activism with only the stars of the fickle vagaries of history to steer by. Yet here she was, smack in the middle of the place that had bridged a tumultuous arc through time.

As they entered, Grace was reminded again of the antiquated lighting in the hallway she had walked with Jeff and Megan, dim and unfocused, lending a grayish aura to the cavernous space of the older building. By contrast, as she and Matt walked into the lobby of this modern place, everything was crisp and stark and bright.

They passed through security and jammed into a crowded elevator that took them to the second floor, and then hurried toward an open door of a room with light flooding out. The raucous din of camera equipment being set up and media people chattering met them as they went inside.

Grace squinted from the television lights washing through the room. About thirty chairs were set up in rows, and reporters were scrambling to get a good one.

"I have to set up over there," Matt indicated a space where several photographers were claiming space, and he headed that direction. "See you after."

"Sorry," Grace said as she frantically looked for a place to sit, elbowing past another reporter she didn't recognize and sliding into a seat.

Frank Wakefield, the Dallas chief of police, walked in and stopped near the podium as the noise began to settle. A small entourage of men and one woman, appearing somber and authoritative, stood behind the chief. He was flanked by Detective Ned Moore, whose downcast eyes and hands thrust deep in his pockets displayed his discomfort. Jerry Philmore, Ned's young partner, lagged a step behind the detective and glanced around the room wide-eyed, as if searching for the nearest exit.

Grace had never interviewed Chief Wakefield, but she had been around him on several civic occasions. She always thought he was a perfect central-casting chief. He was tall, graying and serious, but with a penchant for the dramatic. Immaculately dressed in his well-pressed uniform and military-shined shoes, he stepped to the podium. The camera lights made the blue pop in his eyes. He tapped the microphone and cleared his throat.

"Good morning," Chief Wakefield began. "Because of the intense public interest in the disappearance of Dallas businesswoman Bonnie Vincent, and the many media inquiries we have received, we have called this press conference to give you an update on the situation. Standing here with me are Detective Ned Moore, who's the lead on this case, and his partner Jerry Philmore."

Ned Moore took a half step forward and nodded. Philmore smiled, looking down at his shoes.

"Two days ago," the chief continued, "we learned of the

disappearance of Bonnie Vincent, the public relations executive for the Pearson Accounting firm. Detective Moore is carrying out an intense and thorough inquiry to determine whether or not foul play is involved. At this time we have no reason to believe there is."

Grace rolled her eyes and shook her head, the image of Holthaus and his homely sneer flashing through her mind.

"Meanwhile," the chief continued, "an all points bulletin has gone out advising law enforcement agencies across the country to watch both for Bonnie Vincent and her vehicle—a white, late-model Acura. We want the citizens and business community of Dallas to know we are bending every effort to find her and return her safely to her husband and her employer. And now, your questions..."

All the reporters clamored for attention, and Chief Wakefield pointed immediately at the Associated Press bureau chief, Steve Terwilliger. Steve was a Dallas veteran who had covered the Kennedy assassination for the daily newspaper just six months into his career. He had been gathering human interest feature material when the motorcade happened past the point where he was interviewing on-lookers—near the book depository in Dealey Plaza. After the gunshots and pandemonium, he had somehow managed to squeeze into a pool car with the United Press Association's inimitable Margaret Thompson where she and another reporter were fighting over the tethered car phone.

Being with a veteran group of reporters who sped to Parkland Hospital was a stroke of fortune for Terwilliger. The stories he wrote for months afterward earned him a Pulitzer, and when the Associated Press bureau chief retired, the news service went after him aggressively. They not only considered him an accomplished news-gatherer, but they also knew he had the most extensive non-government file on the assassination—six locked four-drawer file cabinets full of quotes, tapes, articles, photos and documents hidden somewhere in a public storage facility.

Now Terwilliger was the best-known journalist in the

city and nearly always got the first shot at such a press conference. "Chief Wakefield," he led off, "you said there is no foul play. What has led you to that conclusion?"

The chief nodded and turned immediately to Ned Moore. Grace thought he seemed too eager and relieved to relinquish the spotlight. Ned stepped uncertainly to the podium, tugging at his collar. He was in his early to mid-forties, Grace speculated, but his receding hairline and the inexpensive, outdated clothes that hung on him sloppily made him look older.

"I believe Chief Wakefield said we have no reason to believe there is foul play," cautioned Ned in a crusty voice, emphasizing the word "reason." As he spoke, Detective Moore squinted first into the TV lights and then gaped oddly, wide-eyed, at the reporters, like a quarterback expecting to get blitzed. Grace thought a press conference must be a new and unwelcome experience for him. "I say that simply because there is no evidence to support a foul play scenario," Ned continued. "There were no signs of struggle at the home or office, and we have no witnesses who saw anything unusual the last time they saw Bonnie Vincent. She's disappeared, plain and simple, and since her car is missing we don't know if she left under her own power, or someone else's. We will continue to treat it as a missing person case unless we have reason to believe otherwise."

"I understand she travels in her job," Samantha Haverty, a radio reporter, jumped in. "Have you checked her travel itinerary and with PDs of other cities she travels to?"

"We have," answered Ned Moore. "Nothing."

Grace liked the no-nonsense directness of this detective. She half-stood, waving her hand wildly, and Chief Wakefield pointed at her.

"Detective Moore, have you questioned Bonnie Vincent's husband, Mr. Holthaus?"

A slight smile crossed Ned's lips. "Of course we have. As far as we know, he was the last person to see her."

"What did he tell you?"

Before the detective could answer, an excited woman rushed into the room. She paused, scanning the crowd of reporters, and then ducked to avoid the cameras, tip-toed her way to the front and whispered something to Terwilliger.

Chief Wakefield and Ned Moore both frowned at the intrusion, but Ned continued. "What did Mr. Holthaus tell us? That she left for work at her usual time, following her normal routine. Mr. Holthaus first learned she was missing when they called from work to find out why she hadn't shown up."

"I'll bet he did," Grace whispered under her breath to no one in particular. A newspaper reporter next to her eyed her warily.

Suddenly, Terwilliger and the woman scrambled past the rest of the press corps and sped toward the door. As he hurried by, Grace grabbed Terwilliger's arm. "What's going on?" Grace whispered.

"Holthaus," Terwilliger said as he turned toward the exit. "He's going to make a statement."

"Where?"

"Their home. Washington Street condos."

A buzz ran through the group of reporters and they all scrambled for the door, with the chief and Ned glancing at each other helplessly. Grace stayed behind, stalling, motioning across the room for Matt to wait. He nodded and began dismantling his camera equipment.

As the chief and his entourage left with Ned Moore and Jerry Philmore following, Grace rushed up to the detective and grabbed his arm. Startled, Ned stopped and stared at her inquisitively.

"Grace Gleason, Detective. TXDA-TV," Grace spoke softly so no other reporters who might have stayed could hear.

"I'm not doing interviews," Ned said in a clipped manner, his face tense and slightly flushed. "You media guys had your chance, and you ended the conference."

"That's okay," Grace assured him and thought she

noticed that he relaxed a bit. She gave him her friendliest sorority girl smile. "I'm going to drive over to that circus at Holthaus's place. I simply wanted you to know I'm positive he's responsible for his wife's disappearance," she said as casually as she might tell someone what she had for lunch.

Ned's eyebrows went upward and his mouth opened in an amused half-grin. "You've got the case solved?" he asked, his tone partly amused, partly sardonic. "You know Bonnie's whereabouts?"

"I don't know where she is," said Grace, feeling a little sheepish. "But I'm afraid she's dead and he's responsible."

Ned frowned at Grace. She could tell from his baffled expression that he didn't know quite what to make of her. She knew her first impression was often brash, and she had worked hard at infusing her manner and words with a ring of sincerity and innocence. She hoped now she could succeed at making the detective want to hear more.

"Ned—can I call you Ned?" Grace plunged on. "I knew Bonnie and Udo in Austin before they moved here. Not real well, but enough to understand what kind of people they were. Udo never treated her right. I don't understand why she stayed with him, but I also know she wouldn't have run out on him. Trust my instinct and watch the guy."

Ned Moore had a reputation for not dwelling on the soft side of things when there was hard-nosed work to be done. He rarely stayed around to hear people's theoretical speculation when he could be out collecting evidence, sorting through clues, solving things. His directness and disdain for game-playing had come to him honestly from his South St. Louis upbringing where toughness and dirty hands were highly valued. Because his family was one of the few non-Italian, non-Catholic families living in the section known widely and, not-so-fondly, as Dago Hill, young Ned and his older brother Carl were drawn into constant scuffles with the Menotti boys, and the Carduccis, and the DeRosas. They grew tough. They learned to hold their own in a fight, and eventually the others left Ned and his big brother Carl alone.

Their father was a stonemason, and there was plenty of work. Nearly every block of all St. Louis neighborhoods boasted homes built of brick. Carl and Ned learned the trade from their dad at an early age, but Ned wasn't very interested. While Carl worked with their father after school for spending money, Ned sneaked out and played sports. He was in the land of Berra and Garagiola, where baseball was more a religion than a sport, and Ned turned out to be a natural hitter.

"I like playing baseball, Dad, and I'm pretty good," he boasted at the dinner table. "Even the Italian guys want me on their teams."

But Ned suffered his father's barbs. "I can't believe I've got a son who's lazy and not preparing for a future like Carl here," he scolded.

Ned confided to his brother that he was more intrigued by his grandfather's profession—law enforcement—than mixing mud and stacking stones.

"Why would I want to carry a hod around when I could pack heat?" he laughed to Carl one morning on the way to school.

"Pack heat?" Carl scoffed. "Who are you, Clint Eastwood?"

"I like Clint Eastwood," Ned defended. "He's tough like Grandpa."

Ned's mother's father was one of those grizzled old veterans of the St. Louis force. He had pounded a beat in North Saint Louis County for more than twenty-five years. After his granddad retired, Ned seized on any opportunity to sit and listen to the old man's stories about chasing bank robbers and raiding shot houses in the projects. Ned told anyone who would listen that he wanted to be a cop.

That ambition nearly didn't come to fruition. His grandfather could have helped pave the way for him, but the old man died suddenly when Ned was fourteen. As his eighteenth birthday approached, just before high school graduation, Ned had to make a choice. There was no money for college, so he had to decide between taking up the masonry trade or joining the military.

"What should I do?" he asked his high school counselor a week before commencement.

"Well, the service seems like a possible route into the profession your grandfather inspired in you," the counselor advised.

So the older Moore brother, Carl, who had worked side-by-side with their father throughout his teens, continued on in the trade. Ned, who had opted out of hard labor in favor of playing sports, chose the United States Navy.

"I've never been anywhere," he told the Navy recruiter.

"Good reason to join," the recruiter said. "We'll send you around the world and back, but you have to be okay with sea duty."

"Sir, seeing the world from the deck of a ship appeals to me a helluva lot more than digging trenches and maybe getting shot at," Ned mused. "Or pushing papers around some office at an Army base in Podunk, Oklahoma."

Ned began his basic training that summer. He plunged into it enthusiastically, and he performed above average. Some of his fellow recruits hated boot camp. Most of them were soft and lazy, having spent their high school days camped on their asses playing video games. Ned was in great condition from playing sports and helping his father on occasion, and he passed the Navy's physical training test the first day he arrived at Great Lakes.

He seemed to thrive on the physical activities, the skills tests, marching and drill, and weapons firing. He responded to every new task put in front of him and his fellow recruits with enthusiasm, as if it was an exciting adventure.

"It's like trying to hit a new southpaw in town who has a smoking fastball," he told one of his mates at mess one evening.

"Huh?" his fellow swabbie squinted at the eager trainee

from St. Louis.

"Yeah, or fielding a hard-hit liner at your feet with the game on the line. I like a challenge, always have."

"You're nuts, Moore," his friend laughed. "You're going to volunteer for something and get your ass shot off."

The recruit division commander, whose job appeared to be to demean and demonize his minions, was roundly hated among Ned's class. Yet to Ned he seemed no more gruff nor scary than his own father was when the old man's hackles were raised.

As Ned neared the completion of basic, he scored high on the final grueling "battle stations" exercise that tested everything he had learned packed into a twelve-hour simulated shipboard emergency.

"It seemed fun to me," he told the astonished commander when it was over.

The eight weeks of basic had flown by, and Ned was eager to sail. He enlisted in the fireman apprentice training program, attended a course in shipboard operations and was transported to the amphibious assault ship USS Guam.

"That suits me just fine," he told Carl when he called home with the news. "I joined this man's Navy to have new experiences."

Ned hadn't known in this time of relative peace around the world that President Reagan was about to send him into harm's way. It was by this happenstance of fate that he saw his first hostile action.

The Guam, as the lead ship of Amphibious Squadron Four, participated in the invasion of Grenada. Ned was one of fewer than ten thousand United States military personnel sent to fight the battle known as Operation Urgent Fury.

Ned's duties aboard the Guam included a variety of functions focused on the mechanical operation of the ship, from repairing and maintaining equipment to refueling operations.

Before the Guam arrived at Grenada, Ned distinguished himself when he found an oil leak aboard the ship and recruited an impromptu crew to fix it. Ned's quick actions in quelling the dangerous leak would later win him a Navy League Award. The citation noted he had "...averted a potential disaster as the U.S. Navy went to war."

He seemed drawn toward the dramatic, but he also handled adverse situations as routinely and unemotionally as changing a light bulb.

"Do you know what job I like the most?" Ned asked his fellow apprentice Harry Devaney. They were taking a smoke break on deck as the Guam steamed toward the tiny Windward island near Venezuela.

"Yeah. Liberty," Devaney joked.

"No, asshole. Standing watch."

"Jesus. You're kidding."

"No, I like it," Ned laughed. "Plus, getting to take part in damage control during emergencies."

"You're talking out of your butt crack."

Ned continued, "And drill. I like it when we have drill."

"You're completely insane, Moore," Harry laughed.

"I guess those duties make me feel closer to my granddad, you know? Closer to the law enforcement and discipline that made up his entire life."

Ned and Harry had no clue on that night, as they sailed through the Caribbean Sea chatting about Navy life, that they would soon be listening to the deafening sounds of pitched battle.

The ship's commanding officers were in the dark about their mission until less than two days before the invasion, and the battle was imminent before enlisted personnel such as Ned and Harry knew the full story. When they responded to two o'clock reveille in the wee morning hours of October twenty-five, 1983, they swarmed with other swabbies and marines to the mess deck. Ammunition was being staged for transport to the other ships of their amphibious group, and they would soon be launching helicopters flown by young marines into turbulent weather and testy opposition forces.

Ned was excited and happy to be seeing action, but for the weeklong operation he was too busy doing his job to revel in it. The American force met some stiff resistance and lost some lives, but it was a short-lived and popular success.

The Grenada invasion was the first of a series of deployments for Ned. Immediately after Operation Urgent Fury, the Guam sailed to Beirut as part of a multi-national peacekeeping force during the Lebanese Civil War.

The two sailors, Ned and Harry, now best friends, watched smoke rise above the ancient city late in the afternoon from the deck of the Guam.

"I guess we'll be loading up with refugees tomorrow," Harry said, pulling on a cigarette.

"It's hard to believe such a beautiful place is a magnet for war," Ned complained.

"The whole world is going to hell," Harry grumbled. "I can't wait to get out after my four-year hitch."

"You're getting out?" Ned exclaimed in surprise.

"My high school sweetheart and a good career in retail sales management are waiting for me back home," Harry responded. "That experience in Grenada had the direct opposite effect on me than it did on you, buddy. You relish the sailing and the military action, but all it does is make me homesick."

"Your time isn't up yet, pal," Ned laughed. "Let's enjoy ourselves while we can. I can't understand how anyone wouldn't love this life."

In a brief span of time, a young but battle-hardening St. Louis native had visited two parts of the world he could never have imagined seeing a year earlier. He was on his way to a path toward advancement to Petty Officer and a career that would take him to many nations and U.S. ports.

After eight years, Ned's journey found him in the Norfolk Shipyard, a Chief Petty Officer assigned as the regional engineer responsible for shore maintenance activity in hazardous spaces—cargo holds, pump rooms and duct keels.

Because of the dangers of fires, explosions or other accidents in such areas, Ned's position carried enormous responsibility for the lives and safety of many sailors.

Ned kept up with his family through occasional telephone conversations with his brother; he wouldn't have much to talk about with his parents. On Carl's twenty-eighth birthday, Ned called and they chatted for nearly an hour. "I really like the Navy, Carl," he said, as they were about to sign off. "I like the responsibility and the respect they give you. I think I might just stick around for a twenty-year career."

"You could always come back to St. Louis and help me build fucking brick walls," Carl growled and then laughed.

"Don't hold your breath, big brother. Happy birthday."

Ned's career strategy was waylaid by another turn of fate with a telephone call from Harry Devaney. During their time together, on shipboard and at liberty, Harry had heard all of Ned's stories about his grandfather and his friend's boyhood fantasy of law enforcement. Now Harry delivered news that his pal from St. Louis couldn't ignore.

"Hey, old Buddy, I just got wind that the Dallas Police Department is hiring," Harry said.

"So?" Ned asked, trying to sound nonchalant about news that was more than arousing his interest.

"A guy I know over there said they're giving favorable treatment and training to recruits with military backgrounds. Hell, with your record and your ambition, you'd be a natural. And we'd pick up as buddies where we left off."

Ned could live out his boyhood dream after all. In a matter of months, he said goodbye to the Navy and hello to Dallas.

"I like this city," he exclaimed one Saturday afternoon two weeks after moving there as he and Harry rolled some lines at the Classic Bowling Lanes. "The winters are mild and the women are spectacular."

"Speaking of which," Harry said, taking a sip from his long neck beer. "There's someone Melinda wants you to meet."

Harry and his wife Melinda introduced Ned to one of her college friends, and three months later Ned proposed to Martha Jones. Like Ned's mother, Martha was pretty and shy and all he could want in a wife and potential mother of his children.

Ned moved up fast in the Dallas PD. His superiors gave him high ratings on skills and work ethic. He was praised in write-ups for his no-nonsense value system and dedication to getting criminals off the streets.

When Ned made detective, he was assigned to the vice squad. He jumped into the action with zeal; it was a welcome departure from responding to domestic squabbles and arresting two-bit hustlers. Busting drug rings and hauling in pimps for exploiting underage girls made his work more rewarding, and he was good at it.

Two years later, working homicide, Ned's partner requested a transfer to the canine division. Ned's new partner, Jerry Philmore, had been a detective for only a few weeks, and Ned considered him raw and naive. Barely three weeks later, they were assigned to a missing person case—one that Ned told Jerry could mean real trouble.

As Ned and Jerry reviewed the case that first day, the elder detective sternly counseled Jerry against speculation. "We can't jump to conclusions, Jerry, until we have all the facts," he warned. "No matter what the signs tell us, we might be wrong, and in the Dallas political climate we're in right now, we have to be dead solid certain."

"Udo Holthaus seems to have a shady side to him," Jerry offered.

"True, but that might only mean that his wife had taken all the abuse she could and walked out, not that the man did her in," Ned cautioned.

Now he was getting his ears bent by a reporter whose suspicions matched those he and partner Jerry Philmore had already discussed. Ned considered Grace's comments patiently and a twinkle gleamed in his expression as if he were about to give the reporter an education. "Don't worry, Grace," he said in the firmest manner he could muster, "we're watching Udo Holthaus. But we need a few things before we can come down on him too hard."

"Such as?" she seemed eager.

"Such as a body," Ned said, adding, "and proof of a murder. And when we have that, maybe some evidence that tells us who did it."

He turned to go but then paused thoughtfully and turned back. Grace had a surprised and disappointed look that made Ned grin, as if he had silently predicted her reaction. "I'll tell you what, Grace," Ned continued. "If...when...you solve this missing person case, call my partner Jerry here. He's been a detective all of three weeks and can use the experience."

Ned tossed her a "don't bother me again" look and motioned for Jerry to go with him. Grace had almost forgotten Philmore was there. He had remained silent and all but invisible, hanging in the background like a busboy waiting for orders from the waiter.

Jerry shrugged helplessly at Grace and nodded acknowledgement of his partner's signal to follow, like an obedient toddler following his daddy.

"See you around, Grace," Ned said over his shoulder as he walked away, chuckling quietly. She felt disappointment as she watched the detectives exit, but only for a fleet instant. Udo Holthaus's condo was twenty minutes away, and she had to be there for the show.

CHAPTER 4: No Longer Missing

MANY OF Udo Holthaus' and Bonnie Vincent's neighbors peered out of their condo windows, gazing aghast at the sight on their street. Several emerged from their front doors and drifted curiously toward the chaos descending on Number three-oh-five at the end of the block. Two couples who lived in houses across the street stood on their front lawns, sharing looks of grim disapproval as the onslaught of reporters' cars and television trucks interrupted the solitude of their usually placid subdivision and the predictable routines of their lives.

The media hounds invading the neighborhood parked their vehicles wherever a curb space allowed and sprinted toward the front yard where Udo Holthaus stood, solemn and uncomfortable, waiting for them all to congregate and settle. He looked haggard, his eyes dark and tired, his shoulders slumped more than usual.

Camera lights went on and flooded his face, and microphones were thrust at him like a sword in a duel. Blinking from the brightness and straining to smile, Udo spoke nervously in a halting, stammering cadence with a tremor of emotion.

"Thank...thank you all for coming. If...anyone...knows anything about Bonnie's whereabouts," he stumbled, "please come forward. Bonnie...Bonnie doesn't deserve anything bad. She...she's a beautiful, loving person, and I can't imagine anyone would want to hurt her. Please, if you had something to do with her...her disappearance, have some mercy and step forward. Return her to...to her loving home and husband."

Udo appeared to break up and covered his eyes with one hand. *A peculiar performance,* thought Grace, *given his experience as a newsman.* To her, it seemed rehearsed.

As Udo finished the statement, a dozen reporters shouted at him. He held up his shaky hands and pointed at one.

"Mr. Holthaus, where were you when your wife disappeared?" asked Grace's rival from WAFF television.

"Right here, after breakfast two days ago," he said, clearing his throat. "We...we left home at the same time in separate cars. That's the...the last time I saw her."

"Where do you work, sir?" asked the Associated Press's Terwilliger. Grace considered it a strange question, since Steve surely would have known the answer.

Udo hesitated, his gray eyes staring into space. "Oh, uh...uh...at the state department...department of motor vehicles," he sputtered. "Just up the street from where Bonnie worked."

The instant Udo said the words, every sense in Grace's body sprang alive. The hair seemed to crawl on the back of her neck. She ran her mind over his answer, re-traced the words in her memory and felt the spine-tingling sensation intensify. "Mr. Holthaus, did you say worked?" she stepped forward and out-shouted several other questions.

Holthaus turned toward her and his gray eyes widened, as he realized for the first time that the reporter he had known in Austin was there. "Pardon?" he asked, frowning sourly.

"Worked!" Grace punctuated, feeling the adrenaline pump through her body like steam through a pressure cooker. "You said she worked at Pearson. Don't you mean works?"

Udo stood silent, stunned for a moment, appearing to scramble for a response. "My...my wife has disappeared," his answer gushed out, sounding alarmed and panicked to Grace. "Right now she doesn't work anywhere until she returns. I...I just want her back, and whoever knows where she is needs to step forward. That's all. Thank you."

The pace of Udo's closing words had accelerated more and more, like a child quick-stepping toward the high board at the city pool. He turned toward his front door, cast a frown back over his shoulder at Grace and then hurried inside, slamming the door behind him.

A collective murmur ran through the cluster of reporters at Udo's abrupt dismissal. Several moved toward their cars, and photographers were dismantling their lights and packing their cameras into nylon cases. Grace stood stock-still, too stunned to make notes. She glanced across the lawn and noticed that Steve Terwilliger was also standing motionless, staring back at her, his bushy eyebrows raised in what she took to be enlightenment and praise.

The stories ran that night, and after that the Bonnie Vincent missing person case faded away like yesterday's sports scores. Two days later, the lives of Grace Gleason and Ned Moore and Udo Holthaus unexpectedly aligned in a spectacular collision course.

The sun was casting a hint of daytime over rooftops. The flashing lights of three police cars created an eerie sight in the dimness inside the massive concrete parking garage of the Dallas-Fort Worth International Airport.

A seven-year-old sedan was barreling through the entry gate toward the garage with its lights on and flasher affixed to the roof on the driver's side. Ned was driving, and Jerry Philmore was sitting shotgun. Ned gave a quick look at Jerry leaning forward against his seat belt, staring anxiously through the windshield like a prisoner about to be executed.

Turning back to his task as they sped into the garage entrance, Ned said, "I've been on the force for sixteen years—six as a detective—but every time I get to a scene like this it's the same damned excitement all over again."

"It's pretty exciting, all right," Jerry said. "But it's your driving that's scaring the crap out of me."

Ned ignored the comment and went on, "I don't care what it is—hell, it could even be a routine drug bust—the disruption puts a charge in the air."

Philmore turned and looked at his mentor and took a deep breath, trying to relax. "You get a real kick out of this part, huh? Not knowing what we're going to find."

Ned steered around the first turn with the vehicle's tires protesting and gunned it up the ramp toward level two. "That arson case we worked last week—it destroyed that business, right? But to me the charred remains were a blank canvass—a total mystery to be figured out. I like that kind of challenge."

He pushed the sedan around another turn and they hurtled toward level three. "But it's these homicide cases that really energize you—a body in the woods or tossed in a dumpster. There's nothing repulsive or tedious about that, just a string of puzzles stretched out in front of us waiting to be solved. When I was a kid, I remember my grandfather telling me there's nothing more exciting or rewarding than someone else inviting you into their lives 'cause they need help. I think about what he said every time I start a case." He smiled. "Almost makes the low pay worthwhile."

The two detectives screeched to a halt behind one of the police cars and jumped out, the steam of their breath visible in the frosty air. Ned looked around and shivered, and then with Jerry on his heels he hurried to a white Acura ringed by several uniformed officers and an airport security guard.

As they approached, a sergeant named McPherson turned and greeted them. "Hey, Detective," McPherson said to Ned, ignoring Jerry.

Ned acknowledged the sergeant with a nod. "That her car? Bonnie Vincent?"

"Plate checks out," Sergeant McPherson said. "No sign of her."

Ned and Jerry pulled on latex gloves and walked to the car. Ned peeked through the driver-side window and squinted inside, then walked around the car and carefully opened the front passenger side door, looking in. He opened the glove compartment and rummaged through some papers, and then opened the back door and looked inside—up and down, back and forth.

"No sign of struggle, no blood visible," the detective

said, shivering a little from the cold and excitement. He went behind the car and tried the trunk, with Jerry following his every move, observing.

"Locked," Ned noted.

"Want us to pop it?" McPherson asked.

Ned nodded. Sergeant McPherson went to one of the squad cars and returned with a screwdriver. He inserted it into the trunk lock and snapped it with a slight grunt. The lid partly opened, and McPherson stepped back as Ned pushed the trunk lid up like a swimmer testing the water with a toe. Ned recoiled. Detectives are no strangers to discovering dead victims, but Ned looked momentarily startled to see a nude female body crammed inside the Acura trunk in a fetal position. He nodded at Medical Examiner Brad Nessler who had just arrived. Nessler reached in, pulling back the woman's hair. Ned and Jerry stood behind him, gaping over the studious-looking man's shoulder at the naked corpse.

"No blood at all," Ned said, motioning to Jerry who scrambled a pad and pencil out of his pocket and started taking notes. "Just that nasty, purplish bruise on her neck."

Nessler pulled a pair of tweezers from his pocket, reached in and extracted something from the victim's mouth. He slowly unfolded a pair of woman's panties, bowed his neck in reaction and frowned, then carefully placed them in a plastic bag. As Ned retrieved a small flashlight from his pocket and shone it into the trunk, the medical examiner began snapping photographs. Two officers started to string yellow crime scene tape around the area. The activity attracted the curiosity of people who had arrived to park, and then of several reporters who had learned there was a story brewing at the airport and had arrived in a flurry.

"Who found the car?" Ned called out from behind the trunk.

The airport guard stepped toward him. "I did, about twenty minutes ago," he told the detective. "We got the APB so were running a check on cars that had been parked here a while, looking for a white Acura. I ran the plates, and when it matched your bulletin I called it in."

Ned turned to Jerry. "Have the car dusted. Looks like we might have a murderer to track down. Possibly a rapist, too."

"Or maybe a vampire?" Jerry chimed.

Ned frowned, his head cocked, and he glanced around to determine who else had heard the remark. One of the officers was chuckling and looking in their direction, but the remark seemed to have gotten past the rest.

"Sorry," Jerry quickly apologized. "I just...it looks like a bite mark, see?"

Ned had already alerted his superiors that the new detective needed to get control of his social side. "I like the guy, Lieutenant, but what Philmore has in the street smarts department, he lacks in personal discipline," he had said one evening when he was leaving the building and the head of the division stepped out from his office to ask about Philmore's progress. "I'll have to mentor him in those areas as well as detective work," Ned went on. "He'll need to learn when to stifle those thoughtless, spontaneous remarks he makes. And not just because they made him look foolish. Someday a casual comment at the wrong time might jeopardize an investigation or an arrest."

"Maybe you should cut him a little slack, Detective," the lieutenant said flatly, turning back into his office. Ned grimaced at the comment but didn't respond.

Jerry was the newest detective in the division. When a decision had been made to expand the detective ranks and stay abreast of a rising crime rate, he was one of the young patrolmen identified to shore up the ranks. After just three years on the force, not only had he performed meritoriously in several dangerous situations, but he had also tested extremely high in critical thinking, logic and reason. And he had eagerly accepted promotion to detective status.

About that same time, Ned's partner transferred, and

the department supervisors considered Ned's veteran tenure a good match for a green rookie. They assigned Jerry to work with him.

Ned pulled Jerry close, lowering his voice as if not wanting to embarrass the junior detective. With the flashing lights of the patrol cars reflecting on their faces, he spoke sternly. "I may not be a grizzled old veteran," he lectured Jerry, "but I've been on the scene for a few years, and you've only been my partner for eighteen days. Why not keep your mouth shut and watch. Maybe you'll learn something, okay?"

Jerry nodded, blushing deep crimson. Ned watched the young man's face fall as the words sank in, and so he relaxed, laughed and slapped his partner's shoulder good-naturedly. Jerry's relieved expression seemed to say he appreciated his mentor's understanding.

As they were speaking, an ambulance had pulled up. Two medical examiner transport team members were emerging from it. They pulled a gurney from the back and pulled it toward the Acura.

"Let's go see Udo Holthaus," Ned said to Jerry. They walked hurriedly, purposefully toward their car, and as they passed the pack of reporters Grace stepped out from the group.

"Ned. Is it Bonnie?" She said it quietly, trying to keep out of earshot of the other reporters.

"Probably," Ned answered. "I can't say officially until we get a positive identification. But off the record? It's the woman on the posters."

He started to move on, but then he paused, looking pensive. He walked back to Grace and asked, "You said you knew her, right?"

Grace nodded yes, her interest heightened.

Detective Moore stood still for a moment, scratching his head, appearing to be contemplating. Then he abruptly looked straight into Grace's eyes as if making a pact. "Okay," he said. "I have to go talk to the sergeant about his report. Listen to me,

Gleason. I do not want you to go over there and interfere with the M.E. transport team before they remove the body. You do, and those officers will cuff you."

Grace thought Ned said it with far too much finality. She looked for a wink or some other sign, but there was none; Ned offered a slight grin and walked over to the sergeant, turning his back on her. Grace was certain she understood his meaning, but she also knew he was right—that if she crossed the crime scene line, any of the officers could arrest her if they wanted to. *How could I be sure,* she wondered, *that they knew the detective actually wanted me to have a look?*

Grace left the other reporters stealthily and moved to an area near the Acura, taking pains to stay behind the crime scene tape as she planned what her move should be. She made a tentative motion as if she were about to duck under the tape, but an officer stepped hastily toward her, held his hand out and shook his head with a warning in his expression. She was relieved to see that he hadn't reached for his handcuffs.

She saw the transport team move to the trunk and wrap the body in a sheet. Grace strained to watch, careful not to bother the tape. As the team lifted the body slightly to get the sheet around it, she stretched even harder and managed a brief glimpse before they could cover the victim's face. The sight sent a shock through her. Gaping at the gray-bluish face with its pasty eyelids closed and mouth hanging half-open, Grace stepped back, horrified, her hands clasped over her mouth. She pivoted almost automatically toward Ned, who had turned to glance briefly over his shoulder in her direction.

She nodded yes to Ned with her hands stifling a cry and her eyes as wide as the dawning Texas sky. She knew she wouldn't sleep again until she had more information.

CHAPTER 5: Finally, A Good Story

IT WAS SHAPING UP to be a frenzied year for America in the news, domestically and abroad. The economy and stock market had tanked, and a housing crisis that had gripped the country continued, unresolved. The country was at war in the Middle East and kept a wary eye out for another attack by terrorists.

In Dallas, the city and county elections were beginning to crank up and had already grown contentious. Meanwhile, a reporter named Gleason was struggling mightily to gain traction on the news staff of WTXS television.

Grace realized she had pushed the station's news director as far as she could without his losing patience and giving up on her. And yet she knew she was capable of much more than the station's management had permitted her to do so far.

She was working in her cubicle when she noticed Lloyd Hamilton approach Mitchell Court at his desk nearby. It was a familiar sight; Lloyd nearly always favored Mitchell over his fellow reporters and rarely stopped by her desk for anything.

"Mitchell," she heard Hamilton say, "the autopsy report came in on the Bonnie Vincent murder. Looks like she died from strangulation. I want you to get over there and interview the medical examiner."

Grace felt the words like a gigantic slap in the face. Her brain told her to stay silent, but her emotions wouldn't permit that. She jumped instinctively out of her chair, as if someone had shot her out of a giant rifle.

"Wait a minute, Lloyd," Grace protested, walking halfway to Mitchell's desk, her instincts shouting at her to sound helpful and not confrontational. "That's my story. I'll do it."

"Who said it was your story?" Lloyd responded

defensively. "Because you covered a press conference?"

The comment rankled her. *Stay calm,* she told herself.

"Plus, the remote on the discovery of the body," she retaliated, feeling marginalized by the slight but endeavoring to stay composed. "I've been following this piece from the beginning, and you know it."

"We were short-handed," said Lloyd, crossing his arms and sticking out that familiar, stubborn lower lip. "Now we're not."

Mitchell had been listening, looking amused. For months, he had watched this fencing match between the news director and his fellow ambitious reporter. Although he had been at TXDA for five years and was considered by management to be the fair-haired boy, Mitchell had told Grace a day earlier he was pulling for her.

They were reviewing some footage for a story, and suddenly he stopped the tape. She looked up, curious.

"I want you to know something," he said, catching her off-guard. "I think you're a savvy newswoman." He laughed when the comment made her turn scarlett. "I'm serious, Grace. You're thorough, inquisitive and normally unflappable. If I'm ever the main guy here, I want you on my side."

Lloyd had hired Mitchell away from a small station in San Antonio. He had distinguished himself as a first-class business reporter with a series on a complicated business rivalry. The pitched battle between a San Antonio media giant trying to revolutionize the concert recording industry, and competing companies claiming patent infringements, had intrigued Mitchell. He did his homework, networked for contacts inside both warring parties, and became an expert on what became a national story. The network picked up Mitchell's series as well known concert performers became caught in a whipsaw between the various companies fighting over their recording rights.

It could easily have been a drab story. But Mitchell

made it clear that mega-millions of profits involving some of the entertainment world's top stars were at stake. His characterization of the fight attracted the interest of the industry, from the popular "Entertainment News Scene" program to the *Hollywood Daily* newsmagazine.

Mitchell reported on the complex business topic with such understanding, objectivity and clarity that he caught TXDA management's eye, and Richard Stone advised Lloyd to make him an offer when they had an opening.

"It's more than his fluid and informative writing style," Richard told Lloyd when they discussed Mitchell's possible candidacy. "He has a sort of authoritative, mature on-camera presence that will one day make the young man a surefire anchor."

When Lloyd drove to San Antonio and offered the job, Mitchell eagerly accepted. "I've been wanting to move to a larger market for quite a while now," he told the news director. "Dallas will do fine."

"What about your wife?" Lloyd asked. "Any problems with her moving?"

Mitchell smiled. "Sheila likes to shop. Like I said, Dallas will do fine."

After they had moved, settling near the Galleria Mall at Sheila's insistence, he often met her after work at Casa Poco, a small Tex-Mex restaurant near the shopping center. "I know they think I'm a good reporter," he told Sheila two weeks after the move as he sipped a margarita before ordering dinner. "But the thing that helps me the most is that I have a sort of knack for creating an affinity for my management."

"Affinity for management?" she puzzled.

"It's like a relationship skill. In corporate circles they call it managing up. I don't try for it, and I don't think it's anything you can learn. You just have it or you don't. It helps me with the general manager."

"What about Lloyd Hamilton?" she quizzed, appearing intensely interested in all aspects of her husband's work.

"Lloyd? He seems to like my reporting skills. But more importantly, I think he's just proud that he's the one who hired me."

As Grace and Lloyd argued in the newsroom over the Vincent assignment, Mitchell held back and watched the parry and thrust between his news director and a fellow reporter. Grace had a feeling her colleague was cheering for her, given his vote of confidence the previous day. Bickering with Lloyd, she remembered Mitchell's words and hoped he would side with her.

He did.

"Lloyd, let her have the interview," Mitchell said, glancing sideways to catch Grace's reaction. "I don't mind. I've got to cover the Dallas Trust Bank merger today, anyway."

Lloyd's shoulders slumped, and he turned toward Grace and nodded in surrender. "All right. I don't want you twisting the guy around, Grace," he instructed. "No speculation. Straight questions, straight reporting. Nothing more."

Grace beamed and watched Lloyd start walking back toward his office. He had only gone a few steps when she turned and mouthed "thank you" to a widely grinning Mitchell Court.

It was nearly six o'clock that evening, and rush hour was well under way in Dallas. Streetlights were coming on, and cars were streaming through the city as executives, office workers and laborers closed their brief cases and toolboxes and began to crowd onto the surface streets and freeways that took them home.

The main parkway feeding into Brookwood Acres was always jammed, but once Jeff Gleason reached the huge iron-gated entrance to the neighborhood, it was clear sailing down Brook Close, then right on Brookwood Place and finally left on Brook Drive and the cul de sac where Grace's car sat in the driveway.

"I'm home," Jeff called as he entered the kitchen from the garage. The television was blaring in the den, and as he entered the room Grace bounced out of her chair and kissed him lightly. She put a finger on her lips and motioned him in, returning quickly to her chair.

Jeff followed her in. He looked around for Megan, but he imagined she was sequestered in her room with her stereo blaring behind closed doors, the hallmark of all teenagers. He set down his brief case and sank heavily into his recliner as he realized it was Grace's voice on the television news.

"I'm here with the Dallas County medical examiner, Brad Nessler." Grace was saying. *"Have you determined the cause of Bonnie Vincent's death?"* She held a mike in front of her interviewee as "Medical Examiner Brad Nessler" was superimposed on the screen.

"Yes we have. Bonnie Vincent died from strangulation."

"Were there any signs of a struggle?"

"There may have been a struggle. In addition to the strangulation bruising, I found what we believe is a bite mark on the side of her neck."

"Can you match the bite mark with dental records?"

"That remains to be seen. We're searching for a match, but we're still trying to determine if there's enough definition to be able to do that."

"Was there anything else unique about what you found?"

"I couldn't determine the exact time of death because the cold temperatures of the last few days had an effect of preserving the body. Also, there was something quite a bit unusual for a case like this. It appeared that the body had been scrubbed clean."

"Any idea who might do such a thing? The profile? More likely a stranger? Or someone who knew her?

"In the majority of cases like this, it's usually someone who knew the victim. In this particular case, who can be sure?"

On screen, Grace turned and looked directly into the camera.

"That's the medical examiner of Dallas County with the

latest on the Bonnie Vincent murder case. I'm Grace Gleason for channel seven on-the-spot news."

Grace tossed the remote to Jeff who switched to a basketball game already in progress.

"Unbelievable," Grace said, disgusted.

"What's wrong? You did a good job," Jeff responded. "Why do you always have to be so hard on yourself ?"

"They edited out my final comments," she complained.

A "here we go again" look crossed Jeff's face. "Let me guess—the part where you asked Holthaus to confess?" he said, not bothering to stifle the caustic tone.

Grace didn't appreciate the sarcasm and frowned at him. "I simply said if the normal profile was people who knew her, we would be taking a look at those closest to Bonnie, including Udo Holthaus. Damn that Lloyd Hamilton."

"Yeah, damn him for keeping you from getting his station sued," Jeff's lawyer instincts and argumentative nature always seemed to creep into conversations about her work.

"At least he hasn't taken me off the story," Grace said, lightening up. "Honey, I told you I'd start getting meaty assignments."

Jeff turned from the ball game and gave Grace a somber look, as if something was bothering her. She failed to notice, for her attention was turned to the front door bursting open. Megan popped into the room, buoyant and cheerful. Grace loved the way her daughter brightened up any space she entered and the positive vibrations that always seemed to emanate from her.

She had noticed Megan's bright aura from the time of her first words, and she tried to temper her pride with an understanding that all parents probably believe their children are special. When Megan reached her sophomore year, she displayed constant enthusiasm for studying, classroom projects and the extracurricular activities she invariably volunteered for. Grace couldn't deny, even to herself, that this girl was someone special. A stunning beauty had developed—her honey blonde hair, blue-green eyes and lithe figure made her a perfect candidate for cheerleader, school play leads and boy magnet.

Many times during the next year, Grace and Jeff discussed the need to keep their daughter well grounded as all of this popularity swirled around her, but in the end their worries proved unnecessary.

"I guess our concerns were ill founded," Grace told Jeff one Friday night when Megan was at a post-football game slumber party and they dressed for bed. "Megan has zipped through her junior year."

"She seems to handle herself with such maturity," Jeff agreed.

"What's really neat is that she wants to please everyone around her, most importantly her teachers and us," said Grace. "Listen to us. Aren't we pitiful? Our daughter is spoiling us rather than the other way around." They laughed together.

Life was sweet for young Megan until one day, the summer before her senior year, when Jeff and Grace dropped the Dallas grenade into her life and extinguished the excitement of her senior year plans.

For the first time ever, Megan became strident, argumentative and depressed. Grace knew she should have seen it coming, but even so, the pitch of Megan's objections to the move was so vociferous she seemed to become a different person.

Her responses to requests were sharp and negative. She lost interest in her appearance, letting her silky long hair grow dull and stringy. Her usually impeccable dress became sloppy.

Although it was summertime, she had never let herself go like this until the Dallas crisis hit the Gleason household. Megan shunned her friends, opting instead for sitting in her room with the door closed with her stereo turned up to high.

Nothing that Grace and Jeff tried—discussing, reasoning, pleading—pulled their daughter out of the disappointment of missing her final year with her friends and familiar surroundings.

"I promise we'll find you the very best school, honey," Grace told her, "with the activities you want to participate in the most."

Jeff chimed in, "We'll find the friendliest neighborhood with lots of kids your age. And we'll get you a cool used car to drive to school."

But they knew these desperate promises couldn't compensate for the hole they were punching in Megan's dream life.

They had broken the news in mid-July. As the month wore on, the animus failed to subside. Megan objected to Jeff's insistence that she continue to join them for dinner. She was still, deep down, Megan, and so she obeyed. Yet dinner was the most bitter, unhappy time of day for all three of them as Megan sulked and picked at her food and failed to join into any conversation.

Finally, Grace decided she had had enough. One evening in late July, as they finished another wordless dinner, she reached out and took Megan's hand. Megan recoiled, yanking her back, but Grace persisted, hanging on.

"Come walk with me," Grace said, more an order than a request.

Megan's face wrinkled with indignation. "No," her response was curt and defiant. "May I be excused?"

"You may not be excused," Grace answered firmly, wanting to laugh at Megan's innate politeness poking through the gruff exterior. "You and I are going for a walk."

Megan opened her mouth to object, but Grace stood up and, continuing to grasp her daughter's hand tightly, pulling her toward the door.

"We'll be back in half an hour," Grace announced to the stunned Jeff. He nodded, his face reflecting an effort to be supportively somber but his dark eyes fighting amusement at the sight of his wife tugging Megan along like a toddler.

They walked slowly through the neighborhood with Grace continuing to hold her daughter's hand in a viselike grip, ignoring Megan's petulant side-glances.

It was a soft evening. The sun was down, but the final remnants of its light seemed to hold off the enveloping darkness for one last, grateful gasp of daytime as only summer evenings can. The echoes of children's laughing voices and the sounds of their skateboards and bikes were fading around the neighborhood as the calls of mothers beckoned them home.

The air was filled with the full, sweet aroma of honeysuckle. A trace of leaves burning, probably illegally, reminded Grace of her old neighborhood outside Chicago when screen doors slammed across backyards and barking dogs announced a final foray outside before they were shuttered for the night.

Grace had always loved this time of day best, as shadows grew too long to last and sounds and smells lifted her nostalgia to its highest point. But not on this night. As she clung to her daughter's hand and they walked through the subdivision like two old enemies playing out a cold war, a dread swept over Grace that she hadn't known since the phone calls announcing her parents' deaths.

They reached the little vest-pocket park near the neighborhood clubhouse, and Grace parked on a small wooden bench that overlooked the pond where she and Megan had fed the ducks together for years. Megan flopped down beside her, brooding. They sat for long moments, the silence shouting out at Grace.

"I'm not smart enough to know what to say to you," she began, "and to be honest, I'm scared that I can't help you get past this. I've had my share of disappointments in my life, Megan. I didn't have such a great childhood, you know? But I can't begin to know how you must feel right now—what the disappointment must be like."

"It sucks," Megan snapped.

"I know. It does. Sometimes life stinks and you just have to deal with it."

Megan looked straight into her mother's eyes, tears

brimming in her own, disbelief and bitterness covering her smooth young face. "I don't want to deal with it," her normally musical voice was sated with harshness. "You can fix it, Mom. You can tell me we're going to stay in Austin."

Grace shook her head no, emphatically. "We've made the decision. We're moving to Dallas. It's best for your father and for me. I know you don't think so right now, but it's the best decision for you, too. When your final year flies by and it's time for you to go to the college of your choice to pursue your life dreams, we'll be in a great position to make that happen for you."

She sucked in a deep breath, her voice trembling slightly, fear nagging like a persistent disease."

"I don't expect you to accept what I'm saying right now. Maybe you never will. But I'm asking you to stop this campaign of animosity that is so unlike you it's killing me inside. I'm asking you to tell your friends that you'll twitter them every day, post on their Facebook walls, call them every weekend and catch up, and to let us help you embrace your new city."

She paused, waiting. Nothing.

"We'll do all we can to help you be happy there. But right now, I'm asking you to stop being a child–to be a woman and accept what's going to happen."

With those words, the fear became too overwhelming, and Grace began to cry. Megan stared in disbelief. Grace Gleason had always been a rock, a pragmatic boulder who could steel her emotions against the immovable force of any adversity. She had teared up briefly only a few times in Megan's presence, but never really sobbed.

Now, this determined, feisty newswoman and stern pillar of the household's stability was blubbering uncontrollably beside her daughter.

The bitter shell in Megan's face seemed to melt. As her mother's sadness and desperation erupted, Megan cried with her. They were in each other's arms, sobbing together, for minutes.

Finally their weeping began to subside, but still they

held each other, soundless, with Grace's wet face buried in Megan's shoulder.

"I'll try, Mom," came the words Grace had longed to hear. She knew in the overwhelming rush of that moment that her true calling was always to be there for this incredibly special girl.

The argument between Grace and Jeff over the medical examiner interview drifted away as Megan burst into the room, slamming the door behind her. "Hi, Mom. Hi, Dad," she chimed. She dropped her book bag next to the couch and flopped down.

"You're in a great mood," Jeff said. "I thought you were in your room. Where've you been?"

"With some of my friends," Megan answered.

Friends. Grace was elated to hear Megan utter the word. For two months after their move, despite their newfound, uneasy pact, all Grace had heard were her daughter's mumbled complaints about missing her Austin friends and not meeting anyone interesting or fun at the new school. Grace knew Megan was trying to adjust, but at certain times, in the moment, her grief and missing seemed to take over.

During those testy months, several times when emotions were especially high, Megan reverted back to grousing about moving her there. Grace tried to impose a steady and reasoned reaction on those outbursts. She knew that picking an argument might entrench her daughter's resistance to the probability that sometime soon, as she met people in her new school and they liked her, Megan 's allegiances to Austin would gradually drift away like jet contrails in the sky.

Grace and Jeff had loosened the reins a bit right after they moved in, hoping it would help. They gave her latitude to visit her new schoolmates' homes after school, sometimes have dinner with them and vice versa, even sleep over on occasion.

"You're a senior now, and you've earned some leeway," Grace told her when Megan asked permission for the overnight after the football game. "You've proven yourself to be responsible countless times."

And, Grace thought, *you desperately need to fit in here with only one year left in high school.*

Friends. Grace had not realized until that moment how continually tense she had been over Megan's dilemma. When Megan said the word, Grace felt springs uncoil. And now that Megan had been accepted into a circle of schoolmates, Grace was thrilled that their efforts to help their daughter weather this trauma were finally paying dividends.

"Come on, Megan," Grace said cheerfully, her irritation at the Brad Nessler story editing forgotten like last year's movie star. "Let's go fix dinner."

Megan offered up her best teenage nose-wrinkling. "Mom, can't we order pizza? I have a lot of homework."

Jeff seized on the suggestion. "Good idea," he said. "I'll call and go get it."

Grace nodded, "Start your homework, Sweetie. I'll make a salad."

Megan gathered her books and bounced up the stairs toward her room. Grace started toward the kitchen.

"Hey," Jeff said, stopping her with a look of incredulity. "A frigging bite mark?"

"You got it," she laughed over her shoulder as she turned again and went into the kitchen, feeling better about her family than she had in a year. "A frigging bite mark."

Grace and Jeff each had a glass of Pinot Grigio before the pizza arrived, and a second with the pizza. Typically, Megan had asked to have her food in her room while she finished her homework. Grace preferred to have the three of them together for a meal—even takeout—as rare as it was for their schedules to mesh. Yet she wasn't about to discourage Megan's attitude toward schoolwork.

They sat eating pizza and getting tipsy together at the kitchen table. As they ate, their discussion moved quickly beyond Udo Holthaus, Examiner Nessler and bite marks. Jeff was working on a fascinating case involving Naval training exercises in the Gulf of Mexico that environmentalists claimed were causing harm to marine mammals. He was assisting a senior partner who would take the environmentalists' arguments to the Supreme Court. Meanwhile, Grace was working with a newly hired cameraman, Matt Robertson, who was in his thirties but looked fresh out of college. He was already one of the best photographers at the station, she thought.

Their relaxed and easy conversation, wide-ranging and aware, was reminiscent of how they had whiled away their leisure time in college, drinking coffee at the student center or having a quiet hamburger together at one of the off-campus bars. These days, the demands of careers and parenthood and the chores of life stood squarely in the path of taking time to nurture such moments. They were both soaking up a rare plunge into the kind of conversation that had led them to the altar.

Hours later, after the table had been cleared, Jeff was in bed, stripped to the waste, reading a stack of legal briefs. Grace came in from the bathroom wearing the red babydoll chemise Jeff liked so much. She hadn't worn it in months. He looked up from the papers, staring at her over his reading glasses, his interest already appearing to intensify.

A little hazy from the wine, he watched her walk to the bed, carefully following her fluid movement. "Wow," he said. "Lady, you might be nearly forty, but you haven't lost that sensuous aura you had when we first met."

"Megan's sound asleep," she announced. She climbed into the bed. "It's so hard to believe she's about to graduate. We're getting old, Jeff."

Grace rolled over close and hugged him.

Jeff stopped reading the briefs and put his arm around her, kissing her lips softly. "I'm sure we can handle it," he said.

"Think you can handle me, cowboy?" she teased.

Jeff slid the stack of legal briefs off the bed and pulled her closer, returning her kiss, his hand sliding under the chemise and gliding over the smooth line of her back. She had always liked his touch on her skin, surprisingly gentle and tender for a man so athletic and masculine, arousing her.

"It's been a while, but I think so," he chuckled. "I've known how to handle you since college."

He kissed her longer this time, with passion, and she kissed back, lightly running her tongue along his lip and half-climbing on top of him, her leg across his thigh.

"Remember those times," she laughed, her voice sparkling and tender with the memory, "when we tried to do it in your Chevy? Those parking and sparking nights at Portman's Landing? We were shameful. Your hormones were running ten thousand miles a minute."

"You were pretty hot yourself," Jeff recalled. They laughed together, lying back, looking at the ceiling, remembering in unison.

Jeff turned to her, furrowed his brow in mock seriousness, and added, "We were crazy."

"Crazy with lust, maybe," she laughed again. We were red-blooded kids."

A light bulb of memory seemed to switch on, and Jeff's voice cracked with humor, "Remember the time we did it in the front seat and you got so excited you honked the horn with your knee?"

They laughed together again, lost in the hilarity of the experience.

"And I mean, honked it and honked it," he continued.

They began laughing hysterically, and as she caught her breath, Grace climbed on top of Jeff and bent down to kiss him again, deeply. She helped him pull off his shorts, and she stayed astride of him as she pulled the chemise over her head and he caressed her breasts. She reached behind her and found him, stroked him gently, then pulled the sheet up over them. Their lovemaking was slow and sensual and sweeter than it had been in a long time.

Later, they lay on their backs in each other's arms, together but lost for a time in their own private thoughts.

Jeff finally teased, "Not bad."

She laughed at his old joke, the hundredth time she had heard it. "I'll 'not bad' you, Jeffrey Gleason."

He propped up on an elbow and rubbed her neck. "How long has it been?" he asked.

"My God, weeks. We've been so busy."

"Why do we let so much stuff get in the way of this?"

Grace shrugged, shivered and pulled the chemise back on. "We're adults," she answered. "And parents. We're not doing it in the back seat of a Chevy anymore. Sometimes we get caught up in the PTA and our work and forget what it felt like back then."

A minute or two went by. They held each other without speaking, as they used to do. But she could tell something was on Jeff's mind; he seemed locked in an internal debate. She gave him a wary, inquisitive look, hoping that whatever was bothering him didn't ruin this infrequent and welcome tenderness.

"Grace," Jeff said, pulling on his shorts. "I didn't get a chance earlier to tell you something."

He watched her eyes. She waited, skeptical.

"You won't like it."

She sighed, leery, guarded. "What is it?"

"I've got a job offer. A really good one. Partner in a firm."

"What do you mean, not like it? Jeff, that's wonderful. A partner," Grace burst, immediately excited. "It's so sudden. Are you going to take it? What firm is it?"

He hesitated and grimaced, and his expression stopped her cold, like jumping into a pool in March.

"It's a California firm," he told her. "Remember that old law school buddy of mine—Myron Waters? He's out there now and recommended me. We'd have to move to San Francisco."

Jeff's words stunned her. It wasn't cancer or bankruptcy, but even so, she felt it drive a blow deep in the pit of her stomach. She greeted the news with silence.

"What do you think?" he insisted, in the way that lawyers persist in the courtroom, badgering the witness, trying to prod their agreement to a premise.

Grace took a deep breath, trying hard to understand why Jeff would initiate such a conversation.

"My God, we just moved here less than a year ago because you wanted a bigger firm," she protested. She searched his eyes for a hint that he might take her off the hook, not make her the heavy. "Look what we just went through with Megan."

"She can finish out the year here," he said, his voice flat and determined. "By the time I get settled in the job out there and we find a place to live, she'll be in college."

"I'm not moving again just as my career's starting to take off." Grace hated the words, felt disloyal and selfish for saying them, but he should have felt the same for broaching the proposal.

Jeff pressed on. "This isn't about you. They've got television stations in San Francisco. Grace, the work I've been doing on energy accounts has opened my eyes. Environmental law—that's where the opportunity is. And that means California. This is my chance to take a giant career step. It would mean equity in the firm, bigger cases, better bonuses."

She felt the anger welling up—didn't want it to, but couldn't stop it. She felt like screaming at him, punching him, questioning his love. Instead, she sat without speaking, staring at Jeff's expressionless face. Every response she tried to offer choked in her throat.

"You wouldn't hold me back, would you?" he asked, cruelly she thought.

She waited, grasped onto her emotions. Then, in a careful and measured tone, she said,

"You can take any job you please. Everyone will salivate

over hiring a smart lawyer who has already established a track record. You can't expect me to drop my career to tag along so you can further your own."

Jeff's face began to flush. "Shit, Grace," he said, and she dreaded the rising emotion in his words, "I thought you'd be happy for me. Where's the loyal, devoted wife I used to know?"

"Where's the proud, supporting husband I'm supposed to have?" she snapped back. She wondered how so gentle a night could have turned so sharply.

What is it, she wondered, *that makes two people who should join at the hip take flight on their own separate paths, unyielding, married suddenly only to their own egocentric notion of how the world should look*? Jeff had always seemed to fly formation with her right up to a point that might have made a difference, and then pull back, unwilling to step into her dream and embrace it. It was his dream, always, that called him.

She rolled out of the bed, pulled a robe on and stomped out of the room, having no idea where she was going.

Except that she knew where she was not going.

"I'm not moving to Cali-damned-fornia," she tossed at him as she went out the door.

CHAPTER 6: Ratings, Lloyd, Ratings

RICHARD STONE hadn't started his career in broadcasting. Right out of college, he had hired on as a reporter for the *Miami Tribune* and moved up to political columnist and then Washington bureau chief. In late 1990, during the build-up to the Gulf War, he asked to go there and report.

He first mentioned the idea to his managing editor, Charles McGonigle. On Charles' monthly visits to the capital city, they always had late afternoon cocktails at the Round Robin Bar on Pennsylvania Avenue. It was late summer and still steamy. The two newsmen started on their second martini as they discussed the looming Middle East crisis.

"Why in hell would you want to go to that God-forsaken part of the world, when you're becoming a factor in our most important city at the ripe age of thirty-five?" asked McGonigle.

"I'm not sure," Richard responded. "But something is attracting me to what's going to happen over there." He laughed. "I haven't had a nice, long vacation in a while. Maybe it'll be a way to get some travel in."

"Plenty of beach, that's for sure," McGonigle chuckled, then scoffed, "Shit, Richard. You can't even be sure we're even going to get in that fight."

"Oh, we'll get into it. A friend of mine knows the Air Force guy in South Carolina who's on his way to Qatar right now to build our base of operations. We're girding for a campaign. I'm not supposed to know that, and you aren't either."

Richard was certain after Iraq's invasion of Kuwait in August that an international response was imminent and that news from that region would be the focus of American news. Going there to report would be a star in his news crown.

He won his paper's approval. When Operation Desert

Storm hastened the expulsion of Iraq the following January, Richard had already established himself as a serious player in the coverage of American troops there. Although he was there as a print journalist, a Miami television station began to air his reports, and their network took notice not only of his news coverage, but his incisive reports of the United Nations operation's political ramifications.

When Richard returned to Washington after the brief encounter with Saddam Hussein's motley troops had wound down, the network hired him immediately as a political analyst. He bounced around from one network position to another, never quite attaining top billing. But his work on many important stories—President Clinton's impeachment, NATO's attack of Serbia, the Bush-Gore disputed election and the attack on the World Trade Center—won awards and kept him a viable force on the national news scene.

Richard had demonstrated strong managerial skills in his reporting days in the Middle East. He had used his personality and connections to strike out on his own, out-maneuver the pool reporters and locate sources to help him get the best coverage. Back home in the U.S., his coverage of important business stories, most notably the mutual funds scandal of 2003, demonstrated a strong ability to analyze the complexities of the business world.

Meanwhile, his on-camera star quality was beginning to flag as advancing age affected his photographic good looks and turned his dulcet tones gravelly.

"I'd like to try my luck at news management," he appealed to Charles McGonigle, who had been made president of Newsmaker Corporation headquartered in Washington. They were having drinks in their usual booth at the Round Robin, now a weekly ritual.

"That's a real surprise, Richard," McGonigle said. "I thought you were in love with the front side of the camera."

"How about it, Charlie? Can you help me?"

"I've always said you have the business acumen to

become a strong executive," Charles told him. "Yes, I'll help you, old pal. But you're going to have to pay your dues."

"Name it."

"The ratings are sagging at our Dallas station. North Texas is an important market for us. We've been trying to figure out how to solve the problem. You go out there, shore up the ratings, and when you've accomplished that you'll be headed for a position of much greater importance in our New York headquarters office."

Lloyd Hamilton had often told anyone who would listen that he dreamed of anchoring a top-five market station or one of the networks. But when Richard arrived on the scene, he made it clear to Lloyd that the news director had reached his full potential.

"I'm not going to be here long," Richard told his older news director in their first meeting. "We're going to get these ratings fixed my first year, and then I'll move on."

"Then I'll have a shot at GM?' Lloyd sounded cheerful.

Richard shook his head. "Not going to happen, Lloyd. Corporate will bring in someone young with an MBA and ambition to match."

Lloyd's shoulders sagged. Later that day, he related the conversation to assignment manager Wallace James. "Maybe he wasn't trying to discourage me," Lloyd said brightly. "It might have been his way of issuing a challenge."

Wallace laughed. "Don't kid yourself, Lloyd. The news business is changing. This guy is ambitious and aggressive, and he'll mess with our comfort level to get what he wants out of all of us. Then he'll turn the keys over to someone who doesn't know a news story if it kicks him in the ass."

Three weeks passed quietly. Then one morning, right after an assignment meeting, Richard Stone summoned Lloyd.

Richard's office was not huge, but he had managed to cram two decades of news business memorabilia into it. Lined around the walls were signed photographs of newscasters and anchors he had crossed paths with—Rather, Sawyer, Walters and even an aged Cronkite. There was a smattering of signed photos of celebrities and politicians posing with him, shaking hands, mugging for the camera at various functions—John Kerry, Hillary Clinton, John McCain, Brad Pitt, Jerry Seinfeld, Bret Favre and a number of others lesser-known.

Stone's desk and the bookcases behind it were piled high with awards, gifts and trinkets from years of press club banquets, newscaster conventions and celebrity events. The new general manager at TXDA had experienced a load of stations, networks, news services and benefit golf tournaments. This collection in his workspace was a testament to the reputation he had made as a difference-maker in the industry and a well liked public personality.

Richard skimmed through a ratings book, flipping the pages with authority. He didn't look up or speak when Lloyd entered and slid quickly into the chair across from his boss. Lloyd tapped his fingers nervously on the desk and looked around at the collected memories. He appeared cowed and intimidated by the trappings of the office.

The general manager continued to read for several minutes. Finally, he looked up at Hamilton. "I just got the book on the February sweeps," he said.

"I saw them already," Lloyd said, beaming. "We're still the number one news station."

Richard gave him a stifling glance and returned to the book. "We're hanging on by our fucking fingernails," he shot back. "We've lost market share to channel five for two consecutive quarters."

Lloyd squirmed and tugged at his collar. His attempt to paper over the obvious had been thwarted. Richard Stone apparently could not be bluffed.

"What are you doing to get this turned around, Lloyd?" Richard pressed. "I have a corporate office to answer to."

Lloyd leaned forward, obviously straining to be positive. His eyes cast upward, seeming to search his brain for a response that might impress his superior. "We have a great series on corruption in the county budget office just about buttoned down," he offered eagerly.

Richard frowned and sat back in disappointment. "Damn it, Lloyd, the *Morning Sentinel* has already run that story for two days. Unless you've got an angle everyone and his uncle doesn't already have, you'd better give me something else." He returned to the ratings book, appearing deep in thought. "What about this Vincent murder?" he asked, looking up quickly. "Nobody else seems to have much of a handle on it."

"We're working on it," Lloyd responded.

Stone's facial reaction and rapid-fire questioning said he was losing patience with Hamilton's plodding responses. "You didn't seem to think it was much of a story at first."

"It was a missing person case," Lloyd seemed defensive, letting insecurity creep into the whining sound of his answers. "Of course we want ratings, Richard, but you didn't want me to get us sued just because we've got a young reporter who likes to speculate, did you?"

Richard leaned forward again and gave Hamilton a penetrating, powerful stare. "You said it right the first time, Lloyd. We want ratings. We need ratings. If we don't get them, we lose our number one spot. Someone's going to be out of a job, and it's not going to be me."

Lloyd squirmed some more.

"Do you have any problem with a woman on that story?" Richard continued. "This isn't the first time you've gotten crosswise with a female reporter, I'm told."

"Sometimes these girls come out of journalism school and let their emotions run their brains. Grace'll be okay."

"She seems like a go-getter to me," Richard insisted. "This story could get red hot. Maybe you'd better turn that tiger loose and see what she comes up with."

Lloyd got up, nodded, turned for the door and escaped as fast as possible. His quick pace and lack of a friendly goodbye seemed to say he was relieved to be getting out of there.

"Ratings, Lloyd. Think ratings," Richard called after him as he disappeared.

CHAPTER 7: Blind Alleys

A WEEK had passed since Ned Moore and Jerry Philmore discovered a cold body in the airport parking garage. They had exhausted their Dallas leads and turned their attention to Austin and the past of Udo Holthaus and Bonnie Vincent.

Spooley's Bar was a small neighborhood haunt in a strip mall dotted with dollar stores, consignment shops and ethnic restaurants. As Ned and Jerry stepped inside, the contrast between the brilliant day outdoors and the darkness inside stopped them cold. They blinked rapidly to readjust.

Ned motioned for Jerry to follow him. He stepped unsteadily toward the long bar where a pleasant woman with bleached blond hair pulled glasses from a carrier and loaded them onto shelves. She greeted the two with eyes reddened from smoke, but her voice was musical and clear.

"What can I get you?"

Ned flashed his badge. "Ned Moore, Dallas Police," he said.

"You the gents who called Spooley?"

Ned nodded.

"Hold on, I'll get him," she responded and disappeared into the back.

Spooley was short and portly, his thick hair almost white. He welcomed them with a smile that puffed his reddish checks out and narrowed his eyes behind rimless glasses.

"Let's sit over here," Spooley led them to a booth. "Want anything?

"No thanks," Ned answered. Spooley glanced at the barmaid, and as they slid into the booth she hurried a cup of coffee to her boss.

"What can I do for you?" Spooley asked, still friendly.

- 84 -

"Like I said on the phone, we want to ask some questions about Udo Holthaus," Ned answered. "We're told he was a regular here."

Spooley hesitated and the smile faded from his lips. "Is it kosher? I mean, this ain't your jurisdiction, is it?"

"It's connected to an investigation we've got going in Dallas. The Austin PD knows we're here."

"I heard Udo's wife got murdered. You don't suspect him, do you?"

"We're covering all the bases. You know, gathering some background. He was in here a lot?"

"Nearly every day after work." Spooley sipped at his coffee. "He'd come in, have a couple of pops, bitch about work or whatever—he was a grouchy sort—and then head home or over to a strip joint. He liked them tittie bars."

"He ever talk about his wife?" Ned asked.

Spooley hesitated, thinking. "Don't remember him ever mentioning her until..."

"Until?" Ned pulled a small note pad and pen from his coat pocket, laying them on the table.

"He came in here one night not long before they moved away. Really pissed off. Bitching about this argument he had with her over a job offer she got in Dallas."

"What'd he say?" Jerry asked.

"He had already had three or four snorts. He ranted that she thought he was opposed to it because of chauvinism or some damned thing. He got loud, banging his drink glass on the bar. I tried to calm him down a little."

"What'd you say?"

"I said I didn't understand why he objected to it—sounded like a great deal to me. He really got frosted. Said he had a fucking career of his own. Said he had worked his ass off making peace with Austin after he got out of the Coast Guard and started classes at the university. Said everybody made fun of his weird German accent but by God, he showed them—got a good job managing the television news. That was about the gist of it. He got pretty wild."

"Anything else?" Ned asked, jotting down some notes on the pad.

Spooley thought for a moment. "Not really. Oh yeah, he said it chapped his ass that he'd have to start over in a new city. I laughed at that."

"Why?"

"Because I knew what was really eating at him. 'You sure it's not because you'll miss the bars you crawl here in Austin?' I asked him. I was always ragging on him about his fascination with those places. I remember pulling his chain, asking, 'You ever tell your wife about those horny stripper places you go to when you're not here getting blitzed and complaining to me?' He got this arrogant look on his face, said they have men's clubs in Dallas and it wouldn't take him long to learn that city."

Spooley stopped and thought, sipping the coffee. "That's the last time I saw the guy. And now I hear that pretty wife of his got killed."

Ned offered his hand and Spooley shook it, showing the puffy smile.

"Thanks," Ned said. "You've been real helpful."

They slid out of the booth and started toward the door, and Spooley followed.

"You think the guy did her in?" Spooley asked the detectives.

"Not sure," Ned answered, turning toward the barman. "Oh, those strip clubs he went to. Ever mention a name?"

"Sure," Spooley said. "The one he talked about all the time is called the Pink Puppy."

Ned nodded. "Thanks again," and the two detectives re-emerged into the blinding light of day.

The drive to the Pink Puppy took ten minutes.

Bert Brusca, the owner, was a flashy character well known for his brushes with the law and with the priggish city council. Brusca's dancers pushed the local limits on what they could expose and what kind of dances they could perform. Neighborhood groups kept constant pressure on city hall to keep a chokehold on "The Puppy," as the establishment was commonly known.

Brusca motioned the two detectives toward two chairs and sat down across his office desk from them. He wore an open-collared, patterned silk shirt that exposed heavy chest hair. A single gold chain one-half inch wide spanned his thick neck.

"I've got Mitzy Allen coming in to talk to you guys," he said. "She's sort of my queen bee around here—keeps track of the other dancers, makes sure they show up, don't cheat me, all that shit. She would know more about that Holthaus guy coming in here than I would."

They heard a light knock and the door immediately opened. The gorgeous face of Mitzy Allen was heavily made-up and framed in long, blond hair. Brusca motioned her in. She wore tight shorts and a top that showed her bare midriff. The strong scent of Lovely wafted through the air around her. She was thirty-ish, but as she crossed the room and sat next to Ned, she displayed the toned, long legs and tight behind of a college girl.

"Detective Moore, Dallas PD," Ned said, half-standing. He motioned toward Jerry. "This is my partner, Detective Philmore. He's going to ask you a few questions."

Jerry looked at Ned, startled, and Ned smiled.

"Nice to meet you detective," Mitzy purred as she shook Jerry's hand, appearing amused at his discomfort.

"It's a pleasure, ma'am," Jerry sputtered. Mitzy glanced at Brusca with a half-smile, obviously amused at the young detective's embarrassment.

Jerry pulled a small pad and pen from his pocket, his hands slightly shaking.

"We won't keep you long," he told her. "Mr. Udo Holthaus, a former customer. You know him?"

"I remember him," she answered. "He was one of my

trouble-makers."

"How so, Miss Allen?"

"He was a regular, you know? Always came in with a snootful thinking he could throw his weight around with the girls—get them to break the rules, go in the back or out to his car with him, that sort of thing. The girls didn't like him, but they tolerated him."

"Why was that?" Jerry asked.

"Because of who he was. Big muckety-muck like that on a TV station could make it hard on Bert here, if we didn't treat him nice, you know?" She paused. "Plus, he threw money around like it was Christmas. The girls aren't stupid. They could string him along and ding his credit cards with gusto."

"Anything else?"

"We have a lot of assholes who come in here. But the girls hardly pay any attention. This guy was different. He was so strange—with that weird foreign accent and crappy personality—they talked about him a lot. Some were even kind of scared of him."

"He ever cross a line?" Jerry asked, and seeing her inquisitive reaction, then added, "You know—force himself on a girl or stalk her—anything like that?"

She shook her head no. "All the girls knew about him. They knew not to take chances or get too chummy. I tried to keep an eye on him when he was here. He usually left before the place got busy. Tell the truth, we were kind of glad to hear he moved out of town."

Jerry glanced uncertainly at Ned, then back at the dancer. "One last question. Did he ever talk about his wife?"

Mitzy stared inquisitively for a moment. "Not to me," she answered. "Don't know about the other girls. I could ask around."

"We appreciate your time, Mitzy," Ned jumped in, standing. "You too, Mr. Brusca." He handed Mitzy his card. "Call me if you find anything out."

Outside, Ned heaved a hard sigh. "I'm glad as hell to be

out of there. Jerry, we didn't get much, but at least we're dotting all the I's."

"Do you think we should interview Udo's general manager while we're here?" Jerry asked.

Ned frowned. "I called him yesterday and he didn't add a thing. But let's swing by there and look him in the eye, just to be sure."

Later that day, Grace rushed into the Dallas Police Department building. It was a hectic scene, with lawyers, police officers, reporters and citizens streaming in and out. Grace hurried through security and walked to the elevator with a purposeful stride.

The detective division was on the third floor, and the elevator was excruciatingly slow. As she stepped out she glanced around to get her bearings. Although the building was new, bright and vibrant, everything inside it seemed old—the desks, the file drawers, older computers—as if when they moved from the old Lamar Street building they had picked up its insides and plopped it down unchanged into the shiny new structure. The walls were covered with bulletins, news articles and photos, and every desk in the place was stacked high with files.

Ned Moore shared a corner of the office with Jerry Philmore and two other detectives. Grace was surprised as she arrived to find Ned alone. He was talking on the phone with a file folder open in his lap. He looked up and saw Grace coming in with an expression of anticipation on her face, looking eager to talk.

"Yeah, okay, I gotta go," the detective said hastily. "The press is here." He hung up and slapped the file shut as she approached.

Grace craned her neck to peek at the file, and Moore shoved it into a drawer.

"Anything interesting?" she asked.

"Nothing you'd care about," Ned answered bluntly.

"What's up, Grace?"

"Just checking in," she answered. "I was wondering if there's anything new on Bonnie Vincent?"

Ned leaned back and put his scuffed-up size twelve brown Oxfords on the desk. "You're all over this case aren't you?" he said. "Seems like it's more than just another story to you."

"I knew Bonnie," Grace said. "I liked her. She was a class act. I don't know a single person who didn't think she was way too good for that scuzz-bag husband of hers. And yet she stuck by him. That says a lot about the kind of person she was. I can't get rid of this gut feeling that he's mixed up in her death somehow."

Ned hesitated, squinting at her, and then looked toward the doorway and leaned forward, lowering his voice. "Can we talk off the record?"

"Of course," she said, a bit taken back.

"I got burned once by a mouthy reporter. I really have to trust you one hundred percent on this," said Ned, punctuating the statement to give it utmost importance.

Grace hesitated, thinking, wondering what brought on this change of heart. "Absolutely," she assured.

"Then let's go get some coffee," he said. He pushed back and stood up, watching her. She nodded, and he opened his desk, holstered his pistol and pulled on his ugly window pane sports jacket.

On their way out, they encountered Jerry Philmore coming in; Ned's partner seemed puzzled at first at the two of them together, but then shrugged, turned and started to follow them. Ned stopped Jerry with a look. "Philmore, call the desk sergeant about that matter we were discussing, will you? I'll be back in a few minutes."

Jerry looked puzzled, as if wondering what matter he was supposed to call about. But before he could ask, Ned was already walking out, grinning like a practical joker.

The Dallas Diner was a homely little eatery in a run-down part of the city. As Ned and Grace approached it in his sedan, she noted how seedy the surroundings were, with litter everywhere, weeds protruding from enormous sidewalk cracks and once-gleaming building fronts permanently soiled by years of assault from smog, soot and rust.

The windows of nearby vacant storefronts were covered with plywood that had been splintered and punched in by prostitutes and junkies who climbed through them to find a dark haven for their illicit activities. And by vagrants claiming the space at night for shelter.

The diner was the only building on the block that had received a modicum of attention from its ownership. Ned parked at the curb by a "no parking" sign. His car was a familiar sight there, and no one would bother it, least of all a patrol officer.

Grace took a long look at the establishment as she got out. She had read a story in the paper about this place—about its glory days before the neighborhood deteriorated. Despite its age, the diner had become a community icon over the years. It was kept in relatively decent shape to host a daily clientele of mixed backgrounds and interests who stopped in for the breakfast special or the lunch plate. It was the kind of place where Ned met informants over coffee and hamburgers back in the corner booth.

Grace had never seen it. She didn't want to venture into the area also known as a panhandler hangout by day and a homeless sanctuary at night.

Ned guided her back to his usual corner booth as a middle-aged waitress whose name tag said "Sallie" followed with a coffee pot and two mugs. Her face was deeply lined from hard living and worry. The peroxided hair that framed her dull green eyes was straw-stiff and tangled. Grace guessed that Sallie was younger than she appeared.

Ned pointed to the booth and slid in across from Grace.

"Detective," Sallie rasped the greeting in a voice ruined

by cigarettes. She nodded and smiled faintly as she put down one of the mugs in front of him and filled it to the brim.

"How's it going, Sallie?" Ned smiled up at her with an expression of affection reserved for those you've known a long time.

"Can't complain, Detective. I wouldn't get any sympathy anyway." Her cackling laugh at the often-used line rang through the diner, obviously so common a sound that none of the regulars sitting at the counter bothered to look up. "Coffee, Miss?" she asked Grace.

"Please. Cream and sugar," Grace smiled back at her.

"How're those boys?" Ned asked Sallie.

"One of 'em is always in a ditch," Sallie sighed and then scurried away quickly, demonstrating that she knew not to tarry when police work was to be done.

Ned took a sip and squinted across at Grace. "Maybe if we talk a bit, we can help each other," he said in a hushed and confidential tone. "Off the record, remember?"

"Okay."

Ned paused, having some kind of internal argument, then, "We like Holthaus for Bonnie Vincent's murder."

The words grabbed her attention. *Yes!* She thought.

"We don't have enough hard evidence yet," Ned continued, "but the circumstantial evidence points right at him. He had the means and the motive."

Grace was startled by how straightforward and trusting Ned was with private department information. She quickly assumed he had contemplated this discussion for a while and had a motive she didn't understand. "Can you nail him?" she asked.

"It's the damndest case I ever worked," the detective looked puzzled. "Everything was scrubbed clean. Not just the car and her, but the day she disappeared he rented a carpet shampooer and got a bunch of bleach and scrubbed down their condo."

"On one of those forensic cop TV shows, I saw them run

a test that could reveal blood evidence even if it was cleaned up," she suggested in an inquiring tone.

"There's TV and then there's real life," Ned said. "Sure, we've got something that can help us identify blood evidence in some cases. Chemical called luminol—the same stuff that makes those lightsticks glow at concerts."

"How does it work?"

"Badly, sometimes," he chortled at his joke. "Seriously, we can apply it to an area and when it comes in contact with blood hemoglobin it triggers a chemical reaction. You turn the lights down, you can get a pretty spectacular show. The problem is, there are other things that can cause the same reaction—like residual bleach from a thorough cleaning, or even dog piss if it has traces of blood in it."

"Not very encouraging," Grace said.

"That's not all. It can destroy other evidence, too, so we don't walk in like cowboys with luminol guns blazing. It makes great television drama, but it's not always the right answer. In this case, whatever the killer used to scrub the place down made the whole condo glow like Paris on New Year's Eve."

"That's no help at all."

"We're really having to scramble to find evidence, but I think we'll get it."

"Udo was covering his tracks?" Grace asked.

"It looks that way," Ned agreed. "Not just at the condo. We can't find a single witness who can say they saw her car pull into the parking deck. Yet you and I know she was crammed in that trunk, naked as a jaybird and scrubbed like a baby."

They paused as Sallie returned with the coffee pot. She poured refills and hesitated, as if wanting to tell Ned more about the sons he had inquired about, but then apparently thought better of it and rushed off.

"I heard you found a loaded gun under her car seat," Grace ventured.

Ned's eyes opened wide in amazed reaction. "Who the hell are your sources?" he growled.

She grinned. "You're not the only bird in the sky, Detective." She felt pleased that Ned seemed annoyed and impressed at the same time that she had dug up the information on her own.

"There was a gun," he admitted, "registered to her husband, but we don't see any connection to her death. And there were no fingerprints on the car. The only real evidence we have is the mark on her neck. If it's a bite mark and we can find a match, then it might be enough to get it to trial.

"So?"

"The forensic dentist we're working with said whoever bit the victim had a big gap between his teeth," Ned confided.

"Holthaus has a gap in his teeth," she said.

"Him and about fifty million other people," Ned laughed. "Actually, the kind of space in his bite isn't as common as you might think, according to the examiner. He also said the mark was put on the victim very near the time of death. Even so, unless that mark proves conclusively that it's a bite and not just a bruise, and unless it can pan out as a match with our boy, or unless we luck into some more evidence...if Udo did it he might have committed the perfect crime."

"I told you he was sneaky," Grace confirmed.

Ned nodded and downed a slug of coffee. "Did you know he lost his job?" he asked.

"I heard," she nodded. "He had been canned before his phony plea on television. Know why?"

"No one over there is talking," Moore answered, frustration in his response. "They're hiding behind the Employee Privacy Act. But it was probably because he wasn't showing up. When I interviewed Bonnie Vincent's therapist, she told me that he hadn't told his wife. She must have thought he was going to work every day. He even lied to the media, remember? In his statement at his condo he said he worked at motor vehicles."

"What was he doing with his time?" Grace asked.

"We ran a check on his and Bonnie's charge cards. Udo was using them at strip bars, buying lap dances and champagne for the girlies. Ran up some huge bills."

"Strippers," Grace said thoughtfully. "Do you have names?"

"Yes, but they're not cooperating."

"Mind if I try to put the media squeeze on them?" asked Grace, excited about the prospect of chasing down another lead.

"Actually, they might be more willing to talk to a woman," Ned agreed, "and certainly more to the press than to me. Cops aren't exactly at the top of their A list. You might try a dancer over at the Saucy Lady. That's where a lot of the charges were run up. She might be willing to talk to you."

"What's her name?"

"Destiny," Ned said sheepishly.

"Destiny?"

"The girl goes by the name of Destiny Desire," he told her.

"Where do they get these names?" Grace hooted.

Ned laughed with her and looked at his watch. "I have to get back. I've got another case that's really heating up."

"I'll get us a check," Grace said, raising her hand to signal the waitress.

Ned reached across and pulled her arm down, shaking his head. "We're covered," he said.

Ned got up and walked toward the door. Feeling guilty, Grace dropped a two-dollar tip on the table and followed the detective out.

Outside, Grace squinted from the contrast between the muted lighting inside and the brilliant daylight. She extended a slender hand and as Ned shook it, Grace realized that she hadn't noticed how huge his were—products of brick masonry, baseball, shipboard duty and age.

"Thanks, Ned," Grace said. You've been a big help."

The detective held onto her hand, his voice businesslike and serious. "This isn't a one-way street. I've only shared this information with you because my case isn't going anywhere.

You might have a chance to pick up something that will help us expose the guy. Or, on the other hand, exonerate him."

She nodded, and then remembered something. "Wait," she said, reaching out and touching his arm. "You said Holthaus had motive."

"After we found Bonnie's body, I interviewed most of her family. Her father told me that several months before Bonnie died, Udo increased her life insurance a million dollars."

She whistled. "A million. That's worth pursuing."

"Could be," he answered. "But motive and opportunity won't help if there's no hard evidence. If all I have is a circumstantial case, I'm hamstrung. Our illustrious district attorney is famous for not bringing cases to trial if they're not dead solid."

"Because losing a big, visible case would be bad news for his political career?"

"Exactly," Ned said. He looked solemnly into her eyes. "I've told you way more than I should have. But I did it for one reason. I hope you'll keep dogging the guy. Maybe he'll slip up."

They walked toward the car. A beggar approached from the corner of the building. His filthy clothes were in tatters and his unshaven, haggard face lent added sadness to the dramatically blood-shot hollows of his lifeless eyes. Grace knew she couldn't guess his age if a fortune was riding on it.

The ageless, expressionless figure extended a hand. Grace reached for her purse, but Ned stepped in and pointed a meaty finger as if to say, "Back off." The panhandler retreated to his corner and slid down to a crouch position, staring at the sidewalk.

As Ned cranked the engine and they pulled away, Grace peered back at the pathetic figure crouching by the diner. "You should have let me give him some money. I can never get over wanting to help them," she told Ned.

"He'd have drunk it away in half an hour," Ned said. "Or stuck it in his veins. I learned a long time ago there are too many lost souls to save." He glanced over at her. "Just help one.

Help Bonnie Vincent."

"Lloyd Hamilton keeps telling me to drop it," she complained, "but I'm not going to quit."

"Good. I'll support you when I can. But Grace, be careful."

"I'm not intimidated by that creep."

"I mean it," he warned. "Don't take any risky chances. If Holthaus killed his wife, he wouldn't hesitate to kill again."

CHAPTER 8: Digging Up Dirt

BONNIE VINCENT'S older sister, Elizabeth, lived in the Premier Townhouses in a middle-class section of the North Dallas suburbs called Cedarcrest. She had moved there after her four-year, childless marriage to a stockbroker had failed.

In Katy, a Houston suburb, Elizabeth's oil company executive father and homemaker mother had been part of the city's country club scene. Their social status seemed more important to them than nurturing their childrens' needs, but Elizabeth appeared to relish the freedom. She moved through her school activities and among her friends in a manner that most would describe as mature beyond her years.

"Oh my God, how lucky are you?" remarked her best friend Tammy Womsley at cafeteria lunch the second school day of their junior year at Katy High. "My parents smother me with rules. Yours let you do your thing."

"Except when I have to baby-sit Bonnie," Elizabeth retorted.

"She's only four years younger than you," Tammy observed, "so that won't last much longer."

"When she's old enough to look after herself, I'll be in college," Elizabeth pointed out.

"Your mom and dad are gone all the time. How does that affect your little sister?" asked Tammy.

Elizabeth looked at her friend as if she had asked the meaning of life. "I have no idea," she responded blankly.

Elizabeth was Miss Everything in high school. She was elected head cheerleader and Homecoming Queen. She was selected as the school yearbook editor and was class salutatorian. Her parents lavished her with praise and privileges, as if she were an only child. By the time Bonnie came along, the newness of parenthood had worn off for her parents, and she was forced to settle for Elizabeth's hand-me-downs, including her five-year-old car when Bonnie graduated from the University of Houston.

By that time, Elizabeth had graduated from Baylor with a BA in business administration, was working as a teller in a Dallas bank and had become engaged. Her life was a fairy tale, and she rarely had any contact with her younger sister.

"Bonnie graduates next month," Hal Vincent mentioned in early May on his weekly phone call. Her father never missed contacting her at exactly six every Saturday afternoon.

"I know. I got her invitation," Elizabeth answered.

"Are you coming down for it?" he asked.

"I'm going to try," Elizabeth said, "if I can clear my schedule."

"I was thinking...you said last week you were going to trade cars? What if I buy yours from you?" he asked.

"What on earth for?" Elizabeth gasped.

"You've taken good care of it. It's like brand new. Your mother and I would like to give it to Bonnie as a graduation gift."

"For God's sake, Daddy," Elizabeth laughed uproariously, "you should get her a new one. Giving her my clothes and textbooks when she was in school is one thing, but my old sedan for graduation? That doesn't seem right."

"She's driving that piece of crap that's about to fall apart," he argued. "She would appreciate getting your car. I know she would."

Elizabeth's protests went unheeded, and she gave in. She had the car serviced and detailed and delivered it to her parents the night before Bonnie's baccalaureate. After the service, at lunch, she watched her younger sister as their parents presented Bonnie the keys. Bonnie seemed delighted, beaming at her parents and Elizabeth.

On her first day back after returning to Dallas, Elizabeth cooked dinner for Martin, her fiancé. As she stirred the spaghetti sauce and he sipped a beer, she admitted feeling awkward about the gift.

"The thing is," she said, sounding frustrated, "I couldn't tell if Bonnie's reaction was pretense or real."

"You never have been able to read her," Martin reminded. "It seems to me she got caught between her popular, high-achieving big sister and then little Ellie."

"I know, but Ellie was so much younger that I was away at college when she came along. And Bonnie was already a teenager."

Martin nodded. "You talk to Bonnie—what—at holidays and birthdays? How could you possibly have known how she was reacting to being disregarded like that?"

Elizabeth's marriage was gone, and so was her sister. On a chilly evening several weeks after Bonnie's death, Elizabeth was going through the motions of fixing dinner. Misery shadowed her face as she washed the lettuce for salad.

It was a routine she had performed cheerfully when she was cooking for two. In those days, she would rush home from the bank to get there before Martin arrived, make some potatoes and fish or steak and uncork a nice bottle of wine. "Sweetie, you're a fantastic cook," he would say after devouring her latest dessert concoction and downing a second glass of wine. Elizabeth would beam at the compliment.

Now, years after she had discovered Martin's affair and left him, and with grieving her sister Bonnie's horrible death still fresh in her memory, the joy in Elizabeth's countenance was gone.

She heard the car pull up in front, heard the beep of the car lock and clicking of heels on the walk in front. She walked to the living room and peeked around the lace curtain on the front door.

Outside, Grace looked up and down the street, surveying the elegant buildings, turned and walked up to Elizabeth's door trying to form an approach in her mind. She rang the doorbell, but there was no answer. She rang again. Suddenly, she flinched as she saw Elizabeth's face looking out through the curtains with a frightened expression. Grace gave her a small wave and friendly smile and talked to her through the door.

"Elizabeth Vincent?"

Elizabeth stayed motionless. "Yes," she answered, her voice muted through the glass.

"I'm Grace Gleason."

"I know. I've seen you on the news." Elizabeth acknowledged, still not moving.

"Bonnie and I were friends in Austin. I'd like to talk to you. Can I come in?"

Elizabeth opened the door a crack, looked up the street with alarm in her eyes, and then turned her attention to Grace. "I'm about to have dinner," her voice wavered.

"Sorry about the time. I'll only be a minute. Please."

Elizabeth heaved a sigh, undid the chain lock, opened the door cautiously and motioned Grace in. She quickly relocked the door and led Grace to a sofa. "Excuse the big mess. We've been pretty busy," Elizabeth explained.

They sat for a moment without speaking. Grace knew she couldn't imagine what Bonnie's sister had been going through. "I can't tell you how sorry I am about Bonnie," Grace said. "She was a wonderful person, Elizabeth. The best."

"How did you know Bonnie?"

"I worked in television in Austin when they were there," Grace explained. "We moved to Dallas after they did, and I only saw Bonnie once after that, several months ago. But I considered her a good friend."

"The police don't seem to be getting anywhere," Elizabeth sighed, sounding dejected.

Grace nodded, "I'm following the story, but it has been a dead end. I was wondering...do you or anyone in your family have any information that hasn't been shared? Something I can follow up on that will keep Bonnie's death in the public eye and pressure the authorities to pursue it harder?"

"We've agreed not to do interviews," Elizabeth answered coldly.

Grace grimaced. She had expected the response, yet she was disappointed. "Okay," she said. "But can we talk off the record?"

Elizabeth stared at the floor, failing to respond.

"I don't know what your relationship with Udo Holthaus is," Grace persisted, feeling desperate to establish a rapport with Elizabeth. *Time to show my hand,* she thought. "I have to be honest with you. I know him. He's a snake. I can't shake this feeling that he's somehow mixed up in her murder."

Elizabeth's eyes rose to meet Grace's. She sat up straighter and appeared to soften a bit. Grace could tell that she agreed.

"We got some information that Bonnie had a hefty insurance policy," Grace continued. "Aren't you concerned about him getting that kind of money from her death without even knowing who the killer is?"

There was a long pause. The evening of Bonnie's funeral in Houston, when all the guests had left the reception at the Vincent house and Elizabeth was alone with her parents, they had discussed how they would move forward. They agreed to ignore the clamorous requests for press interviews and quietly hire a lawyer to pursue legal avenues that would hamstring Udo Holthaus's attempts at getting Bonnie's insurance money. On the heels of Bonnie's murder, they were already certain Udo was involved.

Elizabeth was faced with her first test of their agreement. "This is strictly between you and me?" Elizabeth asked finally.

"Absolutely," Grace said without hesitating. She could tell from the way Elizabeth was warming to her that Bonnie's big sister needed someone to trust.

"I'm serious," Elizabeth pressed on, her manner calm but insistent. "You can't use any of this for a story." Her eyes probed, and Grace nodded yes. Elizabeth seemed to relax. "You're right about Udo—he was an awful husband," she revealed. "He treated Bonnie like dirt and she took it. My parents have hired a civil lawyer to contest the insurance policy. We plan to show there's enough reasonable doubt to point to him as Bonnie's killer and keep him from cashing in."

Without warning, Elizabeth started to cry. Grace imagined she had done so many times those past days.

"I didn't mean to upset you," Grace consoled, feeling guilty, "but I had to come. Will you and your parents talk to me on camera if the lawsuit is filed?"

"We'll have to see," said Elizabeth, still crying. "Bonnie deserves our help. God knows she didn't get it when she was alive. It's as if no one noticed her. I got all the attention before she came along, and after little Ellie was born Bonnie got lost in the shuffle. She made a success of her life in spite of us, not because of us. And now this..." Her voice broke off.

Grace reached out and took Elizabeth's hand, softly but firmly. "Can I keep in touch with you? For Bonnie's sake, Elizabeth?"

There was gratitude in Elizabeth's eyes as she tried to dry them. "Call me Liz. Yes. I promise if there's anything new from the family I'll let you know."

Everything was frenetic around the Dallas County courthouse the next morning. A constant river of people hurried in and out, tending to the daily business of millions of residents. Inside, in the DA's office, his secretary answered a telephone ringing. "District Attorney Hubert Turner's office," her manner was crisp and businesslike.

Across town, Grace was sitting in the newsroom scanning through images on her computer as she held the phone to her ear with her shoulder. "Grace Gleason from TXDA television," she said. "Is he in?"

"I'll see," the secretary said. "Hold on, please."

When he came to the phone, District Attorney Turner's

greeting had an air of pomposity. Grace had heard the newsroom talk about him—his patronizing attitude toward reporters and explosive reaction when the news coverage was unfavorable. Grace had called him before with brief questions, but never anything of substance. This time, she expected him to be difficult.

"How's that busy little reporter?" she heard him begin. She felt he sounded like a teenager trying an opening insult on for size.

"Busy," Grace answered, annoyed and immediately feeling combative. "I'm wondering why you haven't brought any charges in the Bonnie Vincent case?"

"Charges? Against who?"

"Everyone I talk to says there's motive and opportunity to implicate her husband."

"There's precious little evidence," Hubert shot back. "With what the police have pieced together, I wouldn't be able to get a shop-lifting conviction. You can quote me on that."

Still scrolling through computer images, Grace pulled up a news screen with a photo of the D.A. and a headline: *Dallas County DA May Run For Mayor.* She tried to start reading the article silently as she talked. "Can I come interview you for the record?" she asked.

"You just got all the interview you're going to get," the D.A. responded bluntly.

"You've got the bite mark, a probable match," Grace quarreled. "Holthaus hid the fact that he was out of work and ran up his wife's credit cards at dance clubs and massage parlors. He not only scrubbed her body clean, but he also scrubbed the apartment and didn't leave as much as his own fingerprints anywhere. And he was the last one to see her. Plus, you haven't even revealed whatever other evidence you guys have. What more do you need?"

"Sounds like somebody thinks she knows how to do my job better than I do," Hubert jibed.

"Let's just say you're not going to get my vote," Grace countered.

"Did I say I was running for anything? You need to stop believing every rumor you hear. I have to go. I know you're doing your job, but you just have to let me do mine."

Hubert Turner's flip attitude was quickly fraying Grace's nerves. "Yes, but you're not doing..." she tried to continue the argument.

But Hubert interrupted her by hanging up.

Grace was left with a resounding click and dial tone. "Hang up on me, you pompous ass?" she frowned. She slammed the phone down and pulled up the on-line article, reading aloud. "Sources close to the D.A. say he will throw his hat in the ring soon."

She sat staring at the online article and mulling over her options. There was still the stripper, Destiny Desire. Tomorrow she would try to corner her.

Destiny Desire grew up Dana Garman in Pine Bluff, Arkansas. Born when her mother was fifteen, Dana never knew her father—he skipped out when she was two weeks old.

Dana's mother immediately met an older man, Thurman, who promised to take care of them, and the drunken, stormy marriage lasted several years until the fights and arguments became too intense. Thurman set them up in a rented bungalow on the edge of town and left them on their own.

A procession of men moved in—Kenny, a mechanic, then Mike, a roofer and finally Howard, who had no job that Dana could ascertain. Each of them had a unique personality but one thing in common: they partied incessantly with Dana's mother, whose cocaine habit was supported by Thurman's alimony checks. None of them stayed longer than a year, and the only time they paid attention to the blossoming daughter in the house was when they were drunk or high and sneaked into her room after her mother passed out, trying to grope Dana while she slept. She learned to keep her door locked.

Dana had her first sexual experience with the senior star of the football team when she was a ninth grader at Pine Bluff High School, a child in a woman's body.

She confessed it all to her best friend, Becky Jo Lessler, the next day.

"Jeez, what was it like?" asked Becky Jo.

"It hurt. He was rough and in a big hurry," she whined. "We were in the towel room of the gym after the coaches and players had all gone home. I think he was worried someone would come in there. I didn't really like it at all in the few seconds he lasted. But you know what?"

"What?"

"I liked the part beforehand."

Becky Jo scrunched up her freckled face. "Beforehand?" she puzzled.

"He got so hot and passionate when we were kissing. And he started panting like a Saint Bernard when we undressed and he ran his hands over my body. It made me feel special."

"Do you love him?" asked her obviously intrigued friend.

"I guess so," Dana answered. "Trent says he's really attracted to me, and I totally like it. I mean, he's a senior and a big football star, right? But you know, I stand there in my room looking in the mirror, and I can't figure out what it is about me that turns him on."

"Are you fucking kidding?" Becky Jo screeched. "I'd give up chocolate to have an awesome face and body like yours."

There were plenty of other boyfriends during her sophomore and junior years, all with hormones racing, eager to get Dana into the back seat of their cars or in her bedroom when her mother was out living it up. They introduced her to beer, pot, condoms and oral sex.

When she was a senior, with her mother immersed in a depraved lifestyle and providing zero supervision, Dana met an older man who noticed her milling around a convenience store.

She was looking at the candy bars, trying to decide which to buy, when he sidled up and watched, amused, over her shoulder.

"Which one's your favorite?" he asked nonchalantly with a laugh in his voice.

"I can't decide," she said, catching her breath from the surprise of being approached. "I like them all."

"All of 'em?" he chuckled, and she nodded.

The tall, smoothly handsome, slick-haired stranger scooped up about a dozen different bars and motioned for her to follow him.

She did, and as they reached the clerk she gasped as he pulled a fat wad of bills from his pocket, peeled off a fifty and handed it to the clerk.

As the clerk bagged the candy, the man said, "Keep it," and smiled at Dana. "That's my SUV out front. Want a ride somewhere?" he asked her.

She stood tiptoe to see over the shelving and through the front window, straining to get a glimpse of his car, and then hesitated.

"Sure you do," he answered for her. "But first, how about a drink to go with that chocolate?"

"Okay," Dana said, striving mightily to catch her breath.

"Ma'am," he told the clerk, "take a big slush drink out of that change for this little gal." The clerk frowned at the brash man making overtures to one of the local high school girls, but she shrugged and rang up the drink, sticking the change in her smock pocket.

The man handed Dana the bag and guided her to the drink machine where she poured a slushee. This knockout high school girl, usually coolly and in control around the dorky boys who followed her down the hallways at school, was reacting nervously to an older man who appeared to be successful and confident.

Dana followed the stranger outside. As they got into his car, sparkling clean and leather-smelling, he asked, "Where would you like to go, sweetie pie?"

"Nowhere, really," Dana answered, blushing. "I live right around the corner. Don't get mad. I wanted to see the inside of this beautiful car. It's awesome."

The man leaned across the console toward her and said, "I'm not mad, little darlin'. My name's Tom. I'm a manufacturer's rep from Dallas. I cover this Arkansas territory every week. And honey, you're about the cutest thing I've seen since I hit town. Come have dinner with me tonight." It didn't sound like a question.

"Sure," she said without hesitation, her breathing abnormally quick.

"I'll meet you right here," Tom told her, adding, "Wear something pretty. We're going to a very nice place. He leaned in and kissed her lightly on the cheek, then reached across her and opened the door. As she climbed out, he told her, "Seven o'clock."

Dana arrived early and stood waiting in front of the store, watching nervously as cars drove by. She looked surprised when he showed up. As she jumped in with enthusiasm and he headed the SUV up Interstate 530 toward Little Rock, she appeared even more taken aback.

"Where are we going?" she asked as the city limit sign faded behind them.

"Pine Bluff doesn't have any good restaurants," Tom told her matter-of-factly. "You're too damned good looking to waste on the shit they serve up in this one-dog town. We're going first class tonight."

Dana relaxed at the man's flattery, and as she sat back, her eyes closed, enjoying the ride and listening to an old Journey song on his CD player, his hand found her knee and rested there for the entire hour-long trip.

Tom showed up every week, took her to dinner and then to his hotel room.

Three months to the day from their first meeting, as

they lay in bed after sex, he said, "I want you to move to Dallas where I can see you more often."

She had already virtually dropped out of school, checking into homeroom at eight a.m. and then ducking out with friends. By the time the school discovered their absence, they were shopping at Taylor-Mart or hanging out at a beer joint outside of town where nobody checked IDs nor asked questions. The school's guidance counselor called parents to inquire about their truancy, but Dana's mother was never home, or if she was, she was passed out.

When Dana agreed to the move, she didn't bother to tell her mother. She simply packed her belongings and took off with Tom. By then, she had learned he was married, but she didn't care.

"I'm in love," she told Becky Jo just before leaving. "Tom's going to get a divorce, and then we'll have a life together. That's enough for now."

Tom found her a small apartment and a job in Dallas. He knew the owner of a dance club called the Saucy Lady, he told her, who promised Tom that Dana could skip the audition and start dancing immediately if he liked her looks.

Suzie Sinn, who told Dana her real name was Susan Sheridan, was the first person Dana met at the dance club. Unlike some of the strung-out, bitchy girls working there, Suzie was friendly and assumed the role of a mentor to the new dancer from small town Arkansas. Suzie wasn't one of the drug-taking alcoholics. A single mother five years older than Dana, she was studying cosmetology in the mornings and dancing at night to pay her tuition and rent.

"My aunt," she told Dana, "is supportive and watches my kids nights while I'm working to make a future for them."

The evening before Dana was scheduled to start, Suzie sifted through a wardrobe helping her pick out an outfit.

"You need a name, too," Suzie said. She thought for a moment. "Well, those guys will all think you're desirable. How about Dana Desire?" Dana smiled brightly at the suggestion.

"No," Suzie interjected, "Destiny. Destiny Desire. That's who you are."

The day after Destiny's debut, Suzie invited her to her apartment and taught her some dance moves.

"I really enjoy having another woman to share with," Destiny said, "especially someone who was the first to help me learn my way around the Saucy Lady. I only had one close friend in school. But you seem more like a big sister to me."

They spent what spare time Suzie had together, often in the afternoons when Suzie waited for her children to return home from school. After the new friendship was two weeks old, as they drank tea on the porch watching for the school bus, Destiny told the story about how she had met Tom.

"He treated me great," Destiny said. "I had never been taken to expensive restaurants before, or given nice presents. He gave me this bracelet—see?" She flashed a sterling silver Daniel Orosco-designed bauble for Suzie to admire.

"So old Tom was a married dude, huh?" Suzie asked. "How'd he break it to you?"

"There was this place we used to go in Little Rock, before I moved here," Destiny related. "It was this really neat motel where you drive into a garage, shut the door with a remote control and walk right into the bedroom—just like going in your house from the garage."

"Jesus," Suzie said. "That sounds real sleazy."

"No, no," Destiny protested. "It was very cool. Anyway, we went there a lot—to sleep over, you know? One night we were eating takeout and watching TV in that place, and Tom just put his hand on my face and said 'I'm married,' just like that. Then he started to cry."

"He sounds like a doozie."

"I thought it was sweet. He told me that he was crying because he had made a mistake and he would have left his wife a long time ago if it wasn't for their kids. Then he cried some more. So I told him it was all right, and we made love."

"Honey, you're the most naïve little gal who ever came

to the big city from Slippery Rock."

"Pine Bluff," Destiny corrected.

"Whatever. So what happened to lover boy?"

"One day, right after I moved here, he told me his wife had found out about us and he couldn't leave her."

"Jeez. So he ditched you?"

"He had three kids. He told me he loved me, but he couldn't see me anymore. They moved to someplace in Arizona. I never saw him again."

"The bastard," said Suzie.

"Oh, no," Destiny objected. "He was the nicest guy I ever met. He apologized and everything for lying to me. And the night we said goodbye he gave me two thousand dollars—you know, to help me get by until I saved up more of my own money. He could've disappeared and left me cold."

"I don't care," Suzie said. "They're all bastards."

"They're not," Destiny protested. "They're not all bastards. Most of the men I've met at the club are really nice guys who want us to treat them special."

"I love you to death, honey," Suzie laughed, "but you're so God damned green it hurts. Any prospects for a replacement?"

Destiny shook her head no. "We can't date customers, of course. The only other guys I meet are at the health club where I work out. It's odd, those guys all staring at me," she said. "I think it would be a blast to let them know what I do for a living—that they could see a lot more of me for the price of a drink and a few Washingtons to stick in my G string. But in a funny way, it's a turn-on."

"As much a turn-on as making all these yahoos who come to the club good and horny?" Suzie asked, giggling.

'It's magnified," Destiny responded in seriousness, "because those workout guys might think I'm a dental hygienist or hair stylist for all they know. They know nothing about the life I live four nights a week."

Early the next morning, activity at the Dallas Fitness Center was frenetic. Most of the machines were in use, and some of the members, both men and women, milled around toweling down or stretching, waiting for the next machine in their routine to become available.

Destiny was on a treadmill, wearing a skimpy sports bra and short shorts. She glanced around the room as she speed-walked. She was attracting plenty of attention from the men who worked out on equipment nearby. As they viewed their own flexed muscle poses in the floor-to-ceiling mirrors, they grasped at opportunities to peer at the reflection of this sexy woman perspiring through her routine.

Dressed for a workout, Grace wandered through the rows of equipment and straining bodies until she spotted Destiny. Grace had planned this master stroke. A visit to The Saucy Lady the night before, coupled with stopping here and signing up for a trial membership, had set it up. Grace hoped that Destiny would believe it was a chance meeting, at least until she could gauge the dancer's willingness to talk to her. Besides, she had meant to check out this exercise center ever since she had moved there. The idea of a daily workout before going in to the station appealed to her, especially since childbirth had softened her naturally slender physique.

Grace waited for the heavyset older man, wheezing and panting on the treadmill next to Destiny's. He wouldn't last long, she thought. She was right; five minutes later he huffed and puffed to a slow walk, then cooled down at a hangdog pace for several minutes and stepped heavily off the conveyer. His cotton sweat suit was soaked with perspiration, and his face had turned crimson. Grace wondered if she would need to employ cardiopulmonary resuscitation. As the portly man turned to leave, he gave an embarrassed, apologetic look at Grace and headed for the locker room. She wiped down the sweat that he had ignored on the handrails and stepped on.

After several minutes of slow walking, Grace turned up the speed, and as she did she began to match Destiny's pace.

The stripper glanced over at her and appeared pleasantly surprised. "Hey, you're that channel seven reporter," she chirped.

"Hi. Yes, that's me."

"I'm..."

"I know," Grace interrupted. "Destiny Desire, right?"

Destiny registered surprise, her eyes widening. "How'd you know? Have you caught my act?"

"I saw your picture on the wall at your club," Grace explained. "One of the waitresses told me you work out here. I need to talk to you."

Destiny shut off her treadmill and started to towel off, eyeing Grace with suspicion.

Grace turned her machine off, too. "I've been covering the story about Bonnie Vincent's murder," she said.

The dancer lighted up. "That's where I've seen you." She struck a pose and started imitating. "This is Grace Gleason reporting for channel seven on-the-spot news. I'm not making fun of you. I think you're terrific."

"Thanks. I'm trying to run down some things about her husband, Udo Holthaus."

Wrinkling her brow into a frown, Destiny said, "The cops came in asking us all about him. The boss doesn't like us talking to them about customers. But I'll tell you, Grace. He comes in there all the time. He's kind of a sad guy."

"How long do you remember him coming to the Saucy Lady?"

"A long time," Destiny seemed eager to talk about it. "The girls think he's gross, but they treat him great because the son of a bitch throws money around like some millionaire. Lap dances, champagne cocktails, sex." A touch of panic crossed her face at uttering the comment. "Don't get me wrong. I don't turn tricks, but some of the girls do to support their...well, their bad habits."

Grace wondered if Destiny's eagerness to qualify her sex comment was authentic, but she realized it didn't really matter. Udo Holthaus, and his sordid habits, was her only concern. "He's there every day?" she asked.

"Pretty much. Usually in the evening. Sometimes the afternoons, too. He gets drunk, has his fun and then disappears before the late-night rowdy assholes come in."

"Thanks a lot. I appreciate your candor."

Destiny's eyes widened. "I can't believe the guy is that poor murdered woman's husband. Do you think..."

"Sorry, I really can't speculate," Grace cut her off.

"But do you..." Destiny pressed, obviously eager for some gossip.

"Maybe I'll see you again," Grace interrupted as she turned and walked briskly away before Destiny could complete the question. The dancer looked puzzled, but as Grace disappeared through the doorway, Destiny dismissed the subject with a shrug of her shoulders, toweled her forehead one more time and turned the treadmill back on.

Returning to her locker, Grace felt strangely energized. Destiny Desire had confirmed her suspicions. *I might try to catch you at your game, Udo Holthaus,* she thought.

CHAPTER 9: Danger at The Saucy Lady

THE SAUCY LADY club was a dark and calamitous cavern set back on a side street off the busy Northwest Highway. The club shattered the air with high-energy music blaring at a near-pain level of one hundred and twenty decibels, accompanied by bursts of raucous laughter and a ceaseless din of glasses and bottles rattling.

Despite the club's lack of class, The Saucy Lady's dancers had the strongest reputation in the city for attractiveness, and so it was a popular destination for conventioneers, bachelor partiers, businessmen and college students.

It was barely past dinner hour the evening of Grace's meeting with Destiny Desire at the Dallas Fitness Center. Suzie Sinn was gyrating on the stage in front of two grinning, middle-aged men in white shirts and loosened neckties. She was wearing only a sequined G-string, silver garter and four-inch silver high heels. As she squatted in front of the two eager customers, each of them slipped folded bills into her thong and gaped at her barely covered crotch grinding in front of them.

Nearby, Udo Holthaus sat at the bar, sipping a Scotch and ogling Suzie. Swaying and wriggling to the beat of the pounding song, she danced provocatively over to Udo, kneeled down and swiveled her torso close to his face.

He stuffed several dollars in her garter, baring the big space in his bite with a wide grin and leaning closer, watching intently. She smiled back at him, turned around to writhe her ass in his direction, and then danced away to another part of the stage where some college-aged young men wearing blue jeans and sneakers were pounding down beers. As she danced in front of them, they shouted encouragement.

"Great bod," yelled one.

"Shake those titties, babe," blurted another as he turned and high-fived his buddies giddily as she teased them with her sexy movements.

"And now, gents and ladies," the unctuous voice of the club announcer boomed over the speakers, "let's give a hand to another saucy lady, Miss Destiny Desire."

The star attraction always stops a club cold for a moment. Chatter dies down, the clinking of glasses and bottles ebbs and heads turn.

The Saucy Lady manager had decided this fresh and pretty Arkansas girl was their new headliner. She attracted unusual attention whenever she danced, collected the most tips and fielded more requests for lap dances than most of the other dancers. She was, her boss had decided, a top draw.

Destiny sauntered out on the stage, smiling widely to enthusiastic applause. She was wearing a see-through negligee with a bra and G-string visible underneath. She grasped the pole and did a spin around it, and then started to dance, first slowly sliding the negligee off as she grasped and circled the pole slowly, then reaching behind her back and unfastening the bra, letting it fall to the floor.

Udo leaned forward on his bar stool, his interest intensified, as Destiny danced away from the pole.

Suzie left the college boys who were not tipping and moved back toward Udo, dancing slowly in front of him, extending her leg and pointing alluringly toward her garter. He stuffed more bills into it, but he barely looked at her. His attention was directed totally at Destiny Desire.

A small crowd of men who had been milling around the club or sitting at tables in the back began to gather near the stage. Udo swiveled around and reacted crossly as they crowded in to get a better look at the object of his attention.

Meanwhile, Destiny moved across the stage to the two white-shirted businessmen and they stuffed dollars into in her G-string as she leaned over them and shimmied her breasts.

Udo and the gathering group stared at her, and nearly half of them wandered around the bar toward Destiny's new location, straining to get a better view.

A topless waitress pushed through the cluster of drunken oglers and stopped next to Udo with a tray of drinks. She took one off and set it in front of him. He threw some bills on her tray, and as she started to make change he waved her away. She nodded a dispassionate "thank you" for the tip and worked her way down the bar.

During all of this activity, Udo had not taken his eyes from Destiny.

Finally, the music stopped. Destiny and Suzie stooped to gather dollar bills from the floor that had been tossed at them and then descended the steps to the bar level, slipping their bras back on.

Destiny pulled Suzie aside. "Listen, honey. Do me a favor, will you?" she said with a tone of urgency.

"Sure. Just as long as it won't cost me money."

"Actually, it'll make you money," Destiny promised.

"Then count me in."

"See that guy over there—the half-drunk asshole that was feeding you dollar bills?" said Destiny, pointing out Holthaus.

"I know who he is. He's in here all the time," Suzie nodded, uninterested.

"You can use the money, right? For you kids?"

"Yeah..." Suzie was guarded.

"Go ask him if he wants a lap dance."

"Why don't you?" Suzie sounded skeptical. "He's always asking for you. What's wrong with the guy?"

"Nothing, I swear," Destiny said. "He's okay. He can get a little rough, and you might have to pull his hands off you a few times, but you can handle him. And he'll tip you great. I've danced for him before, but I feel a little creepy when I'm around him, for some reason. Suzie, I'd do it, but I don't feel like putting up with any crap tonight. Besides, you need the money a lot more."

"Well...Okay. But he'd better tip big like you say," Suzie said.

"Count on it," Destiny said. "You can hit him big time for a champagne cocktail, too."

Suzie moved toward Udo Holthaus while Destiny disappeared through the dressing room door. Suzie was in her bra and skimpy thong and carried a small bag. Udo appeared annoyed at first, seeing that it was Suzie and not Destiny approaching, but when Suzie sat on the stool next to him and put her arm around his shoulder, drawing her face close to his, he began to show more interest.

"Hi, honey. Having a good time?" Suzie purred.

"It's getting better," Udo said.

"How about a lap dance?" she asked, getting closer.

"Why? What's so special about your lap dances?" Udo asked, taking a swig of his drink.

"Why don't you come with me and you'll find out how special they are. Do you like my body?"

"I've seen worse."

Suzie straightened up on the stool, pouting. "There are lots of guys in the bar I can go talk to, guys who appreciate me. Come on. What do you say?" She pulled on Holtaus's shirt. He stood up but weaved unsteadily.

He propped himself against the bar and nodded. "Sure, baby. Let's go." Udo grabbed his drink off the bar, and Suzie led him by the arm through the club toward a private back room.

"You know," she said as they walked past the bar toward the room, "I could sure use a drink when I'm dancing. I really worked up a thirst up there, and a little champagne would definitely make me want to give you a dance you'll never forget."

"Yeah, sweetheart. Whatever," Udo slurred.

Suzie motioned toward a barmaid as she and Udo disappeared into the private room, a dark recess with a leather sofa and side chair. Cheap motel-sale paintings had been hung haphazardly on the walls. A small end table held a lamp with a muted shade, creating enough shadow to hide blemishes and stretch marks but permitting enough light to let the patrons see through their drunken haze what they were paying for.

"Let's take care of the technicalities first," Suzie said in a businesslike manner. "It'll be fifty bucks, up front."

Udo dug a hundred out of his wallet and handed it to her. "Make it worth my while."

Suzie took the bill and stuck it in her handbag. The barmaid arrived with two champagne cocktails on a tray. She set them on the table and Holthaus tossed a credit card down.

"Here, doll, put a little something on there for yourself," he said eagerly, as if becoming immersed in the sordid atmosphere of his surroundings. "Not too much, now," he added and laughed his raspy cackle. Still standing unsteadily, hanging onto his Scotch, he reached toward the barmaid. She pushed his hand away, nodded and smiled at Suzie before hurrying out. Udo flopped down on the sofa, and Suzie swayed to the music, slipping her top off. Udo leaned back and half-closed his eyes, a drunken smile on his face as he watched her dance seductively toward him.

While Udo Holthaus was getting inebriated and throwing money indiscriminately at strippers, Grace sat in her parked car across the darkened street and watched men go in and out of the Saucy Lady Club. She had arrived more than an hour earlier, circling through the parking lot and searching for Udo's car. Her senses were reeling from the fear and excitement of being in this unfamiliar space, not wanting to be seen yet driven to know if her adversary was there. She felt her heart surge when his car came into view, and she instinctively wheeled out of the lot and across to the other side, where she waited.

What are you doing here? she thought to herself, and several times she reached for the ignition but couldn't turn it. She waited longer. Every time the door opened and another customer exited, she felt the ambiguous electric charge of hope and dread that it would be Udo Holthaus.

Finally, as she was contemplating leaving for the fourth time, the front door opened and this time Udo appeared, walking like a toddler still learning his mobility skills. Grace watched him wander for a moment as he got his bearings, searching for his car and then finding it. As the dome light ignited inside it from his remote key, Grace cranked the ignition, revved her car and rushed across the street into the Saucy Lady lot. She pulled her car next to Udo's and rolled her window down as he opened his door.

Udo stopped and gave her a hazy, incredulous stare. "What the fuck do you want, Gleason?"

"Having a good time in there, Udo?"

"What kind of time I'm having is no God damned concern of yours," he blurted.

"Maybe it is if you're supposed to be mourning the loss of your wife," she said bitterly. "Do you remember her? Do you remember Bonnie, Udo?"

"Screw off, bitch. Maybe I came here to get my mind off losing her."

"Sure. Like you got your mind off telling her you lost your job? Or forgot to tell her about the strippers and whores you ran her charge cards up with?"

"What? I don't know what the hell you're talking about," he said.

"Yes you do, Udo," she retorted angrily. "You know exactly what I'm talking about. Bonnie found out about everything, didn't she? She found out how you lost your job. Played fast and loose with all the women. She knew, didn't she?

Two men emerged from the club laughing and smoking cigars, and Udo froze, watching them as they walked past. They stopped talking momentarily and cast curious looks first at Udo and then at Grace, but without speaking moved on toward a far corner of the parking lot and opened their car door with the "beep-beep" of a remote.

Udo watched them drive away, then slammed his door,

drew closer and leaned in near Grace. He staggered a bit and caught his balance on the side of her door. Grace recoiled as the heavy stench of liquor on his breath engulfed her.

"You do-goody fucking bitch," Udo growled. "I don't need you to tell me how to live my life. I'm warning you. You'd better quit following me around."

"Or what, Udo?" she said.

She was a little afraid, but this was the man she had promised herself, and Ned Moore, she would try to expose. Grace was determined not to back down from the monster until she had confronted him. She had hunted him down without giving it much thought beyond a nagging, indefinable need to hear him admit the truth. That she was stepping into murky and dangerous territory hadn't quite fazed her yet. But now she was struck by an intense form of fright she had never experienced as Udo reached suddenly through the window, gripped the back of her neck and yanked it roughly as she tried desperately to break free. The strength of his fingers digging into her nape astonished her.

"I can deal with nosy whores like you," Udo snorted in a tone so inhuman that Grace cringed.

"Let...go...Holthaus!" Grace shouted as a mental image of Bonnie Vincent fighting him off flashed through her mind. With as much force as she could gather, Grace grabbed Udo's hand and pulled it from her neck, sliding almost completely sideways in her car so that the center console dug painfully into her side.

Udo wobbled backward as she pushed his arm away. He caught himself before falling. He stood next to her car, tottering back and forth, looked in at Grace uncertainly for a moment as if plotting a move. Then he gave her a dismissive wave of both hands and staggered back to his car.

Incensed, Grace leaned out of the window and screamed at him. "You gonna deal with me like you dealt with Bonnie, Udo?"

Udo tumbled into his car, started it up, threw an acid

look back at Grace and squealed out of the parking lot.

Grace sat shaking almost uncontrollably, gasping deeply. Her neck burned from his fingers digging into it, and her ribs ached from crashing against the console. Her mind was racing like a centrifuge, and she tried to fight off tears that were coming in torrents.

"My God, Grace, you idiot," she shouted as she trembled and sobbed. "What are you doing? Are you crazy?"

Grace had acted out of calculated but blind instinct. She was confident in her suspicions, but despite her previous contacts with the man, and with his wife, Grace knew little of what made Udo Holthaus the man he had become.

He had grown up an odd and ungainly small-town Texas boy with an insecure, gap-tooth smile. His mother and father had been brought separately to America as children. Their parents had settled in the German community of Fredericksberg, Texas, where relatives lived. The small village near Austin had been founded by Germans fleeing economic hardship in their homeland in the 1800s.

Udo's parents grew up speaking the unique Texas German dialect—a curious mix of Teutonic accent and Southern drawl—that had been spoken there for generations. They met, married, and raised their two sons, Heinrich and Udo, in that same provincial setting, speaking the odd vernacular and subjecting them to strict demands for obedience and conformity.

Udo witnessed his father's frequent beatings of his mother throughout his turbulent school years. Because his older brother had left home as a teen to escape the mayhem, Udo was essentially an only child.

Twice he tried to run away, but the community was close-knit and there was nowhere to go. He would hide, trying to decide where to flee, but the search parties eventually found him curled up in a barn or deer blind, shivering from cold and fear. When he was returned home, there was penance to pay.

His father's belt stung him many times for his insubordination.

When he was seventeen, Udo followed his brother's lead. He abandoned Fredericksburg, lied about his age and joined the Coast Guard.

His shipmates laughed at the young seaman's aloofness and unusual accent. Assigned to a patrol boat out of Pascagoula, Mississippi, he kept to himself and ignored their teasing. Finally, after six months of abuse, he responded one hot and sunny June day as the crew chipped paint while the cutter put in for fuel at Corpus Christi.

"Hey, kraut head," a fellow swabbie taunted him. "Why not try talking the fucking king's English for a change?"

"Guten tag, mein Admiral," mocked another, offering up a Nazi salute.

Everyone laughed, but Udo continued chipping paint. "Go ahead, make fun," he grunted. "I don't mind one bit. I'm in the U.S. Coast Guard, and I've had seen more strange and exciting places in months than I've experienced my entire life up to now. Norfolk, Pensacola, New Orleans, New York—never have I imagined such places. You can tease me, but I like this life."

Eventually Udo managed to make a few friends, mostly misfits like him, and they partied together on liberty. Despite seeing such cities initially from the deck of a ship moving port-to-port, Udo became intimate with each port of call from its underbelly—bars, strip palaces and whorehouses.

On one occasion, his philandering led to trouble. Drunk and angry, he beat up a dancer in the parking lot of a bar for taking money for lap dances and disappearing backstage. Her screams brought the bouncer, who subdued Holthaus and called the Shore Patrol. The Coast Guard kept it quiet, but Holthaus spent time in the brig and took a demotion for his indiscretion.

All his life, even beneath the cover of a respected news position, Udo Holthaus had been a small-town loner from a strange part of the Texas hill country, in turn intrigued and enraged by the depravity of the dark world he had discovered.

CHAPTER 10: Let's Go to Court

THREE DAYS had passed since her secret agreement with Detective Ned Moore, and Grace felt as if she had been on a roller coaster. A visit to Elizabeth Vincent. The contentious phone call to DA Turner. Her fitness center conversation with Destiny Desire. And finally, the violent confrontation with Udo, In that span of seventy-two frenetic hours she had gathered a wealth of information she had barely found time to store on her computer.

Her neck and side were still sore from the previous night's attack by Holthous as she sat across the desk from her news director feeling irritable and angry. Lloyd Hamilton sat stiffly at his desk, trying to look important. Despite her discomfort, Grace had to stifle a laugh; staffers called this pose his "presidential presence."

"The district attorney called me all teed off," Lloyd said in a solemn voice. "He says you've been pushing him, being unprofessional."

Grace puckered her lips in an annoyed grimace. She knew this rebuke was forthcoming and was ready with her comeback. "Turner's a grade-A number one idiot," she said caustically.

"Grace," said Lloyd, ignoring the retort, "I'm about at the end of my rope. I'm ordering you to do nothing more on Bonnie Vincent unless there's a break. And even then you consult with me."

"Okay," she agreed, trying to look as casual as possible while she gauged his reaction.

Lloyd sat back, surprise registering on his normally solemn expression. "What?" he responded warily.

"I said okay. I get it. There'll be no more coverage on

Bonnie's death unless there's a break."

Few things delighted Grace more these days than springing a shocker on Lloyd and watching the air expel from his balloon. The news director's cubic jaw dropped a bit, and he slumped in his chair, his darting eyes searching Grace's for a catch. "Are you serious?" his normally baritone voice came at her in a high-pitched comedy of disbelief. "You're agreeing with me?"

"I am," she said, fighting to hold back her glee. "I agree that we should drop the story unless something big happens. As long as you promise that I'll get to cover it if there's some new development."

Lloyd leaned forward slowly. He smiled and eased his tone a little, the battle with his cantankerous reporter obviously won. "Now you're talking sense. Thank you," he said in a fatherly tone.

"No, thank you," Grace flashed him her best gotcha smile. "Because, you see, Lloyd, there has been a break."

"What kind of break?"

"I got a call five minutes ago from Elizabeth Vincent," Grace divulged. "Bonnie's family has sued Udo Holthaus in civil court."

"Civil court? For what?" Lloyd's face registered confusion.

"To keep Udo from collecting Bonnie's life insurance," Grace said.

"You're joking."

"I'm serious. So now that means the story's very much alive, and I'll be covering the trial. Right?"

Grace could see bewilderment in Lloyd's reaction. He obviously didn't know whether to look astonished, or angry, or both. After a long pause, with a scratch of his wide chin he shrugged weakly, sending an adrenaline rush through his reporter. The story was hers!

It was unusually warm for eight-thirty a.m. in May,

portending an early start to summer and reviving the arguments on opinion programs about global warming.

Outside the Dallas County Courthouse, the city was preparing for a busy day of jurisprudence. Individuals of all sizes, shapes, ages, races and economic status swarmed in and out of the courthouse. Cars, trucks, buses and SUVs rushed by on South Lamar Street carrying passengers who had no clue that a pitched battle was about to be waged over a puzzling and brutal murder.

Grace couldn't recall when she had been so excited about covering a story. Years, probably. After several months of denials, stalled police work and inactivity in the DA's office, Udo Holthaus's actions on that violent day in February were being called into question. This wasn't a criminal action, but Grace knew she was going to see the man sweat for the crime she was certain, deep to her core, Udo Holthaus had committed.

As she walked vigorously toward the front entrance, she paused when she noticed a taxi pull up in front and Elizabeth Vincent and her family's lawyer, John Boyd, emerge.

Elizabeth was dressed in a conservative, cream-colored suit with a single strand of pearls and no earrings. Despite the dark circles under her eyes which makeup could never fully hide, Elizabeth looked to Grace enormously elegant in the simple outfit and with her long, dark hair pulled up. Grace approached them eagerly, waving to Elizabeth who smiled, seeming relieved to spot a friendly face. As Grace approached Elizabeth, John Boyd started to intervene, but Elizabeth grasped his arm and nodded. Grace took Elizabeth's arm in hers, and they walked together toward the entrance with John a step behind.

"Are you okay," Grace grasped Elizabeth's hand.

"I'm scared to death," Elizabeth confessed, sounding tiny and insecure.

"Are you going to testify?"

Elizabeth shook her head yes. "My dad's too sick. I drew the short straw. My mother and aunt and some cousins plan to be here for moral support."

"I'll be there if that will be any help," Grace said. She pulled Elizabeth closer and semi-whispered, "This is your big chance, Liz. You can ruin this guy."

Elizabeth stopped and turned her green eyes directly into Grace's. "If he doesn't ruin me first," she said, her voice quivering.

Grace pulled Elizabeth even closer in a gesture of encouragement, and they turned to walk again, arm-in-arm. Grace glanced around momentarily, searching for other reporters in the vicinity, wondering how this show of friendship might play among her colleagues. She knew her emotions about this story must be jeopardizing her credibility as an objective journalist. Yet she felt an overpowering urge to protect and support this woman. As they reached the doorway, John caught up with them and took Elizabeth's arm, guiding her away from Grace and inside. Grace stopped and let them go ahead, watching them make their way slowly through security.

Elizabeth turned back with one final, feeble smile, and then disappeared with John Boyd into the cavern of the courthouse for an opportunity for a piece of justice.

"Good luck, Liz," Grace said softly.

The build-up to this trial in the media had been extensive, and every bench in the courtroom was tightly packed. A few people who arrived too late for seats lined the wall in the back and craned their necks to see who was there. Grace rushed down the aisle and slid into a bench in the reporter section. She looked around the courtroom and made some notes. She turned her attention to the table where Udo Holthaus was sitting, looking sour and uncomfortable. Udo glanced back at her for a fleet second, and his subtle scowl sent a shiver down Grace's back.

She quickly looked away and focused on Udo's lawyer, Hamlin McLaughlin. McLaughlin was a short, comical figure, about sixty, balding and paunchy. Grace thought he looked ill suited for a dignified courtroom, with his white linen suit and flowered necktie framed by red suspenders. She had heard all the stories about Hamlin. His silly theatrics in trials to divert a jury from the facts had made the rounds among the media, as had his zany, out-of-courtroom antics.

When word had gone out to TXDA that Hamlin McLaughlin would represent Holthaus, Grace dug up old video of post-trial interviews McLaughlin had conducted, to get a feel for his style. Immediately she could see how flamboyant, flippant and loquacious the man was. But he could give an interesting and incisive interview if the occasion seemed to call for it. *He's crazy as a Mensa,* Grace thought.

As Grace watched the video on a monitor in the newsroom, Mitchell Court noticed and came to watch with her. "You know about this guy?" he asked.

"A little," she said. "I know he has chewed up opposing lawyers when they didn't take him seriously."

"Exactly," Mitchell agreed. "For all his daffiness and unorthodox behavior, he's no dummy. He plays the part, but he has a knack of getting juries to listen to his twisted logic." Mitchell turned to leave but then stopped. "You know he was disbarred, don't you?"

"I heard—for some kind of underhanded deal he tried to make with a potential witness that backfired. Terwilliger over at the Associated Press says Hamlin went to Udo and offered to represent him against the Vincents. Hamlin needed a high-profile case to get help him back in the game after being reinstated."

"That's the story I heard," Mitchell confirmed. "Keep your eye on him. He's a shrewd cookie."

Grace watched Hamlin jerkily thumbing through files he had pulled from his briefcase, She played the conversation with Mitchell over in her mind and promised herself to watch this unconventional lawyer closely.

She quickly scanned the other two men sitting at the

defendant's table. She didn't know them, but she assumed that they represented the insurance company.

Across the aisle, John Boyd and Elizabeth Vincent were waiting quietly at the plaintiff's table. John was sitting back, reviewing some notes on a tablet. Elizabeth had her hands folded in her lap, and she cast a fleeting look back at her mother and other relatives who occupied a bench directly behind her. As they smiled, she turned back and sat very still, staring straight ahead as if waiting for a firing squad.

Grace's attention was suddenly diverted to the chamber door as it opened and the jury filed in behind a court clerk who motioned toward their seats. Grace scanned them briefly, making a note of the appearance, race, gender and approximate age of each of the twelve. As they sat down, the clerk took her position by the judge's bench and waited, hands clasped behind her in military rest position. At a small table next to her, a pudgy, elderly court reporter waited with a bored look for the action to begin.

Within seconds, the judge's chamber door opened and Jackson Montgomery entered. Grace had seen Judge Montgomery in action. He had been the first African-American ever appointed to the bench of a Texas state district court, and he had a reputation for being direct and tough, but fair. The Vincents would get a just and thorough hearing, she thought. But then, so would Udo.

"All rise," said the court clerk in an officious tone, her chin high and her gaze fixed into the empty space in front of her. There was a clamor as everyone in the courtroom rose as one. "The Ninth District Court of Dallas County, State of Texas, civil case number 38405, in the matter of Travis Vincent, et al, versus Udo Holthaus and the Premier Life Insurance Company, Judge Jackson Montgomery presiding, is now in session."

"Be seated," Judge Montgonery advised, his voice deep and demeanor serious. "This action is brought against Mr. Udo Holthaus by Mr. Travis Vincent, Ms. Elizabeth Vincent and other members of the family of the insured, Bonnie Vincent, who are attempting to prevent payment of the deceased's life insurance policy to her husband, Mr. Holthaus, named as the sole policy beneficiary. Are the plaintiffs ready to proceed?"

John Boyd stood. He wore a navy blue suit, with matching tie against the background of a white shirt. Perfectly measured French cuffs, with diamond-studded links, protruded from the coat sleeves. Boyd was tall and slender, tan from golf and beach vacations, his thick hair almost completely gray. "We are, your Honor," he responded quickly and sat back down beside Elizabeth.

"And the defense?"

"Yes, your Honor," the defendant's lawyer stepped out from the table and boomed the announcement. "At this time I move for dismissal, Judge. There is no evidence whatsoever connecting Mr. Holthaus with the unfortunate death of the policy holder, Bonnie Vincent, and the beneficiary payment should be paid as the deceased wished."

John Boyd rose quickly as if anticipating the move. "There's a long list of witnesses who will testify to Mr. Holthaus's motive and opportunity in this crime, your Honor. He remains a prime suspect."

Judge Montgomery leaned forward and surveyed the attornies over narrow reading glasses. "We're not here to argue the merits—or lack thereof—of a criminal charge. The jury has already been instructed that this civil case does not carry the same burden of reasonable doubt as a criminal case. Let's let them decide whether or not Mr. Holthaus is eligible for the insurance benefit. Mr. McLaughlin, your motion is denied."

Hamlin started to speak again, but the judge instantly motioned for him to sit down, and the lawyer acquiesced.

"Who represents the insurance company?" Judge Montgomery continued. One of the men Grace had not recognized at the defense table stood—a young lawyer with thinning hair and glasses that gave him a studious appearance. "Terrance Cooper, counsel for the Premier Life Insurance Company, your Honor."

Courtroom trials, unlike those depicted on popular television programs, are usually tedious affairs, sated with details, dates, times and places. The moments chosen to entertain a TV audience actually occur, but to entertain viewers they are mined from mountains of back-and-forth, he-said-she-said, hours-long questions, answers, speeches and legal arguments.

Grace was already fighting off a little boredom, but as she doodled on a notepad she took a sidelong glance at Udo. She was startled to see he was fixing his gaze directly at her. She felt her senses tingle as she sat up a bit straighter. As she was about to look down, feeling self-conscious, Holthaus subtly reached up and slowly drew his index finger across his throat. Seeing her eyes-wide reaction, he broadened his homely face into a menacing smile.

Grace looked quickly away, newly alert. She dared not let a snippet of any question or answer escape.

She promised herself to be vigilant as John Boyd questioned the first witness, Medical Examiner Brad Nessler. The testimony especially held Grace's attention because she had interviewed the examiner for TXDA. After the trivia of his background, his credentials and the description of his job responsibilities had been dispatched, the meaty part of Brad's testimony began.

"The cause of death was asphyxiation," Brad told the court in response to John Boyd's question. "Ms. Vincent died of strangulation."

"Were there any marks on the body besides those that led to that conclusion?" John asked.

"We found what looked like a bite mark on her neck," Brad testified, and a murmuring sound rippled through the assembled crowd even though Grace imagined most of them were already familiar with this oddity.

"Was there anything distinctive about it?" John asked the examiner.

"There was a gap between two of the marks made by the front teeth."

"Did you examine the dental records of her husband, Udo Holthaus?" John went on.

"We did examine his records, at the police department's request," reported Brad. "There was a definite gap between two of his front teeth."

Hamlin jumped up, highly animated, and pounded his fist on the table so forcefully that several people seated nearby jumped, startled. "Your Honor!" Hamlin's high-volume voice bounced around the room. "Mr. Holthaus has not been charged with a crime. This testimony is improper and inappropriate."

"I'm going to allow it," the judge said almost immediately, as if knowing what the objection would be. Hamlin sank back into his chair, displaying feigned disappointment.

"Have you established a time of death?" John proceeded with the questioning.

"The victim had been dead for a considerable period of time before being found in the car trunk," Brad answered. "The effects of the cold weather made it impossible to fix an exact time of death—or even an accurate estimate of what day she died."

"But the death occurred at least a number of hours before police found the body?" asked John.

Brad nodded. "I'm sure of that."

John waited a few seconds and waited, watching until the jury members' heads all turned toward him. "So Bonnie Vincent might have died at home and..."

Hamlin jumped up again, interrupting Boyd with gusto. "Objection. Calls for speculation."

"Sustained," the judge said, turning his attention to John. "I gave you a little leeway, counselor, but you abused it," he admonished. Then, to the court reporter, "Strike the last answer. Jury, disregard it."

John continued, "Did you determine whether or not the victim had been sexually assaulted?"

"There was no evidence supporting sexual assault."

"No more questions," said John.

The judge motioned to McLaughlin. Grace could feel her senses awaken with the prospect of seeing this out-of-the-box litigator in action for the first time.

Hamlin rose without hesitation and asked his questions with spirit, in a rapid-fire manner. "You found no vaginal bruising? No semen evidence?"

"No, sir," Brad replied.

"In fact, you were so intrigued and preoccupied with the mark on Bonnie Vincent's neck that you gave the rape possibility short shrift, didn't you?"

The examiner squinted. "We examined the victim for sexual assault."

"That examination was perfunctory, wasn't it? You skimmed over that part?"

John Boyd rose. "Objection."

"Sustained," said the judge.

Hamlin ignored the objection and Judge Montgomery's ruling, instead plunging ahead unabated.

"Mr. Nessler, if you're dead-set certain Bonnie Vincent wasn't raped, how do you explain the panties in her mouth? Isn't that the common behavior of a rapist?"

"Objection," barked John Boyd. "Goes beyond Mr. Nessler's field of expertise."

"Sustained."

"You have no idea," Hamlin went on, undeterred, as though no one else were in the room. "whether or not she was sexually assaulted and then her panties stuffed in her mouth and then..."

"Your Honor!" Boyd protested.

"Take another tack, counselor," Judge Montgomery directed, sounding peeved.

Hamlin looked undaunted. He relished this fox-and-hound game. "You're not one hundred percent certain that the mark on her neck was really a bite mark, are you, Examiner?"

"We ruled everything else out."

"If you're so sure, show me how he did it."

"Pardon me?" the examiner responded, turning toward the judge, confused and astonished.

"Show me how he did it," Hamlin repeated, turning toward the courtroom observers and hamming it up. "Come down here and bite my neck. Come on, bite my neck!"

There was a noisy eruption of gasps and laughter in the courtroom. *Mitchell was right,* marveled Grace. *This guy's a handful.*

John Boyd started to rise to object, then sat back and threw his hands in the air, looking at the judge for some answer.

Judge Montgomery banged his gavel sharply. "Mr. McLaughlin, I'm warning you..."

Hamlin waved the warning off as one might shoo a fly. "All right," he said. "Mr. Nessler, you say you're reasonably sure it was a bite mark. But there wasn't even enough definition to make an accurate match with Mr. Udo Holthaus's dental records, was there?"

"I'd agree that's an accurate statement," said Brad to the smug smile of Hamlin McLaughlin.

Grace had grown to know Detective Ned Moore, seeing him in press conferences, in discussion with his colleagues, and most of all, face-to-face in private discussions. She had come to understand his personality, and she knew his appearance in this trial would feel like a noose around the neck of this private and self-conscious man who loved his work but hated the limelight, in spite of the many times he must have testified.

As Ned was sworn in, Grace could see a line of perspiration on his upper lip and watched him tug at his collar as he squirmed uncomfortably, despite having testified many times. He glanced momentarily toward Grace and gave her a nervous half-smile.

"You conducted a thorough investigation of Udo Holthaus in connection with his wife Bonnie Vincent's murder, didn't you?" John asked him. "He was the prime suspect?"

"Yes," Ned offered a predictably economic answer.

"Did you learn anything from your investigation that caused you to drop him as a suspect?"

"To the contrary," responded Ned. "He had lost his job, but those close to his wife said she wasn't aware of it. He ran up big credit card bills, many on his wife's cards. Those were considered possible motives."

"What kind of expenses were on those bills?" John quizzed.

"Mostly bars and exotic dance clubs."

"Strip clubs?" John sought to clarify.

"Yes." Ned answered.

"Did you conclude from those charges how often he visited bars and strip clubs?'

"Almost every night," answered Ned. "Some days, too."

"Was there anything else that made you suspicious that he might have been involved in his wife's death?"

"He was a voracious reader of detective magazines."

John scanned the faces of the jury members, appearing to watch for their reactions as he asked the next question. "What's so unusual about that? Don't thousands of people read those magazines?"

"Yes, many people read detective magazines," Ned testified. "But we thought it was worth noting that Holthaus especially read magazines giving details about how criminals make it hard for investigators to identify suspects."

Grace and her management had agreed that she would deliver live reports each day during the noon newscast, when court would be recessed for lunch. That first day, outside the Dallas County Superior Court Building, she selected a spot in front of the courthouse and stood with a mike in one hand and a notepad in the other. Matt Robertson had set up the camera and was looking into it, assessing the shot. A small group of bystanders watched. Two of them—animated young men trying to get into camera range behind Grace, mugged immaturely toward the lens.

Grace recounted Ned's testimony about the crime magazines.

"Detective Moore said that some of the articles about committing so-called perfect crimes were even dog-eared, as if being marked to be re-read," she reported. "Moore said that made Holthaus more suspicious than ever. This afternoon the plaintiffs will begin questioning witnesses about the seedy side of Udo Holthaus's lifestyle. This is Grace Gleason for on-the-spot news."

CHAPTER 11: Udo's Obsession

JOHN BOYD planned to rely on the Bonnie Vincent's therapist as an expert psychiatric witness to increase the jury's doubts about Holthaus' emotional state.

Dr. Sylvia Jablonsky had expressed sympathy and understanding for Bonnie Vincent's dilemma in their initial therapy session. But she explained to Bonnie her method of counseling was to strive for absolute objectivity—to refuse to draw any conclusions from first meetings.

"At the outset, I search for clarity," she told her new patient. "I try to ferret out hidden nuances and complexities of relationships and backgrounds before offering advice. Once I think I have enough information, my approach is to teach my patients how to change their behavior and improve the marriage."

In the few sessions they had together, Bonnie divulged feelings she told Dr. Jablonsky she hadn't shared with anyone. Growing up, she related, she had never felt appreciated for her brains and talent.

"While my sisters garnered all the attention for their academic excellence, or their musical ability or activities reserved for the popular," Bonnie said, "I had shrunk into the background. I plodded along making average grades and participated half-heartedly in the extra-curricular activities I was pressured into," until her senior year, she told the doctor. That was when she realized, as a member of the yearbook staff, that she had a gift for writing. The faculty sponsor marveled at her colorful verbs and deft descriptions of the year's events.

"I had finally found a niche," she confided. "One that had gone unnoticed by my parents and teachers."

"And that led to journalism school and a degree," Dr.

Jablonsky nodded.

"Yes. But I could never shake the feeling that I was second-rate," Bonnie answered. "My mother and father never heaped the kind of praise on me that they gave my older sister Elizabeth and my baby sister Ellie."

Her career was much the same, she related.

"I made a living reporting the news, but I never felt successful at it until I met this quirky television news director who took a liking to me."

"Your husband? Udo?"

"He was the first person to mentor and encourage me—even admire me. When Udo proposed, I didn't even care about his odd looks and occasional boorish manners. I thought he loved me for who I was." She paused a long time, fighting for words. "Yet something started eating away at me about our marriage."

"When you still lived in Austin?"

"Yes," Bonnie's lip quivered as the tears and resentment welled up. "Udo would disappear some evenings and return home drunk. When I asked where he had been, he would mumble excuses about business meetings. He continued to help me with my work, but when I tried to become intimate, he would turn me away. I could feel our relationship slipping badly."

"What about sex?"

Bonnie's tears flowed more freely at the question, and she held her stomach as it began to convulse from tension. "Sex was becoming less frequent and more impersonal," she wailed. "It was almost as if he...I don't know, resented being in bed with me. And ever since our move here to Dallas, he hasn't been able to perform sexually at all. So it becomes embarrassing. I never initiate sex anymore, and of course he doesn't either."

Bonnie and her obvious agony over Udo's brutish refusal to participate in solving their problem drew Sylvia to Bonnie in such an empathetic way that she sought counsel from a colleague.

"I have this dilemma with one of my patients," she told Dr. Kirkland Lewis, her mentor, an older psychiatrist, as they sipped bourbon in his office one evening after her session with Bonnie. "She has tried so hard to break through to her husband and nothing has worked."

"That's not so unusual," chuckled Dr. Lewis. "When have you ever had a patient who wasn't distraught over his or her failing marriage?"

"I know, but his seems exceedingly different," Sylvia explained. "There's a degree of desperation that doesn't come from insecurity, phobia, anxiety or any of the other diagnoses you normally might be leaning toward. It's coming from some deeper kind of fear."

"Fear? Of what?"

"I'm not sure. But I want to say...of evil."

Dr. Lewis gave her a subtle, dubious look. "Evil!"

"My client has described her husband and his actions in a lot of detail. She tries to hold back, but it comes flowing out. Kirkland, the man sounds more demonic than a mere sociopath."

Her confidante turned back to his bourbon. "What does the husband say?

"They're not coming in together. He refuses to participate, so she comes alone."

"Also not so unusual," the older psychiatrist commented. "Well, get him to come in. Alone, too, if necessary."

"Yes. You're absolutely right. I should do that," Dr. Jablonsky agreed.

In her next session with Bonnie, the counselor sat listening quietly as her patient wailed about her unresponsive husband. Then she made a suggestion that prompted Bonnie to sit straight up.

"I want to ask him to come talk to me. I'd like to find out more about what's going on from his perspective."

"The idea scares me," Bonnie admitted. "It's all I can do

to talk to you about these things myself. If Udo gets involved, we will have to discuss our problems openly. I can't imagine how he'll react, and I don't know if I can handle possible backlash."

"I think I could help," the doctor had advised.

Bonnie had lowered her head into her hands and sat that way for a long time, crying, thinking. Finally, "Anything to save my marriage," she had said.

"Good," Dr. Jablonsky had responded. "Meanwhile, make a concerted effort to be kind and gentle, to make him more comfortable with intimate comments and touches."

Psychiatrist Dr. Sylvia Jablonsky looked surprisingly youthful for early forties. John Boyd had expressed concern about that impression to his three-member staff several months before the court date as they sat in a conference room and planned the case, discussing potential witnesses.

"She comes across so young," he complained. "I'm not sure I can get a jury to take her seriously enough."

"Listen to you," said his law clerk of two years, Carletta Conrad, whose confrontational, no-nonsense style in these sessions was one reason John had hired her. Carletta was in her third year of law school, but despite her inexperience she seemed able to cut through and understand the core of an issue. "The woman has incredible credentials," Carletta said emphatically. "There's not one thing that McLaughlin can attack her on. Remember what she said in your interview with her–that Holthaus might just as well pack it in and give up the money, because she knew the man from the inside out."

"I'd feel a lot better if she looked her age," John persisted.

Carletta slammed her hand on the conference table, palm down, startling everyone else. "If she were a man, you'd be bragging to all your colleagues that you've got this heavy-hitter who can shoot down the opposition," she argued, adding with mockery, "'Oh, and by the way, he's a virile, young-looking dude the jury will like right away.'"

At that point, all eyes turned to Boyd, and he grinned. Sylvia Jablonsky's youthful appearance would no longer be an issue.

The testimony by Medical Examiner Brad Nessler and later by Detective Moore was building a solid case for John Boyd, the Vincents' attorney. But as in most trials, the testimony from an unexpected and fascinating witness promised to bolster the case in the eyes of impressionable jurors.

Immediately after the lunch break, Judge Montgomery instructed Boyd to call his next witness.

"I call Dr. Sylvia Jablonsky to the stand," Boyd announced.

The psychiatrist rose from her seat in the front row and walked purposefully toward the witness stand. As she strode confidently to the witness chair, head held high, dressed impeccably in a blue suit and low heels, she exuded an air of credibility even before opening her mouth.

"Raise your hand," instructed the clerk, holding out the Bible for her to touch. "Do you swear to tell the truth, the whole truth and nothing but the truth, so help you God?"

Udo and Hamlin half-turned from the judge's bench and engaged in an animated, vigorous exchange, Udo gesturing wildly.

"What the hell?" Holthaus whispered, his eyes burning through his lawyer. "Did you know she would testify?"

"She was on the list, but I didn't worry about it. She can't possibly testify since she counseled with you. I'll get her kicked off, pronto," Hamlin promised.

"Please state your name for the record," instructed the clerk.

"Dr. Sylvia Jablonsky," she complied, as John Boyd rose to question her.

"Judge," interjected Hamlin, rising up and straining to be heard before Boyd could get the first question out. "I vehemently object to the witness. She is here to testify about my client, and she knows full well she is bound by doctor-patient confidentiality."

"Your Honor," said Boyd, "Mr. Hamlin's client is not a patient of Dr. Jablonsky."

"Is that true, Doctor?" Judge Montgomery peered at Sylvia over his reading glasses.

"It is, your Honor. Bonnie Vincent was my patient."

"Did you counsel Mr. Holthaus?" the judge asked.

"As part of my treatment of Bonnie Vincent, I requested that Mr. Holthaus come to see me. We had conversations. I did not bill him, nor did I treat him."

Hamlin stood to object again, but the judge raised his hand. "I'll allow her testimony."

The courtroom came alive with a ripple of reaction. McLaughlin flopped down.

Udo leaned in at him angrily. "You told me the God damned shrink wouldn't be allowed to testify," he said harshly under his breath.

"We can use it as grounds for appeal."

Holthaus' eyes became slits. "Appeal? You said we'd win this thing."

Overhearing the exchange, John Boyd had to stifle a grin before he questioned the doctor. "You are an expert on sexual dysfunction?" he asked her.

"I hold a doctorate in counseling psychology from Hofstra University, Long Island, New York," Sylvia answered in her distinct Eastern accent sounding confident and authoritative. "I have practiced for twenty years in Dallas, the past seven exclusively in the field of sexual dysfunction and marriage."

John Boyd paused for effect, letting his witness' credentials sink in. As he asked his first question, he subtly scanned the jury, watching for clues of their impression of his star witness.

"Dr. Jablonsky," he started, "what was the purpose of

asking Mr. Holthaus to come see you?"

"Bonnie Vincent was extremely frustrated with the lack of intimacy in their marriage," Sylvia answered. "She was concerned that her husband was experiencing some sexual inadequacy that prevented them from being close in other ways."

"How many times did you meet with Mr. Holthaus?"

"Twice. First we explored his background and past experiences. In our second meeting I elicited information about how he was living his life. And its effects on their marriage."

Again, Boyd scanned the jury, this time openly, to let them know he was asking the question for them. "Doctor, in lay terms we can all understand, what did you learn about Mr. Holthaus in each of those areas?"

"He had an extremely unhappy childhood," Sylvia testified. "His older brother left home when Udo Holthaus was ten, so emotionally he was an only child. His mother refused sex with his father, who beat her in response." She cast a quick look in Udo's direction and just as quickly looked away. "He still lives with images of Hans Holthaus punching his wife Nelda with his closed fist, and then taunting his son whose painful birth was his mother's excuse for never wanting sex nor another childbirth again."

Grace glanced at Udo. His neck was growing red, and his lips tightened. He was simmering inside.

"Mr. Holthaus witnessed this scenario many times," Sylvia continued, "and when he was old enough he escaped by enlisting in the Coast Guard. But he took the trauma of those scenes from his childhood with him."

"What about his lifestyle?" John queried.

"In the service he visited many strip bars and houses of prostitution. He took his fascination for that element of life to college with him, then into his work world and right on into the marriage."

"He didn't stop this behavior after he married?" John glanced at the jury.

"No," she answered, "not frequenting the bars, anyway. His marriage was in considerable trouble. He was increasingly experiencing an inability to achieve erection in an intimate setting with his wife. It frustrated them both, and he escaped that reality by visiting these bars more often until they became an obsession."

Grace glanced at the other reporters in the section and they were writing notes frantically as Holthaus' sexual activities were unveiled like a steamy soap opera.

"Did his wife—did Bonnie Vincent know he was visiting men's clubs?" John asked the psychiatrist.

"If so, she didn't share that with me. I was prepared to bring them both in and discuss it with them, but I never got the chance. I learned from the news reports that Ms. Vincent's body was found two days before her next scheduled appointment."

"Doctor, to your knowledge, did Bonnie Vincent and Udo Holthaus discuss separation or divorce?"

"No."

"Why not?" John Boyd asked.

"If they split up, he would lose everything—her devotion, her unprotesting acceptance, and especially her financial support. He had no job and no prospects that I know of. I believe he felt her slipping away, and with her his lifestyle of decadence and unfettered spending. Bonnie was considering divorce."

The lawyer continued to check jury members for reactions as Sylvia answered his final question. He paused for a moment, to let the testimony sink in with them. Then he turned to Hamlin McLaughlin. "Your witness, counselor," he said.

Hamlin sat at his table and rifled through the pages of his legal pad, then stopped suddenly as if he had found what page he was looking for. He had studied the courtroom techniques of the great Clarence Darrow and others, and this was one of the many tricks he had mastered and used often to be sure the jury was paying attention to him and no one else. He cleared his throat. "You're not saying Mr. Holthaus had anything to do with his wife's murder?" Hamlin McLaughlin asked Sylvia.

The doctor hesitated. "No, I'm not saying that."

"My client isn't the only red-blooded American husband to visit strip clubs?" he asked, punctuating the words as if to inject a challenge in the question.

"No," Sylvia conceded.

Hamlin smiled, cleared his throat again, loudly, and rifled through more pages as if searching for the *coup de grace*. "Are you familiar with a study that shows Americans spend more money on exotic dance clubs than on any other form of live entertainment, including rock concerts?"

Sylvia Jablonsky stopped short, appeared to think deeply as if seeking a motive for the question, then smiled. "I'm not familiar with that study," she answered.

Hamlin slammed the pad down on the table. "No further questions," he said.

"Call your next witness, Mr. Boyd," Judge Montgomery instructed as Sylvia Jablonsky retreated to the courtroom aisle and out of the door.

"I call Destiny Desire."

Destiny sauntered toward the stand, glancing around the courtroom and seeming to enjoy the clamor her presence was causing. She had been coached by John Boyd to dress conservatively. She wore a silk blouse accented with a scarf any businesswoman might wear, but her skirt was mid-thigh, showing off much of her well-toned, tan legs and the colorful snake tattoo that ran up one from her ankle to her knee. She walked easily on her four-inch heels, creating a swaying motion in her derriere.

As he watched, Udo Holthaus leaned toward Hamlin McLaughlin. "You can cut this little tramp down to a nub, Hamlin. She's an airhead. Show her for the whore she is."

Hamlin put a finger to his lips, cutting Udo off. By now Destiny had completed the oath and was seated in the witness chair.

"State your name for the record," the court clerk instructed Destiny.

"Destiny Desire."

The response was met with giggles running through the crowd. Judge Montgomery rapped his gavel for silence, but stopped short and instead turned a grandfatherly expression toward Destiny. "Ma'am," he said, "this is a court of law. You have to use your real name."

"It is my real name, your Honor," Destiny cooed. "I had it legally changed, honest."

Judge Montgomery shook his head and made a note. "I'll take your word for it. Proceed."

"Miss...um...Desire, what is your profession?" Boyd asked.

"I'm a dancer at the Saucy Lady Club over on Northwest Highway."

"Do you know the defendant, Udo Holthaus?"

Destiny fixed her gaze on Udo, who remained expressionless.

"He comes in the club," she stated.

"When he comes into your club, how does he spend his time?

Destiny glanced over at Udo again, receiving the same cold stare. "He sits at the bar and drinks a lot, watches us dance, puts money in our garters, stuff like that. He's not rowdy, if that's what you're getting at."

John smiled, "No, I'm just trying to get your honest answer about what you've seen when he came in. For instance, did he ever try to touch you and the other dancers?"

"Objection, irrelevant," Hamlin chimed in.

"These questions go to character, your Honor. I think we'll see a pattern here that will prove a point."

"Proceed," said Judge Montgomery. "But let's get somewhere in a hurry, counselor."

"So...Miss Destiny, did Mr. Holthaus ever make contact with you?"

"A few times I had to keep his hands off me—during the private dances." She squirmed a little.

"Private dances?"

"Yeah, you know—he would pay us extra to go to a private room with him and perform a lap dance. Sometimes he got...handsy. That's a no-no at our club." Some in the courtroom laughed at the comment, and Destiny smiled the surprised way children do when someone laughs unexpectedly at their joke.

"Did he pay for these lap dances often?" John asked her.

"All the time. He liked the attention, I think."

"Were you the only dancer he showed interest in?"

"He told me he liked me a lot, and quite a few times he would ask for me by name when he wanted a private dance. But when he wanted more, one of the other girls would go with him."

"More?"

"Yeah, you know. More than just a dance. I didn't do that, but some of the girls made dates with him."

John Boyd hesitated. Then, "You and some of the other dancers from the Saucy Lady Club visited Mr. Holthaus, didn't you, Miss Desire?"

"Sure. At a hotel room near his condo. He invited several of us over there to party. He was doling out good money and lots of booze."

"When did that occur?"

"Right after his wife disappeared."

Destiny's statement caused a noisy outburst throughout the courtroom, prompting the judge to bang his gavel repeatedly until it subsided.

It was late in the afternoon. Grace was at the TXDA news desk, delivering a story next to the anchorman, Phil Sawyer. The station had added these appearances to her live noon reports because audience response to the story had grown so strong.

"Miss Desire," Grace said into the camera, "testified that she and the other dancers had a big party with Holthaus, drinking, dancing and—to use her word—whatever. When attorney John Boyd asked her to define 'whatever,' she took the fifth amendment. Judge Montgomery agreed to leave it at that, and adjourned the trial until tomorrow morning."

"Thank you, Grace Gleason," said Anchorman Sawyer. Phil turned to another camera for his next report. The camera on Grace went off. She slipped off her chair and walked back to the newsroom, feeling the springs in her neck and shoulders unwind. This action and the stories it generated were stimulating and exciting, but the tension they created took their toll on her energy level.

She sat down at her desk, got a video clip from a drawer, slipped it into a monitor and began to watch thoughtfully, intently. It was the clip from her encounter with Holthaus at his condo.

"Mr. Holthaus, did you say worked?"

"Pardon?"

"Worked! You said she worked at Pearson. Don't you mean works?"

Grace's phone rang, startling her, and she hit the stop button. "TXDA news. Gleason."

There was no sound. She waited. "Anyone there?" Still no sound. Grace sat silently for another moment and then slammed the phone down just as Mitchell Court passed her desk.

"They must have refused you an interview," he smiled.

"Another hang-up call," she complained. "That's the third one today. I know it's Udo Holthaus."

"Those calls could come from a hundred different places," Mitchell countered calmly. "Someone you made look bad on the air. Kids playing pranks. Phone problems."

Grace arched her neck, staring at Mitchell with a piercing glare. "I know who it was, Mitchell. Udo gives me creepy looks every time I glance his way in the courtroom."

Mitchell drew his shoulders up in non-commitment and retreated to his cubicle, leaving Grace with a sour feeling.

An hour later, she sat in the kitchen eating dinner with Jeff. She was still in a foul mood from the hang-up call and Mitchell's lack of empathy. She was sorry she had told Jeff about it, because he wouldn't let it drop.

"I don't want you taking any chances around Holthaus," he said. "Stay away from him."

"I haven't gone anywhere near him," Grace answered indignantly, "since that night at the Saucy Lady. But I know he was making those calls."

"How do you know, Grace? How in God's name could you possibly know?"

Grace was annoyed that the second person this evening doubted her, and she especially despised that one of them was Jeff, not merely because he was her husband but also because of a nit-picky questioning habit he had acquired. It seemed to have intensified since he had moved up the ladder in his law practice, and it carried with it a sort of smugness—the opposite of the non-judgmental understanding she needed.

"I know," she said contemptuously. "I could hear him breathing. I could almost smell him."

"God damn it, Grace. You don't have to do this story anymore," Jeff growled, stabbing at his food with his fork. "Get Hamilton to put someone else on it. Holthaus knows you're trying to put him in jail, for Christ's sake."

Grace took a deep breath and a sip of wine, hoping to allay the contentious turn the conversation had taken. "This is a big break for me, Jeff," she said softly, almost a plea. "I've wanted to do news reporting since I was in the eighth grade. I worked my tail off in college to learn this business, and I'm finally getting some respect. I'm not backing down from this story."

She waited. He waited longer.

"Besides, I'm right," she tossed into the silence. Grace

pleaded her case, her voice and facial expression begging for understanding. "You didn't feel how desperately he gripped my neck that night at the Saucy Lady." As she recalled that incident, she grew angry. "I can see it in the courtroom every time he flashes that arrogant sneer of his. He knows he committed the perfect murder. And I'm afraid he's going to get away with it."

Jeff nonchalantly poured a second glass of wine. He seemed to be gearing up for a battle. "This isn't your fight. Why do you care so much?"

"Because I can't stand it when the bullies of the world like Udo win." She leaned across the table, trying mightily to soften her tone. "Jeff, honey, do you remember the story I covered in Austin when that innocent woman was gunned down in the crossfire of two gangs? She died because she had gone shopping at the wrong time. She had children and a job at the university. They caught the guys, but they got fifteen years and those poor kids got a dead mother."

She paused to drain her wine as if seeking fortification. She pushed her plate of food away, half-finished, as she became more upset. "Bonnie was a wonderful person and good friend. She didn't deserve the fate that bastard handed her. I hate him for it. Don't you understand?"

"We don't even know if he did it or not." Jeff watched her recoil.

Grace pushed her chair back, her eyes wide and moist. "You can't be serious."

"I am," he responded bluntly, his lawyer posture in high gear. "We don't know if he's guilty, and I don't care."

"You can't be saying this," she shouted, her hands in the air. "My own husband."

"Grace, you've gotten in way over your head. We can move to California and forget all about Udo Holthaus. You can still pursue your career, and I'll move up the ladder."

"That's what this is all about?" she bounced back angrily. "You're still considering that opportunity? I told you I'm against it."

"Maybe I'll go out there by myself," he said, his voice rising to match hers. "You can hang around here until that crazy son of a bitch comes after you." He kicked his chair back and stomped out of the room.

As he disappeared, Grace called after him, "Then you could go to my funeral and say I told you so, right?"

She knew he heard her. She waited. The garage door groaned as it yanked open. Jeff's car squealed out into the driveway, and its roar faded into the distance. As she sat finishing her wine, the hostile words of their argument bounced around her head. The garage door returned to the floor.

CHAPTER 12: Brutality

THE DALLAS DINER had become a safe haven for Grace and Detective Moore. Each could slip easily away and meet there, unnoticed and undisturbed, to exchange findings and opinions off the record.

They were in their usual corner booth, discussing the trial. Sallie brought their coffee and shuffled quickly away, apparently accustomed to the pair meeting and comparing notes in hushed tones.

"We have to be back in thirty minutes," Grace reminded Ned. "Is anyone at the Dallas PD laying odds?"

"I'd say it's fifty-fifty," he responded. "The stripper's testimony helped a lot, but the key will be the insurance investigators. They did a thorough investigation, plus they even went back to the condo and gave it a twice-over."

"And?" she urged.

"They agree with us that Bonnie was killed at the condo while she dressed for work—that they argued, probably about his using her credit cards."

"And what the cards were used for?" Grace interjected.

"Right. And maybe about his losing his job and not telling her," Ned added.

"What else?" Grace prompted.

"We think Udo stuffed the panties in her mouth to make it look like a sexual attack from a stranger and then crammed her body into the car trunk and drove it to the airport. More than likely he hopped public transportation and got back home without anyone paying much attention. We searched that entire parking garage. No one saw him at the airport in her car. And no cab driver who worked the area that morning could ID Holthaus's photo."

"You have evidence to support all of this?"

Ned hesitated, reluctant at first. "We're still off the record until the facts come out, okay?"

Grace nodded agreement.

He continued, "We found crumpled up credit card statements with strip club charges. Bonnie Vincent's prints were on them. And remember when I said the place had been scrubbed clean? We found empty bleach bottles and sponges in the dumpster outside with Udo's prints. Brushes from a carpet cleaner, too."

Grace soaked in the information and then checked her watch and panicked slightly. "They're about to call the first witness."

Ned raised a hand for her to wait. "There's something else. You need to be prepared for the worst. I want nothing more than to prove Holthaus did it—I can't stand unfinished business. But we're navigating through some political bullshit that's slowing us down."

"What political bullshit?" she asked. It was the first time she had heard Ned talk about the case in a resigned and skeptical manner.

"I'll just say the higher-ups won't take a chance of getting hosed at election time if we don't have an air-tight case," he answered.

Grace reacted with a look of frustration and then glanced at her watch again. Reacting to the time, she pulled some bills from her purse and put them on the table. Ned sat back, accustomed to getting free coffee, and motioned for her to pay. "Thanks, Gracie," he chuckled. "Let's go to court."

Ned started to get up, but Grace reached out and grabbed his arm, stopping him short. He sat back, waiting, curious. "It's Grace!" she exclaimed, annoyed.

Surprise crossed Ned's face. He looked at her for a second, perplexed, before explaining. "I'm sorry," he said in a sincere tone. "I didn't mean to offend." He paused, searching for words with obvious difficulty. He took a deep breath, and then, "I've never told you about my little girl."

Grace's inquisitive reaction told him to go on.

"Years ago, Martha and I had a daughter. Named her Rose. I called her Rosie. She was the sweetest, smartest thing you could imagine. But she got leukemia when she was very young. She was a brave little thing, always cheerful even when we knew she was hurting. She lived five more years, but then we lost her."

Grace reached across and put her hand on his.

His eyes pled with her for understanding. "You kinda remind me of what she might have been like, you know? I would have wanted her to be like you. Sorry if I crossed a line."

Grace heaved a breath and leaned back, still holding onto Ned's hand. She was on the verge of tears. "It's okay, Ned," she said softly. "I'm honored."

They sat for a moment without speaking. Ned pulled a handkerchief from his pocket and blew his nose. "Come on. Trial time," he said, dismissing the topic.

Court had already been convened when they returned. Grace and Ned tiptoed in, and Ned squeezed into the back row bench while Grace speed-walked awkwardly to the reporters' seating area. Elizabeth Vincent was in the witness chair, appearing edgy and frightened. She glanced periodically at her mother, aunts and cousins sitting in the second row of the gallery, and then she looked across at Grace who gave her a little smile and a nod as she settled into her seat. Elizabeth smiled faintly but looked immediately away to focus on the questions she was being asked.

John Boyd was speaking to Elizabeth in a quiet and respectful voice. "Miss Vincent, you said there were incidents when you thought your sister had been struck by another person or object. Could you elaborate on that?"

She took a deep breath, trying hard to control the trembling in her voice. "Several times when Bonnie came to our house, she had bruises on her face," she began. "Bonnie had tried to cover them up with make-up, but they were so bad she couldn't hide them."

"Did you ever ask her about them?"

"She would just make up some ridiculous excuse like running into a door or falling," Elizabeth answered.

"How many times are we talking about?"

Elizabeth paused, trying to gather herself, obviously becoming distraught over having to testify about Udo's brutality to her sister. "Many times," she said resentfully.

"And on these occasions...many times, you said...when Bonnie showed up with bruises, was Mr. Holthaus with her?"

"Udo Holthaus didn't come to our house much," she said, fighting back tears and fixing a hateful, vitriolic gaze on the villain.

"Did you ever confront him about the bruises?" asked John Boyd.

"Not directly," she responded. "There were occasions when I was at their place and they argued. He would get pretty worked up and Bonnie would ask him to calm down."

"What was his reaction?"

Elizabeth began to cry harder, and the clerk took her some tissues. "His reaction was violent," she began to wail. "He would yell at her and tell me to mind my own business."

"Did he physically threaten you?"

"I would leave before he had a chance," Elizabeth answered. "But I know what happened after I left...what happened to..."

McLaughlin jumped up. "Objection, your Honor."

"Sustained," said the judge. "Miss Vincent..."

"She was my sister," Elizabeth interrupted, anguished. "I wish everyone in this courtroom could hear Bonnie's screams, feel her pain, understand the sweet and gentle life that has been snuffed out. She didn't get any breaks. She tried so hard to please everyone and no one paid attention."

Judge Montgomery leaned toward the witness stand. "Miss Vincent, please," he said firmly, frowning at John Boyd, who walked toward the witness stand, his hand out, attempting to stop her.

Hamlin McLaughlin jumped up, his outstretched arms pleading with the judge.

"Ellie and I got all the attention and Bonnie took it like a trooper," Elizabeth continued, ignoring them, speaking plaintively to the jury. "She built a life for herself..." Elizabeth turned and spoke the last words directly to Udo, shaking, bawling uncontrollably, "...and she didn't deserve this..."

She broke down, tried to continue, but words wouldn't come out. Judge Montgomery extended his hands toward John Boyd. "Get your witness under control."

"Your Honor, I have no more questions," said Boyd. "I think we should dismiss this witness."

Judge Montgomery swiveled to look questioningly at Hamlin McLaughlin, who nodded. Udo lurched back in his chair as if witnessing a missed call at a ball game. As Elizabeth stepped down from the stand with the court clerk taking her arm, Holthaus appeared highly upset, whispering frantically to Hamlin McLaughlin.

As Elizabeth passed Udo's table, her teary, hateful stare seared the air between them.

That evening, Grace and Phil were side-by-side at the anchor desk. Grace was giving her evening report, her delivery uncharacteristically emotional. "...Elizabeth Vincent had the entire courtroom's rapt attention, Phil," Grace related. "She said her sister denied that her husband had hit her, but added that Bonnie Vincent was the kind of person who would have stayed loyal to her husband regardless of how he treated her."

"Did any other members of the Vincent family testify?" Phil asked.

"Bonnie's father is ill and can't testify. The youngest sister lives overseas. They let Elizabeth speak for the family."

"What's on tap for tomorrow?"

"The defense will open with testimony from the

insurance company," Grace answered. "No one expects attorney Hamlin McLaughlin to do more than establish Udo Holthaus as the beneficiary of Bonnie Vincent's insurance."

"Will Holthaus testify?"

"Probably not. If the defense case is as brief as expected, the judge could charge the jury tomorrow morning."

CHAPTER 13: A Threat

THE MORNING AFTER Elizabeth Vincent's explosive testimony, Judge Montgomery was seated at the bench, and the jury was in place. The courtroom was quiet. Burt Redmond, the witness for the Premier Insurance Company, was on the stand being questioned without drama by Hamlin McLaughlin.

Redmond was a portly man, about fifty, with a rotund face made ruddy from too many happy hours. He had worked for Premier for twenty-three years. He was first a young policy salesman and then, after phenomenal success as a regional sales manager and a stint as a marketing director, he was promoted into the company's uppermost management ranks. He had risen to the position of senior vice president for claims administration, and his department was responsible for evaluating and processing claims and authorizing payment of benefits.

Burt didn't normally become involved in individual cases, but the Bonnie Vincent murder had become such a high profile case, the firm's CEO had designated him to "go down to Dallas and see that things are handled right in that mess."

As he sat in the witness chair, Redmond appeared enormously calm and confident.

"Mr. Redmond," said Hamlin, "Premier Life has confirmed the validity of Bonnie Vincent's intent with respect to the policy beneficiary?"

"Mr. Holthaus is clearly designated the legal beneficiary of the policy," Redmond responded in a businesslike drone. "We've confirmed the policy is paid up and properly witnessed."

"Paid up in what amount?"

"One million, one hundred thousand dollars," said Burt to a collective gasp.

"No further questions."

Several members of the jury exchanged glances. Accustomed to lengthy and emotional inquisitions from Hamlin, all twelve watched him with puzzled expressions as Hamlin returned to his seat and exchanged confident smiles with Udo.

John Boyd rose to question Redmond. "The policy was originally written in the amount of one hundred thousand?" he asked.

"Yes," said Burt. "Recently...three months ago today...the policy was increased by one million dollars."

"Did Bonnie Vincent increase the policy?" asked Boyd.

Burt shook his head no. "That was done by Mr. Holthaus."

John Boyd moved toward the defendants' table and stared in Udo's direction for apparent effect. "The Premier Insurance Company has deferred payment because of this lawsuit?"

"Anytime there is a question raised in court," Burt confirmed, "we can't make a payout until that question is resolved."

"And if there's a finding of guilt in this civil proceeding?"

"We would withhold payment," assured Redmond.

Without hesitation, John changed the line of questions. "You were on the team that investigated the murder of Bonnie Vincent for Premier?"

"Yes."

"And you found no sign of a struggle in the condo occupied by Bonnie Vincent and Udo Holthaus? No blood traces, no sign of violence of any kind?"

"That's right," Burt responded.

"Then how could you possibly have concluded that Bonnie Vincent died there, as your report states?"

"Not only was it devoid of any signs of violence," Burt said, "it was also devoid of any signs of life. The entire place was sterile—scrubbed clean."

"How could you tell?" quizzed Boyd, appearing

fascinated but already having heard the answer in deposition.

"Besides being obvious from our inspection of the place?" Burt said. "Police found empty bleach containers in the condo dumpster, sponges with traces of bleach, carpet cleaner brushes. And there was a stiff bleach smell in the condo."

"No further questions," Boyd said.

Hamlin Mclaughlin scrunched up his face like a schoolboy about to play a practical joke. "You guys at Premier are hoping we lose this case, aren't you?"

Terrance Cooper rose. "Objection," he bellowed.

The judge pondered for a moment. "I want to see where this is going," he said.

Hamlin appeared pleased that he won one. "Thank you, Judge," he said obsequiously. "What about it, Mr. Redmond? You would like to see my client hung out to dry, wouldn't you?"

"I don't know what you..." Burt's rosy face was growing even more crimson. His dark eyes darted toward his lawyer, who did not respond.

Hamlin interjected, "Premier stands to pay out a million dollars if Mr. Holthaus is rightfully found innocent by these fine men and women here. But if they decide he might have done it, which he didn't, you can sit on all that dough."

Burt sat up straight, bristling. "My company isn't in the business of..."

Hamlin silenced him with a wave of his hand, moving swiftly on to another question. "Now, about that so-called investigation of the condo, you said there was no blood that you could find?"

"That's correct," responded Redmond.

"Educate us again about how no blood could possibly mean—to anyone in their right mind—that Bonnie Vincent died at home?"

The clock on the courthouse building said noon, exactly. Grace was reporting from her usual spot, with Matt Robertson manning the camera. A group of school children on a field trip with their teachers stopped to watch. Holthaus emerged from the courthouse and lurked in the background as Grace worked.

"The investigator said the lack of blood in the condo made it appear that Bonnnie Vincent didn't die there," she said, looking into the camera. "But when combined with the extraordinary absence of fingerprints, hairs, nail clippings and skin fragments—all of that could only mean either that no one lived there, or that someone had done a good job of cleaning the place to cover up a crime."

Grace caught Udo in her peripheral view and peered his direction briefly as she reported. She was startled by his presence, but she quickly regained her composure and continued. "Redmond said in his fifteen years of investigating crime scenes for Premier Life, he had never seen a potential crime scene so spotless. After the lunch break it's on to closing arguments. Then Judge Montgomery will charge the jury."

Matt turned off the camera and started to pack up his equipment. Grace turned and saw that Udo was still standing there, staring at her.

"Holthaus is stalking me," she told Matt.

"He's weird," Matt exclaimed. "Want me to walk you inside before I go back to the station?"

"Detective Moore is inside," she said. "Holthaus wouldn't try anything. I'm a little afraid of him, but not here in front of the courthouse in broad daylight."

"Okay, Grace. I'll see you, then."

"See you back at the ranch," she said. "Tell Lloyd Hamilton I love him."

Matt responded with a confused look, but shrugged and walked to the station's news van parked on the curb. Grace went back inside the courthouse, but as she got inside the door, she was aware that Udo had followed and had nearly caught up with her. She stopped and turned to confront him. His expression was intensely hostile.

"I want you to stop this crusade against me, Gleason," he snapped a warning.

"What's the matter, Udo?" she answered tersely, not wanting to show her fear. "Are you afraid of the truth?" Her legs were shaking like a loblolly pine in a gale, and she hoped he couldn't tell.

"The truth is that your campaign to ruin my life is rubbing a little raw," Udo said with contempt. "It's about time you stopped."

"Or what? I asked you that once before at the Saucy Lady, remember? You never answered me." Her legs were trying to buckle at the knee, and she planted her feet solidly, farther apart, fighting against the quaking sensation.

"Here's an answer," Udo said, his voice transforming into something sounding like evil. "You have a daughter, don't you?"

Grace flinched almost violently, her eyes widening with astonishment. She could feel the back of her neck tingle and her heart beating wildly. "You son of a bitch..." she hissed at him.

Holthaus cut in, "What is she, about seventeen? Cute little thing?"

"If you ever go near Megan or even think about it, I will make you wish you were dead instead of Bonnie." In her anger, the trembling of her legs had disappeared, but it was replaced by rage in her voice.

Holthaus seemed pleased, chuckling nastily. "Whoa," he said sadistically. "Touched a nerve there, did we? Megan, huh? Sweet name. If I were you, I'd do everything I could to make sure little Megan stays nice and safe." Udo scoffed and strutted almost nonchalantly down the hallway into the courtroom. Grace watched him go, mute, stunned and incredulous.

CHAPTER 14: Partial Justice

THE SPECTER of harm to Megan rattled Grace. She stood motionless for several minutes, angry and frightened. She had tenaciously dogged the man she considered a killer with her coverage of the murder and the trial. Yet in her fervor to perform her job, it hadn't occurred to her that he might respond with vengeance. Having met his ire face-to-face, she remembered how spine-chilling her impression of the man had been when she first shook his hand in Austin.

Udo had made his threat and casually walked away, leaving her horrified and alone. She gathered herself and walked unsteadily down the hallway, unable to retrieve her thoughts from an inescapable confused daze. Udo had uttered one word that had shaken her to her shoes—Megan!

Grace tried to decide on a next move, but Udo had reduced her rational processes to a blinding blur. The sight in front of her, down the hallway, rescued her. Ned Moore was finishing a cell phone call in a recessed area of the corridor. He smiled when he saw Grace coming toward him.

Spotting Ned in her confusion was like finding a brilliant, life-saving light in a darkened cave.

"I think the jury'll be out for quite a while," Ned said as she approached. "I'm going back to the office and wait it out."

As Grace edged closer, Ned's face registered concern at her wide-eyed, terrified demeanor. "Hey, what gives?" he asked, his eyes squinting with confusion. "You're shaking like one of those paint agitators at the hardware store."

"Udo Holthaus bushwhacked me out there," she told Ned tearfully. "He used threats against my daughter to scare me off the story."

Ned cringed. "Jesus Christ. Let me to go talk to him. I'll put the fear of God in him."

"No, Ned," Grace appealed, "It would make things worse, I'm sure. But could I call you if he harasses me again?"

"Sure," he said, fishing a card from his wallet and handing it to her. "I don't give it out to many people."

"Knowing I have it makes me feel better," she said, breathing deeply, searching for calm.

"Good," Ned said. He started to speak, but hesitated. Grace took another breath and looked at him inquisitively, guessing his indecision might be covering up bad news. "Uh, Grace," he continued, "that call I was on...I'm going to tell you something that'll make you feel even worse."

"Perfect," she moaned.

"Those incompetent sons of bitches in the evidence room have misplaced what little evidence we had in the case against Udo." He paused. "Misplaced it...or else were bribed."

Ned watched Grace's reaction. Her mouth flew open in shock. "No!" she exclaimed. "The credit card bills with her prints all over them?"

He nodded.

"The bleach bottles? The sponges? The carpet cleaning stuff? "

Ned nodded again at each question.

"What about his dental records?" she asked, sounding desperate.

"The dental records we can replace," he assured her. "But yeah, pretty much everything."

"I don't understand," Grace sputtered, unbelieving. "How can they do that? Isn't all that stuff locked up and guarded? What about chain of command?"

"It happens. Sometimes intentionally, sometimes not."

"So you've lost your case?" she asked, her shoulders feeling as if the weight of a mountain had crushed them.

"Maybe," Ned said uncertainly. "We have a lot more than a theory, but it's circumstantial. We can't prove the smell of bleach we encountered in the condo when we investigated, except for our testimony. And Burt Redmond's. We're still hoping they'll find the missing evidence, but it doesn't happen very often."

Grace spun and walked down the hall for a few paces, then stopped and walked back to Ned, feeling incredibly frustrated. "I can't believe this," she complained. "We had a chance to solve this case."

"Hey, I'm plenty pissed off," Ned told her, "but they've searched the room. It's not there."

"That's it?" she asked crisply. "Everyone's hard work down the tubes? The criminal case is done?"

Ned shook his head no. "Not entirely done. This has put a big dent in it. Much harder to convince a jury when everything's circumstantial."

Grace shook her head angrily at his answer. She was almost in tears again.

Ned continued, "We've still got the law of probability. And the bizarre behavior of Udo Holthaus. The testimony of the psychiatrist, stripper and insurance investigators. We have Elizabeth's testimony about Udo beating Bonnie up all the time."

There was a long silence, Ned and Grace both staring at the floor. She was feeling more calm.

"The judge said reasonable doubt is harder to prove in the criminal trial, right?" Grace asked.

"It has to be beyond a reasonable doubt," he answered. "We don't have a great shot at a criminal conviction now that the evidence is in limbo somewhere."

Grace brightened, grasping, needing a positive answer on this rotten afternoon. "Even so, the jury might see it our way in this civil suit, right?"

"Udo would end up broke," Ned said brightly.

"And desperate," she responded ominously.

It was almost four-thirty. Grace was in the newsroom when Ned called. "The jury's coming back," he said.

As she hurried into the courtroom, she looked at her watch. Judge Montgomery had charged the jury shortly after one. They had deliberated more than three hours.

Grace looked around as she scurried to her seat. It was packed, as it had been for the entire trial, and everyone was scrambling for a seat to hear the verdict. The observers lined the walls two-deep.

The jury filed in and sat, their faces emotionless. Judge Montgomery entered and the court clerk stepped forward. As Grace focused on Udo Holthaus, with his beady eyes fixed at the jury foreperson, the tension in the room was palpable.

"All rise," the clerk commanded. All complied.

As Holthaus rose, he glanced sideways at Hamlin McLaughlin and assumed a smug and confident grin. Grace felt her body stiffen and the hair on her arms tingle. She wanted to fly across the room and assail him, beat him to mush. Never in her life could she remember loathing another human being a fraction as much as she despised this dreadful man. Her thoughts lingered with amazement at how unusually spiteful one person could have made her. She didn't like it, but she also knew that in Udo Holthaus' case, she would never change.

Judge Montgomery's resounding voice shook Grace from her vindictive whimsy. "Be seated," the judge advised. Her mind was jerked back into the courtroom and the business at hand.

"Ladies and gentlemen," the judge addressed the jury, "have you reached a decision in the case of Travis Vincent *et al* versus Udo Holthaus and the Premier Life Insurance Company?"

The foreperson, a middle-aged woman with short, salt-and-pepper hair and a strong and vibrant voice, responded grimly, "We have, your Honor."

She handed a piece of paper to the clerk, who carried it with a bit of flourish to the judge. He adjusted his reading glasses, read the note and handed it back. The clerk returned it to the foreperson, who stood and waited for her instruction.

"Please read the jury's decision?" requested Judge Montgomery.

"We the jury," the foreperson read, "in the matter of civil case number 38405, find in favor of the plaintiff."

An eruption of jubilation came from the Vincent family and their supporters. Udo Holthaus slumped into his chair and glowered at Hamlin McLaughlin, then cast a sidelong frown at Grace. Terrance Cooper and Burt Redmond stifled a smile at each other, gathered their briefcases and prepared for a quick exit.

The courtroom was in chaos. Judge Montgomery pounded for silence. "Thank you for your service, ladies and gentlemen of the jury. You are dismissed."

He gaveled again and quickly rose and stepped down from the bench and out the door to his chambers. Reporters and onlookers crowded up the aisle and darted out of the courtroom.

Grace paused as she reached Elizabeth Vincent who was weeping and hugging John Boyd. "Congratulations," Grace said as Elizabeth turned and slipped her slender arms around the reporter's shoulders. "I'm glad you can cry tears of joy for a change."

Elizabeth pulled back and looked at Grace with gratitude. "They're tears of relief," she said, trying to smile through her crying. Grace nodded and followed the crowd up the aisle as Elizabeth spun toward her approaching mother and their relatives with her arms outstretched.

Grace rushed back to TXDA and immediately began working on the story. The evidence room loss was a distant memory for the time being. The thrill of seeing Udo's crest-fallen reaction, of hearing the cheers of the Vincent family as the foreperson delivered the decision, the stampede of her fellow reporters eager to tell the story of Bonnie Vincent's victory, were still with her. She knew she must fight through the exhilaration of this partial justice to put the news into a factual account.

An hour after the verdict had been read, Grace was seated at the news desk with Phil Sawyer, delivering the story for the early evening news. But the bliss of this day would be hard to forget. She struggled to contain it as she stared into the camera, speaking the words she had hoped she might. "...Udo Holthaus has been denied his wife's life insurance benefit," Grace reported. "He hasn't been charged with anything criminal, but this jury decided there is doubt of his innocence in Bonnie Vincent's murder, Phil."

"What about the criminal case, Grace?" asked Phil.

"That remains to be seen. I'll be following it closely for our viewers."

"Thank you, Grace Gleason, for your coverage of this intriguing trial. And thank you, viewers, for watching channel seven's on-the-spot six o'clock news."

The camera lights went off. Grace stood up, and Phil reached out and touched her arm. She turned to see a serious look of concern cross his face.

"Grace. Be careful," was all he said.

She was still feeling relieved. Ned's bad news was not on her mind this evening, nor was the murky warning of Udo Holthaus. The Vincent family had lost their sweet daughter and sister, but they had found some peace in at least one court, and Grace's thoughts were with Elizabeth, and through her with Hal and Betty and Ellie, the Vincents she hadn't even met.

Grace's car was parked at the pump at the Gas 'N' Go station. She realized as she gassed it up that she had performed many such daily chores by rote for quite some time. Her preoccupation with Bonnie's murder had relegated every small task to automatic pilot.

As Grace stood staring at the nozzle, absently filling her tank without even remembering the swipe of her credit card, the startling thought struck her that she couldn't recall the last time she had performed this errand. She knew she must have filled up several times in the past few weeks, but she would have to learn where or when from her bills.

This is not a great way to go through life, she thought.

She remained in her newfound state of euphoria and inattention as she finished fueling, climbed back into her car and started to pull out of the station driveway, Without paying much attention to her surroundings, she vaguely realized another car had left simultaneously and seemed in a rush to catch up. She jolted herself alert and searched the mirror. The other car that had exited immediately behind her and was now following her closely was Udo's!

"Good Lord, Grace," she admonished herself aloud. "How could you have been so damned careless not to notice the bastard?"

She panicked and sped up, but his front bumper was tightly on her car's rear.

"All right, Holthaus. Here we go," she shouted. Grace knew she was in no emotional state to try outrunning him, but her life was being driven by emotion and adrenalin these days, and they took over. She whipped around several corners and went through a yellow light. Udo ran it as it turned red, and the persistent man's car remained glued to her back bumper.

Grace became increasingly frenzied. She glanced up at the rear view mirror and then looked left and right for help, but the two cars were racing down a four-lane street with no pedestrians in sight and vehicles whizzing past at high rates of speed. She cranked the steering wheel recklessly, swerving around corners, trying to shake Udo, but he was relentless in his chase.

Shaking from fear and anger, Grace continued to drive with her left hand while she fumbled at her purse on the passenger seat, grasping desperately for her cell phone. Her hand struck its smooth, curved surface and she yanked it from the bag. She slowed down slightly, glancing intermittently through the windshield and at the phone as she activated it with her thumb, pushed the speaker button and speed-dialed her home number.

Grace heard a rapid beep and grimaced.

"No signal? Damn it," she blurted aloud, hanging up.

She spotted a strip mall ahead and slued into it, locating a vacant space at the curb between two parked vehicles. Her car skidded to a stop and rammed the curb hard. Grace picked the phone up again and dialed, looking anxiously over her shoulder for a sign of Udo's car. She couldn't see it, but her instincts shrieked that he wouldn't have given up so easily.

In her preoccupation with dialing her phone, she hadn't noticed the driver of the car on her passenger side emerging from a store and climbing in.

The sound of a busy signal over her phone's speaker sent her senses reeling. "Oh, no, no! Get off the phone, Jeff," she screamed, but her voice was drowned out by the car next to her starting up, revving, and pulling out.

As she punched the buttons to redial Jeff with shaky fingers, her heart seemed to fly in fright as she watched Udo's car pull into the next space. The evil man sat unmoving, casting a maniacal, hateful glare at her. She had never felt so terrorized.

What are my options? she asked herself as she scanned the storefronts, all but one of them dark. She was ready to jump out and run for the lighted store with its neon "open" sign still glittering, but Udo's car door opened slowly. Cringing in panic, Grace forgot the phone call and the store. All she could think about was fleeing.

She slammed her car into reverse and catapulted out of the space, pausing at the entrance to the street as traffic zipped by. She felt a thump from behind. Udo hammered her back bumper.

That psycho! He'll kill me, she thought as she peeled out of the parking lot and back onto the busy avenue with Holthaus in heated pursuit.

Grace drove toward Dallas police headquarters, barreling down South Lamar twenty miles over the speed limit. It was only a few short minutes, but it seemed like tortuous hours.

Screeching around a corner, Grace careened into the large parking lot half-filled with squad cars and police vans. She almost rammed one of the vans as she slammed on the brakes and jumped out, her heart racing like a horse on the track. She watched in terror as Udo's car pulled up behind her and stopped at the lot entrance. Grace shook in helpless fear as Udo's car backed up very slowly for a long and foreboding moment, its headlights nearly blinding her.

The lot lights were not fully illuminated yet. Grace sprinted between the vehicles toward the back entrance, praying the door would not be locked. As she ran, she glanced back again, but her view of Holthaus' car was blocked by a van she was rushing past.

Then she heard footsteps coming toward her. She froze, trying to fix the direction of the sound. She fumbled in her purse for her cell phone, her breath coming in gasps.

The steps grew louder, and the dark shape of a man, backlit and indeterminable, emerged from behind a van.

She froze. *Where the hell is my cell phone?* Her brain was reeling.

The footsteps came closer and the figure crossed under the rays of a brightening lot light.

"Ned," Grace screamed as the detective's face became visible.

"Grace? What the hell?" Ned Moore said, his mouth gaping open.

She rushed to him and threw her arms around his shoulders, trembling. She peered back, scanning the entrance to the lot.

Udo's car was nowhere to be seen.

For two days, Grace lived a nightmare of fear. Then Ned Moore called the third morning and asked her to meet him at the Dallas Diner. She rushed to meet him, and his presence calmed her.

"Maybe we should buy some stock in this place," Grace joked as she and Ned sat in the familiar corner booth.

Ned laughed and did a quick surveillance. "Not if we have to report today's earnings. I think there's a homemade lemonade stand in my neighborhood with better gross receipts than they're generating here."

The breakfast business had waned, and it was still too early for the coffee break crowd. Only two other booths were occupied, and no one was sitting at the counter. The place where rattle and clatter and chatter were common during the busiest hours, was almost scarily peaceful. Even the waitresses, who usually busied themselves filling coffee cups, bantering with customers and shouting orders to the cooks, were lolling lazily around the cash register near the entrance, gossiping and giggling quietly, paying scant attention to their clientele.

"I prefer it like this," Grace expelled a sigh.

She had come to regard this diner, with this man in his corner booth, as a safe and welcome harbor, and today she was especially grateful for the calm. Yet she was edgy, glancing periodically with some trepidation toward the door, lines of concern carved firmly in her brow.

"Grace, relax," Ned pleaded. "We've had you watched for two days. Nothing."

"Holthaus dogged me all the way home," she recounted, the anxiety in her voice seeming oddly out of place in this quiet and relaxed setting. "I thought he was going to run me off the road. Ned, it was two days ago and I'm still scared spitless. I'm afraid to go to work and then afraid to go back home. I won't let Megan go out of the house alone, not even to the grocery store, and she's angry because I won't tell her why. Every time I hear someone behind me or know someone's on the other side of a door I'm going through, that frisson of dread just grabs me. I'm so paranoid that I'm driving my husband crazy."

"Relax, Grace. He's gone," Ned said, almost as an order.

Grace sat forward and fixed her attention on him. "He's gone?" Her hopeful eyes searched his, begging for no hidden catch.

"His condo has been cleaned out and it's up for sale," Ned reassured her. "My contact at the license bureau says he asked for his severance check to be mailed to a post office box. The box was emptied out and closed two days ago. We've checked all his old haunts, including the Saucy Lady. No one has seen him. The son of a bitch has cleared out, Grace."

She considered, but frowned, unconvinced. "He might be hiding, waiting for his chance. You didn't see him, Ned—the hate and desperation in the man's face. I was never really afraid of him until he threatened me with Megan at the courthouse and then tried to run me down the other night. I've been sleeping with one eye open."

"We've stopped investigating until something new comes up," the detective said. "It's not going to come to trial. But Udo Holthaus knows we still like him for Bonnie's murder. There's no way he'll wait around to feel that kind of heat." He reached out and placed both hands on hers, and the warmth of his soft, giant paws ran through her body, soothing her.

His happy eyes fixed on her frightened face. "Grace, he's gone," Ned insisted. "Udo Holthaus won't bother you any more."

CHAPTER 15: A Different Kind of Scare

JEFF LEFT in late spring. "I can't wait any longer," he told Grace on the last day of May. They sat in the screened sun porch and watched the encroaching evening envelop the garden. "There's no way to close this rift. I have to get out to the West Coast and be in the environmental game. And you need to be here."

She sat silently for a long moment, fighting off a nagging tightness in her throat. They had been through all of the fights and make-ups. There seemed little more to say.

"There's no way you can stay here and be happy?" Her voice was tired.

He turned sad eyes toward her. She could scarcely hear his words, "There's no way," but they drove a spike through any hope that they might reconcile.

The sultry, hang dog days of August and September sit upon Texas like a giant, lazy reptile, stifling any chance for movement, unwilling or unable to budge. Children not daunted by the searing temperatures venture outdoors to play, even during the worst heat of day, but most adults opt for the air conditioned comfort of the indoors or the cool water of the pool until the evening promises a bit of welcome breeze. Even the golf courses and tennis courts at midday during these months stand mostly idle.

It is a time to hunker down and wait for relief as the pleasant and fragrant days of spring fade like an ebbing memory.

As the summer wore on, Grace Gleason didn't mind the oppression of the season. She felt happier and more alive than she had in a long time. Udo Holthaus had apparently fled, abandoning his menacing threats toward Grace and leaving no trace. She felt an obscure longing from Jeff's absence, but the relief from fearing Holthaus helped her overcome the ache.

Megan swung into college mode, but not at her originally hoped-for destination of the University of Texas in Austin. The decision that she would enroll in the university's Richardson campus, near Dallas, was compelled partly by the expense of a contentious divorce. But the deciding factors were the possibility of a vengeful man learning that Grace's daughter lived in a distant city and Grace's need to have contact with the remaining vestige of her marriage.

Initially disappointed, Megan's growing maturity and her fading connections with her old Austin crowd eventually led her to accept the decision to attend Richardson.

"All right, I'll go there," she conceded over lunch with Grace and Jeff a week before Labor Day weekend. Jeff had flown in to finalize the divorce negotiations and participate in Megan's college decision. "Provided they accept me. But..." she scanned their faces with apprehension, "...I want to live up there."

"Not a good idea," Jeff reacted. "You should commute from home, where your mom can keep track of you and we can save some rent money."

"Dad, I don't need someone to monitor me," Megan said in a manner so reserved and reasoned it made Grace beam with pride. "I've proven I'm a responsible person, wouldn't you agree?" Megan persisted.

"Well, yes," Jeff stammered, unaccustomed to losing arguments, least of all to his daughter. "But..."

"So," Megan interrupted, "I would like to prove to you and Mom I can take this responsibility to another level. There are secure, patrolled apartments close to campus, and I can find some roommates to share the expense. Please?"

Jeff looked questioningly at Grace, who nodded yes. Megan would live away from home for the first time in her life.

Within three weeks, Megan had moved into an apartment. But a phone call she made to Grace threw her college plans off-course.

"I think I'm running a fever," she told her mother. "And I'm feeling this heavy, achy feeling in my stomach."

"Have you thrown up?" Grace asked.

"Not yet, but I feel like I'm going to any minute."

"Honey, you should come on home where I can take care of you."

"What about school, Mom? And your work?"

"School can wait. When I have to go in to work, I'll see if Mrs. Heilbronner next door can look in on you. She offered as much when your father moved out."

Anna was the perfect role model for a next-door neighbor. With Jeff gone, Grace felt a strong connection to the woman whose first name she still couldn't bring herself to use. They sometimes sat in Grace's kitchen, sipping coffee and commiserating, reminiscing, chatting about the state of the world and gossiping about the happenings of Dallas. Grace enjoyed Anna's company, and she didn't know when she had met a gentler, kinder, classier person in her life.

Anna had told Grace her story in one of those coffee mornings, barely a month after Jeff had left. A widow, she had lived in this neighborhood with her husband for twenty years. Jackson Heilbronner had been a lawyer and behind-the-scenes political figure for the Republican Party, and together they had raised four children.

"We brought them all up to be independent thinkers," Anna told Grace, "and darned if they didn't all become liberals, have our grandchildren and then move to the four corners of the darned globe."

"That's terrible," Grace consoled. "Not the liberal part—the part about your being so far away from your grandbabies."

"I see them on holidays. My sons both live overseas—one in Hong Kong and the other in Dubai, of all places. But my daughters live in California. I considered moving there—even talked to a realtor about putting my big old house on the market. But all of our close friends are here, my bridge buddies and Jackson's old cronies and their wives. And I just couldn't face leaving this place. You know, we built the first home in this subdivision, and we did it with our heart and soul."

"Twenty years of memories," Grace said.

"Well, someday I'll have to give it up. I suppose I'll shuffle off to La-la land and live in a home where my family can visit on Sundays."

"Mrs. Heilbronner," Grace admonished. "That's so cynical."

"I know. Privilege of old age."

Megan returned home on Saturday, and she and Grace spent the weekend watching old movies when Megan wasn't sleeping. She continued to run a low-grade fever, but Grace pumped aspirin and orange juice down her, and she appeared to be improving by Monday. It would be a slow news day, so she might not have to work long hours, but still Grace felt the need to report to work. She checked on Megan, who was sleeping restlessly, and then dressed for work and walked next door, knocking on Anna Heilbronner's door.

Anna answered the door in a robe. Her silver hair was perfectly brushed and her makeup was on, but she had not yet dressed.

"Morning, Mrs. Heilbronner," Grace felt a need to apologize for the intrusion, but she also felt rushed.

"Good morning, Grace. I must look awful. Do you want some coffee?"

"You look fine, and I'm sorry to intrude so early. I have to go to work, and I have a huge favor to ask. Do you remember when Jeff moved out, you said if there's ever anything..."

"Of course," Anna interrupted. "What is it, dear?"

"Megan's sick. She'll be okay, but she's running a fever. It's the flu. I can't beg off work today, and I need someone to look in on her."

"Megan's back home?"

"I brought her home Saturday. She's not very happy. Just weeks after moving into her apartment, getting to know her new roommates."

"Of course I will, Grace. I was going to putter in the garden today. Let me get dressed and I'll park myself in your house and watch television."

Grace felt a rush of relief. "You're a doll, Mrs. Heilbronner." She hugged her and hurried off to work.

The day passed swiftly. Grace and Matt had been sent out to cover a house fire in an otherwise quiet, middle-class Dallas residential neighborhood. Matt parked the TXDA van on the street near the barricades, and Grace went in search of the fire chief while Matt unpacked his equipment. The fire that had once obviously raged, destroying much of the house, was dying.

Small clusters of people stood across the street watching the action, their eyes wide and sad as gushes of water pummeled the home. Occasional crashes of falling joists and drywall added audible insult to the destruction.

"Not sure what the cause was," the fire chief told Grace, "but it looks like it started in the garage. Maybe faulty wiring. We'll investigate it thoroughly, of course."

"Was anyone home?" Grace asked as she made notes.

"That couple over there hugging each other? They're the owners. They're about as upset as I've ever seen. I don't imagine they'll talk to you, but you can ask. Some of those neighbors over there might, though."

Matt set up the shot with a fire truck in the background, firefighters still pouring water on the fire as it crackled and smoldered.

Grace spoke into the camera, its lights illuminating her face and immediate surroundings. "The husband and wife managed to get out safely, but nearly everything they owned was destroyed. They declined an interview, obviously still extremely devastated."

Ten minutes later, inside the truck, Grace and Matt huddled over a monitor as they edited the story. "Nice job, Matt." The words had barely left Grace's mouth when she felt her cell phone vibrate in her pocket. She always turned the ringer off during interviews, and she had failed to turn it back on. "Gleason," she answered. "Yes, Mrs. Heilbronner. My God. Can you take her to Doctor's Hospital? I'm finishing a story and can meet you there. Thank you. Thank you so much. I'll hurry." She turned the phone off and looked pleadingly at Matt, who was still fussing with the video. "Megan is sick, and she's gotten worse. My neighbor has been watching her, but she thinks she should go to the E.R. Can you drop me?"

"Of course," Matt said. "This is finished. Let me feed it back to the station and we'll get going." Matt finished the transmission quickly, and in minutes the van was speeding through the Dallas streets.

"I don't know what happened," Grace muttered. "I thought she was getting better."

"She'll be fine," Matt consoled.

"She'll be fine," he had said. Matt didn't know Megan at all—barely knew Grace much better, and yet she sensed a connection from him that was more than passing co-worker sympathy. Grace stored the emotion in her memory and then shrugged it off for the time being. She needed to focus on her daughter as they sped into the emergency drive-up and Grace jumped out.

"Want me to wait?" Matt asked, leaning across and grabbing the door she was about to slam shut.

"That's okay. Mrs. Heilbronner has a car if I need it. Can you tell them at the station what's happened?"

"Sure. Grace," he continued, "Don't worry." There it was again, that sensation that something had drawn them closer. She nodded. As he yanked on the van door she paused to take in his smile, and then rushed for the emergency room entrance.

The waiting area was frenzied, an uproar of sound and motion. Patients and receptionists were interacting animatedly. Nurses and doctors came in and out, looking at charts, stopping to confer with family members, looking after the frenetic business of medical care.

An EMT crew burst in with an elderly Latino man on a gurney, an IV implanted in his arm and held by one of the crew. A medical team met them and hurried them back through the double doors into the waiting space where life and death are played out daily.

Anna found Grace as she rushed toward the reception desk. "They took her back about twenty minutes ago," Anna said.

"What happened? She seemed to be improving when I left," Grace couldn't help sounding frantic.

"Those pains in her stomach just kept getting worse, and then her temperature shot way up. I was worried," Anna explained.

"Thanks for getting her here so fast."

"My pleasure. If it's okay, I'll wait around with you."

A nurse stuck her head through the waiting room door. "Mrs. Gleason?" she called out.

Grace rushed to her and noted her nametag—Lana Hopkins—a habit of observation she had formed from years at her profession. "I'm Grace Gleason."

Nurse Hopkins smiled, opened the door and motioned Grace through. Grace nodded her thanks to Anna, who retreated to a chair in the waiting room.

The smell of antiseptic greeted Grace as Nurse Hopkins led her to her daughter's tiny room. Megan was in bed, pale and perspiring. A doctor stood at her side, his stethoscope moving across Megan's chest. Grace noted his name on his white coat—Dr. Anish Patel—and then went to Megan's side, smoothed her hair back and kissed her forehead. Megan's skin was warm and clammy.

"Hi, sweetie," Grace tried to sound reassuring.

"Mrs. Gleason, we've done some blood work," Dr. Patel wasted no time with pleasantries, his approach all business. "Your daughter's appendix has ruptured. We need to operate as soon as possible. Nurse Hopkins here has the permissions ready."

His words astonished Grace. A ruptured appendix had not even occurred to her. "Doctor, I thought she had the flu. Doesn't the appendix only hurt on one side?"

"Not always," Dr. Patel sounded annoyed by the delay. "We don't want to waste any time. We'll get her into pre-op while you handle the paperwork. The anesthesiologist is on her way."

Grace felt a pang of panic and drew in a deep breath. Everything was happening too fast to process properly. She gathered her wits and kissed her daughter again. Megan's wrinkled forehead and darting eyes told Grace she was frightened.

"Mom." Megan said shakily.

"Don't worry. They'll take good care of you. I'll be right here."

Several hours had passed since Megan's surgery. On the heels of a busy workday and the stress of Megan's emergency, Grace was exhausted. She was dozing in the chair beside Megan's bed in the recovery room when a night nurse shook her shoulder.

"There's a woman named Anna outside who would like to speak to you," the nurse told her. Grace took a moment to identify time and place. Seeing Megan sleeping soundly, hooked up to an IV line, Grace rallied.

"I left you and Megan alone for a while," Anna told her outside the door, "but I think you need to go home and get some rest. I can stay with her for a while."

"What would I do without you?" Grace praised her friend. "I don't want to be gone when she comes around, but I would like to go home and shower. I should call Jeff, too. I left him a message when she went into surgery, so he's probably having a fit."

"Then go," Anna instructed her. "Take my car for as long as it takes. I had dinner and a nap, and I can stay here all night if you need me to."

Grace fought drowsiness as she drove toward Brookwood Acres, thinking about a world where people help other people, an existence so foreign to many that Grace felt an overwhelming gratitude for living in the country that invented volunteerism.

Megan will be okay, she thought thankfully, and wondered what it would have been like had Jeff been there, his help needed when the chips were in the pot. "He would have been reading briefs," she found herself answering aloud, laughing quietly about people who talk to themselves in their advancing age. A hot shower and some soup was exactly what she needed.

Grace enjoyed every spoonful of the vegetable broth as though it was her last. She regained some vigor and decided it was still early enough in California to catch Jeff before showering. Sitting at her computer, she dialed his number on her video hookup and hoped he was home.

When Jeff answered, he looked uncombed and unshaven.

Grace recalled telling Mitchell Court the day she had the service installed, "The good part of this video calling service is that you can see who you're speaking with."

"And the bad part?" Mitchell had asked.

"You can see who you're speaking with," she joked.

Grace had ordered the service so that Megan could speak with Jeff face-to-face when she came home on weekends. Grace had never used it for anything else, until now.

"Hey," Jeff said sounding groggy.

"Jeff, I'm sorry. I thought you'd be up," Grace said. "It's not that late out there, is it?"

"No, it's okay," he reassured her. "I was reading and dozed off. Is she all right?"

"She's out of danger. Mrs. Heilbronner is staying with her so I can take a shower. Then I'll go right back."

"I'd better come out," he said.

"You don't need to," Grace answered. "I can update you."

"No, I'm coming out," he said with finality. "I can be there early tomorrow."

When they hung up, Grace stared at the computer screen for several minutes. It was not that long ago that they had sat facing each other across a table, or under the covers, or on a park bench somewhere, committing their devotion for a lifetime. It seemed to her an unexplained mystery how all of that mutual emotion had become reduced to a picture over a wire, made significant only by their shared interest in the one good thing that remained from their union.

She felt a hard lump in her throat. She had cried all she ever would over the loss of the life and love they had once had. But at a time like this, the emptiness of divorce returned to trouble her. She shook her head sadly and walked into the bathroom, undressing for the hot shower that she knew would feel healing.

The next day, Megan was asleep in her hospital still connected to tubes. Grace had showered and changed, then returned and sent Anna Heilbronner home with her undying gratitude. She was dozing in a chair next to Megan when a knock at the door jarred her. She saw Jeff poke his head inside and push through the doorway carrying a large bouquet of red roses. Grace looked up sleepily as Megan opened her eyes slowly and managed a weak smile at the sight of her father stealing into the room.

"Hi, Dad," she said, her voice a wisp.

"Hey, Punkin." Jeff nodded and smiled at Grace who was fully awake now.

She got up and took the flowers, setting them on a window ledge.

Jeff went to Megan's side. "How're you feeling?

"Okay, sort of. It hurts," Megan answered weakly.

Jeff kissed her.

"I'm going to miss freshman orientation," she wailed.

Grace had left them alone, relieved at not having to be the only sentinel, at least for a while. She wandered through the corridor, walking off the haziness of sleep, and then found a coffee machine in the waiting room. It was strangely quiet there at this hour. She sat in a corner chair sipping the coffee and flipping through a magazine when Jeff came in.

"She's asleep."

"Good," Grace sighed.

Jeff sat down and looked at her squarely, judgment in his face. "I don't get how it could have gone that long without you knowing," Jeff began his complaint.

"I thought it was the flu. She seemed better."

"Same old story. You weren't there." His lips were tight.

In the face of his accusations, Grace tried her best to maintain an even and dispassionate tone, but she was growing angry. "And you were?" she said, softly and measured. "Don't try to lay a guilt trip on me, Jeff. "

"I thought the whole idea of her coming home was so you could take care of her. Now I learn that Anna is her nurse," his lips grew tauter.

Grace felt her boiling point getting perilously close. She slowed her retort, measured her words with care. "Mrs Heilbronner helped out on this because I had to go to work. If you want to triple Megan's support I'll consider a leave of absence until she finishes college." There was a long pause, resentment festering on Grace's face.

When they were two thousand miles apart, communicating by phone or video, it was easy for the old doubts to emerge. *Did we act hastily? Did we turn our back on something valuable in the heat of argument?* But back together momentarily in a crisis-laden snapshot of time, the brazen reminders of what had pushed them into divorce hell loomed everywhere. Grace was annoyed by the bickering but grateful for its truth.

"Have you re-thought letting her live away from home?" Jeff asked, his voice softer.

Grace repeated the response she had used so many times when they had debated Megan's move. "I'm as close to her apartment when I'm working as I would be if she lived at home,"

"What about that Holthaus guy? Aren't you worried about him?"

Grace waited, her brain working on the unexpected and excruciating question. Then, remembering Ned's comment at the diner, she simply answered, "He's gone." They sat without speaking for a time and then, as an afterthought, Grace turned to Jeff and reassured him. "I'm in touch with Megan every day. I see her all the time. I've never told her everything about him, and I don't want you to, either. She has enough to worry about. Jeff, she'll be okay."

Jeff sat back and gave her a tired nod, and the argument died.

Three days passed. Megan was mending in the hospital. A brilliant, sunny day was dawning in Dallas, and Grace had slept at home for the first night since the near-catastrophe. Jeff had left the afternoon he had arrived, as she had known he would. She was happily pouring a cup for Anna in her kitchen—a welcome return to a pleasant routine before driving to the hospital to learn the schedule of Megan's release.

"Thanks for helping me, Mrs. Heilbronner."

"No problem. She was a sick puppy."

Unexpectedly, Grace sat down and began to cry.

"Oh, come on now, Grace," Anna said, reaching out and patting her shoulder awkwardly. "She's getting better by the minute."

"What if anything happened to her?"

"Nothing's going to happen to that sweet girl."

"Jeff gives me such a hard time. Since he left, every time something goes wrong—even the smallest thing, I..."

Anna squeezed her arm, stopping her. "Listen to me. You've done a wonderful job raising Megan. All kids give you a headache once in a while—that's not your fault. It's their job. That ex of yours can go kiss a snake."

Grace laughed through her tears, wondering what she would possibly do without such a comforting friend. She felt a surge of positive energy. *Time to get Megan well and into college. And to move on with my career.*

CHAPTER 16: Crime Reporter

IT HAD ONLY BEEN seven months, but it seemed to Grace like years since that icy morning in the airport garage when she identified the cold, nude body of Bonnie Vincent. Since that dreadful incident, rarely did Grace cover a crime story—a mugging, wife beating or murder—that the image of Bonnie didn't reappear to her. On such occasions, the bruising on Bonnie's throat, the savage bite mark, the pale bluish lips of the woman Grace had known as vibrant and attractive ran through her senses in a haunting of unimaginable horror.

She tried to shut that terrible picture from her mind, but like the memory of a fatal mistake, she couldn't shake the image.

Grace was certain she knew who killed Bonnie Vincent, and Udo Holthaus was still out there somewhere. His shifty smirk was indelibly inscribed in her memory. Every time she closed her eyes and tried to erase it, all the question marks re-emerged. *Is he psychopathic, or sociopathic, or simply vicious and amoral? Is he living a life of scandal and brutality somewhere, or has he retreated to the shadows like a coward? Will he return? Will he kill again?*

Today that image of a horrific murder and the unanswered mysteries swirled in Grace's head once again.

In the subtle way that winter has of sneaking up on the Lone Star State, autumn introduces a hint of nip to the air in late afternoons. Sometimes, without warning, the fading light evokes memories of the danger that brought Grace face-to-face with evil months earlier.

The days were growing shorter rapidly, and on this early October day the sun was already fading at six o'clock in the Dallas suburb of Richardson. At sunset, the evening smelled crisp and almost frosty, normally promising to usher in a fresh and pleasant prologue to nighttime.

Sometimes, promises deceive.

The parking lot of Richardson's Metro Mall revealed the time of day. A mere scattering of parked cars indicated that most afternoon shoppers had already left and the evening rush hour crowd had not yet abandoned offices and factories and delivery trucks to make their stops on the way home.

Maria Alvarez was an exception. At this time she would normally be *codinar la cena*–cooking dinner–for her four children. But a late run through several stores had taken longer than she expected. Now, loaded down with packages and bags, she lugged them across the lot still not fully lighted by the night-activated street lamps.

She glanced around apprehensively as she hurried to reach her car, fumbling in her purse as she walked, trying to fish out her keys. Her motions of digging through the purse grew more hurried and frantic as she drew closer to the car without finding them. She had read the recent series of stories in the *Al Dia–Dallas* newspaper about women who were car-jacked at malls.

"No ser tonto– va a estar bien." she muttered aloud in a nervous cadence. *Don't be foolish–you will be fine.* As she juggled her packages, her searching fingers located the keys and fumbled with them in a frantic effort to wrest them from the handbag. She finally retrieved them with a look of relief crossing her face, but she was still struggling not to drop the packages as she stumbled awkwardly toward the car.

Suddenly, silently, a lone figure loomed behind her from the nearby shadows and seized her with abrupt force. The attacker threw his arm around her neck in a tight chokehold. Maria screamed and dropped her keys, trying desperately to pull away from her surprise assailant.

Maria's mugger was Johnny McPherson, a two-bit hoodlum who picked his prey indiscriminately, based on his mood, financial needs and horniness.

Johnny had never held a real job. After dropping out of high school two years earlier, he had gone on a rampage of convenience store heists. He was caught once and copped a misdemeanor plea in exchange for time served and probation with drug rehabilitation.

While completing that sentence, Johnny worked some corners selling crack. One evening, at dusk, he encountered a young Hispanic woman walking home alone and discovered how easy it was to nab an unsuspecting Latina, drag her into a vacant building, rape her and take her money. It wasn't extremely lucrative, but repeated on a regular basis the action provided dope and food money, sex and excitement—all the perks a no-account loser could ask for.

"I can tell the illegal ones," Johnny had told one of the druggies he hung out with as they shared a joint. "They're dressed like housecleaners or waitresses, and when they're in public they watch over their shoulders for the immigration authorities."

"So?" his whacked-out friend said, unimpressed.

"So, after you rob and fuck 'em, you say you'll turn them in to the immigration authorities if they squeal. They've got a deathly fear of that agency getting its hands on 'em."

Watching Maria cross the lot, warily scanning the area as she hunted for her keys, Johnny couldn't know that she held a green card, acquired when she married her citizen husband.

Johnny quickly scooped up Maria's keys off the ground without completely losing his hold on her. She dropped her packages as she wrestled to get free.

He violently pulled her back close to him and shook her in warning. "Don't fight me, Chiquita, and I won't hurt you," Johnny commanded, the two joints he had smoked earlier emboldening him and making him impervious to her hoarse, hysterical pleas.

"Por favor, dejame!" she begged him to let her go.

"I've heard those words before, Chiquita," Johnny ranted. "Go ahead, keep begging. It fucking turns me on."

He maintained a strangle hold on the struggling woman, flipped the door key out and inserted it into the driver's side door. He was fumbling to open it, but Maria continued to fight, hitting and kicking at him, making it difficult for Johnny to maneuver the door.

Maria screamed again, even louder this time.

Two young men crossing the lot to their car heard Maria's cries and saw the struggle. They ran full-pace toward Johnny and Maria. They arrived as Johnny had swung the door completely open and was beginning to drag the still-thrashing Maria inside the car with him.

The first of the two men to arrive, built stocky and muscular like a football linebacker, body-blocked Johnny full-steam, knocking him to the pavement with violent force. Johnny's head hit the pavement with the sound of a rock glancing off a two-by-four. Meanwhile, his friend, a tall and wiry young man, latched onto Maria as she was about to feint and propped her against the car hood. As Maria regained her balance, the taller man jumped on the groggy Johnny McPherson's back, twisted his arm in a hammerlock and held him down.

The stocky man who had slammed into Johnny recovered quickly from the collision, stood up, jammed one foot down on Johnny's neck and pulled a cell phone from his blue jeans pocket. He dialed nine-one-one. It rang as Johnny's captors kept their prey pinned face down on the ground, writhing and moaning in pain.

Within minutes, two black squad cars with *"Richardson Police"* emblazoned on the side in neon green, barreled into the lot with their blue lights flashing. As officers jumped out and rushed to the scene, several shoppers picked up their pace and hurried by without stopping, as if pausing to watch might somehow implicate them in the trouble. Meanwhile, several other cars pulled in off the street and stopped near the scene. Their curious occupants jumped out and moved in to get a close-up view of the excitement.

Two of the officers grabbed Johnny, cuffed his wrists behind his back and guided him toward their patrol car. Another policeman motioned for the two rescuers to follow him away from the scene, and the remaining officer, who spoke Spanish, handed Maria her purse and guided her to join them.

Maria stood sobbing and shaking with the officer's arm around her shoulder for support. She rummaged through her purse looking for her cell phone. *"Debo telefono Eduardo y decirle por que llego tarde,"* she told the Spanish-speaking officer. *I must telephone Edward and tell him why I am late.*

The officer nodded, but the chaos around them and the presence of *la policia* made Maria's hands tremble. In the excitement, she was unable to dial the phone. Frustrated, she stuffed it back into her purse and took a deep, tremulous breath.

Maria looked thankfully at the young men who helped her as they began to give their statements to the officers. Giving their names and showing their identification, they told the police they were college students, players on the university football team.

"Deciries gracias por salvarme," Maria said to the officer.

"The lady says thank you," the officer translated.

"No problem," the linebacker said to her, and she nodded understanding. "Is she...you know, legal?" he asked.

"Says she is," the officer responded. "We'll check her ID."

"Let's finish getting your statements," the second officer said, pulling a notepad and pen from his pocket.

"We heard this lady screaming, and this guy was dragging her toward that car right there," said first to arrive and attack McPherson. His short, muscular frame was topped by a blond shock of hair atop a block-shaped head.

"Todd got there first," said his black friend, the taller one. "I saw him sprinting across the lot and creaming that guy. I caught the lady just as she was going down and leaned her up against the car. Then I jumped on this douche bag's back as hard as I could."

"Yeah, DeMarcus is a defensive end, so he's kinda slow, you know?"

The officers guffawed at them. Maria watched the young men give their statements and the officers' response with a puzzled expression. She was taking deep breaths, trying to subdue her trembling as she watched the interaction.

Nearby, the other two other policemen had opened the back door of their squad car and were struggling to get McPherson into the back seat. Johnny was fidgety and uncooperative. He jerked away, fighting against the handcuffs that cut into his wrists behind him, and made a motion as if to run. One of the officers grabbed him again, wheeled him toward the open car door, pushed down on his head forcefully and leaned against him until Johnny sank into the back seat.

"Come on, man," Johnny squawked frantically as he fought against the cuffs. "I was making a citizen's arrest. The bitch is illegal."

"Shut up," the officer warned as he slammed the door shut, dashed around to the passenger side and jumped into the car as his partner revved up the engine. The patrol car sped away, bouncing out of the lot and onto the busy street with its lights flashing.

The two remaining officers finished interviewing the young men and turned their attention to Maria.

"Tenemos que ver su identificacion," the Spanish speaker said. *We need to see your ID.*

Still quivering tensely, Maria dug through her handbag and retrieved papers.

"Joke's on that guy," said the officer, sifting through Mara's identification. This lady's got a green card. Married to a U.S. of A. citizen."

In another part of Richardson, Grace Gleason was

following the TXDA-TV van through a darkening residential street. She would normally be riding shotgun in the van, next to her cameraman, Matt Robertson. But when they had received the assignment to cover a fraternity house break-in, she had decided to drive. It would give her a chance to check in on Megan.

She never stopped worrying about her daughter and wondering if letting her move into an apartment with two other girls had been wise. Grace's work as the TXDA crime reporter was her passion, but Megan was her life. With Megan living away for the first time in eightteen years, Grace knew her daughter's well-being was probably on her mind even when she wasn't consciously aware of it. The emergency appendectomy and Jeff's harsh admonition in the waiting room that night had heightened her understanding of how fragile the arrangement was, adding to her consternation.

Her cell phone ringing jolted her. "Gleason," she answered.

"It's Matt. Just got an interesting text. Attempted kidnapping and probably rape at the Metro Mall. That's three minutes from here if we get green lights. Want to check it out?"

Grace's news sense stirred, and she didn't hesitate, "Of course," she answered.

"I'll alert the station. Follow me."

The lights had been favorable, and they beat Matt's estimate by a minute. The van squealed into the Metro Mall parking lot and screeched to a stop near the scene of the squad car's still-flashing lights. Grace stopped right behind the van and sprang out of her car, carrying a notepad and Blackberry. Matt pulled up the parking brake on the van and jumped down from the driver's side. He sprinted to the back of the van and hurriedly grabbed lights and camera equipment from it as Grace approached the officers.

One of the policemen took a few steps toward her and assumed what looked to her like a military air.

"I need to talk to that woman, officer," she said, trying

to sound friendly.

"No you don't. That's our victim." The officer crossed his arms. He seemed defensive, she thought, wondering if he had been burned by the media at some time. "You guys sure got here fast," he observed.

Grace smiled at him, still trying to appear non-threatening. "We were on another story near here and my camera guy got a text from a source," she explained. "How about the woman?"

"Name's Maria Alvarez. Sorry, she *no habla Ingles*."

"And the two guys?" Grace pushed, wanting to salvage the story.

The officer seemed annoyed, but he walked back and conferred with the two young men who were listening as Maria gave her statement and the Spanish-speaking officer translated. Everyone paused to look at Grace as if on cue, and then they all turned back together again.

The military-like officer returned to Grace, appearing to soften his defensive posture. *Maybe,* she thought, *he has decided I'm no threat.*

The patrolman heaved a sigh, but moved closer, seeming friendlier now. "You're that Grace Gleason woman, aren't you? I've seen your stories. You do an okay job."

"Thanks," she said, smiling inwardly at the lameness of his compliment.

"Sorry," he said, "they don't want any publicity. Nothing personal. Afraid of retaliation."

"Damn it," Grace growled. "Got the name of the suspect?"

"The alleged perpetrator is Johnny McPherson. Nineteen-year-old kid, but you didn't get that from me," he said, using the code of cooperative non-cooperation the Dallas area cops often employed with reporters they liked.

The policeman nodded and smiled and returned to the group. Grace wrote down a couple of notes, moved toward the van, positioned herself so the group would appear in her background, and motioned for Matt to turn on the lights and camera. He handed her a sheet of paper, and she held in front of her so he could test the lights. As she gave it back he handed her a microphone. Grace tugged at her jacket and smoothed her hair, a routine that came automatically from years of seeing what looks good and bad on the screen.

"Hair okay?" she asked Matt.

"Perfect," he answered. "Three, two, one..."

Matt pointed at her and she spoke into the camera. "Phil, the excitement here at Richardson's Metro Mall is beginning to die down. A now-handcuffed nineteen-year-old suspect, Johnny McPherson, is going to police headquarters to be charged with assault and attempted kidnapping.

"This suspect's luck ran out thanks to the screams of his alleged victim—Maria Alvarez—and the actions of two alert young men who called for law enforcement and wrestled McPherson to the ground until the Richardson police arrived.' She motioned toward the group. "As you can see, they are still giving their statements to police. Mrs. Alvarez is okay. The tense moments here are subsiding, and it looks like all involved are a bit shaken but all right. I'm Grace Gleason bringing you Dallas's channel seven on-the-spot news. Phil, back to you."

Grace stood silently. The lights on Matt's camera went off. She relaxed and handed the microphone back to him.

"Nice job, Grace," said Matt.

"Thanks. Stories like this give me the willies."

She followed him to the van, climbed in on the passenger side, opened her laptop computer and started typing an intro for the story as they talked and he packed his equipment away.

When she was starting out, Grace had often labored far too long on stories, debating over single word choices, searching her brain for the right adverb or adjective, changing phrases from one metaphor to another. Over the years, writing the stories had come easier to her until now she could pound out a first draft, polish it here and there for a minute or two, and it was done. She had come a long way, and she was supremely confident in her craft.

"Why?" Matt broke her concentration as he packed away the equipment.

"What?" she responded, still not fully extracted from her focus on the story.

"Why do they give you the willies?" Matt persisted. "You've been covering murders, rapes and car-jackings for a while." He laughed. "Management hasn't been calling you our 'crime go-to gal' for nothing."

"I know, but it's different with Megan in college up here, you know? It seems personal."

Matt nodded. "I'd feel the same way if I had kids. There are too many weirdos running around these days." He got in on the driver's side as Grace closed her laptop and climbed out. He leaned across the seat. "Uh, Grace, how about some dinner?" he asked tentatively.

"I can't," she answered, happy to have the excuse. Not that she didn't like Matt nor think he would be a good match for some lucky woman who was ready for a commitment. He was tall and athletic and handsome in a Marlboro man sort of way. Grace remembered that when she first met him, she watched him work when she knew he didn't notice. She was checking out the professionalism of the guy she would be partnering with, but also sizing him up for looks and character. She liked what she saw—the easy way he had of flashing his perfectly white, friendly smile and making people feel at ease, his polite, homespun manner and the respect with which he treated all women and anyone in authority.

Whereas her ex, Jeff, was slick and glib, Matt was a down-to-ground, genuine man—what some people would call the salt of the earth. When he listened, it didn't seem to her to be for effect or to formulate some clever retort, but rather because he was truly interested in what someone else had to say.

Grace was happy to draw Matt as her cameraman on

many of these assignments. He was a talented photographer, cooperative, energetic, with a good eye for what would help sell the story. And she enjoyed working with him when the chatter was newsy but impersonal. But she didn't need complication in her life, nor did she think she would ever want the anchor of a relationship holding her down again.

She decided to discourage Matt's flirtations without disturbing the chemistry they had on assignments. "I drove myself up here so I could stop by Megan's apartment," she explained, thinking his expression sagged a little. "I like to check up on her when I'm anywhere near Richardson."

"I heard you got a divorce," he ventured.

"Getting," she responded quickly, surprised. "It's filed, but it's not final yet."

Matt flashed the grin she was attracted to. "One of these days I'm going to get you to say yes. To dinner, I mean."

She was taken aback somewhat, realizing his invitation was more than casual flirtation. "You mean a date? This is out of left field, Matt."

He seemed unfazed. "I figure we work together, we like each other..." He let her imagination finish the thought.

This is getting too deep, she thought. "I'm all work and absolutely no play, cowboy," she laughed.

Matt pressed on, "I'm going to stay on your case until you give me a shot."

"You don't need me," she argued, trying her best to keep the repartee light. "I'll bet women fall all over you. Besides, I'm way older than you."

"Right," Matt scoffed. "Four or five years. Big freaking deal."

Grace laughed at his reaction, stepped out of the van and walked toward her car. "See you back at the ranch."

"I'm not giving up, Grace Gleason," Matt called after her. "We're going to have that dinner together."

The overture had astonished her, a bolt from some other planet. Not that she hadn't seen the approving glances when he thought she wasn't aware, or that she hadn't noticed how attentive he was to making her look good on camera. But those could easily have been gestures of professional courtesy or simply old-fashioned friendship. Matt had never spoken up until this moment.

As Grace drove away, the photographer's rugged, farmhand good looks and deep, easy conversation stayed with her for a few minutes. She had been on a few casual dates since her split with Jeff, but never had any of her friendships approached anything serious.

Her work and her daughter were all she could handle.

Who knows? she thought. *Given another time and situation, I might be helplessly attracted to him.*

But not now.

CHAPTER 17: Evil Returns

UNIVERSITY AVENUE was a tree-lined residential street a few blocks from the University of Texas-Dallas campus in Richardson. Most of the homes in the upper-middle-class neighborhood had been built in the 1980s and 90s. A number of small apartment complexes dotted the neighborhood, built new by developers or converted from existing buildings to accommodate the growing university population.

Daylight was nearly gone, and Grace could see the streetlights beginning to flicker on as she drove toward Megan's apartment. Students walking or riding bicycles to and from the apartments gave the early evening a communal buzz as they returned from classes or headed out to the library or to dinner. Most of them were wearing jeans and sneakers and carried book bags. The brisk, cool breeze was starting to whip down from the North, causing them to hunch down into their jackets or sweaters as falling leaves swirled around their feet.

Grace glanced up the street and slowed down as she spotted Megan's building coming into view. It was a small, Spartan, brick fourplex—one of the earliest-built units in the neighborhood, lined wall-to-wall in uniformity with shutter-less windows and a simple stoop entrance at each doorway.

As she reached Megan's building, Grace saw the familiar wooden sign, with the neatly lettered words *University Apartments* lighted by a yard lamp. A small porch light glowed at each unit's doorway, and shafts of yellow rays spilled from the apartment windows onto the neatly kept lawn outside.

Grace parked in the driveway of Megan's unit and got out. She looked around at the surroundings, as had become her habit ever since the Holthaus stalking. Three young students with backpacks were hurrying past as Grace walked by and knocked on the door. One of them looked back at her curiously, as if he knew her but couldn't quite remember how.

Grace was accustomed to being vaguely recognized, and she returned his smile. "She's somebody, I know it," she heard him tell the others.

The other two cast a quick glance back at her, too. "It's that reporter, Grace something-or-other."

"Yeah. Hey, Grace," said the first student, waving.

She smiled and waved back. She never tired of knowing her reporting was reaching so many people.

The door opened. Grace didn't try to hide the thrill of seeing Megan's bright, happy face light up when she greeted her mother. Megan was eighteen now, slender, model-pretty with a musical voice that Jeff once said had the magic to pull the tides.

When Jeff had announced he was leaving alone for California, it took Grace weeks to accept his decision. It would require a much longer adjustment to get past the devastation of divorce. She instinctively understood it would probably take Megan a long time to accept her parents' doomed marriage. Although Grace had tired of the bickering as much as Jeff had, she quickly learned that even when divorce is the best option, it leaves a multitude of doubts for the couple and gigantic voids for their offspring.

After their decision to sever their marriage on that spring evening, Grace and Jeff had sat down the next day and talked to Megan together.

"You guys wouldn't be fighting if I had cooperated with your plan to move to Dallas," she protested.

"Honey, it has nothing to do with that," Grace reassured. "You handled that whole phase of your life with incredible maturity."

"She's right. This is between your mother and me," Jeff supported. "We need to go our own way, that's all. It's not your fault. It's ours."

Still, they sometimes heard Megan crying in her room.

Grace knew that the sadness, and the missing after Jeff left, would have to be part of the process.

Now Grace was the sole caretaker. Dad would become someone who showed up at Christmas with unusable presents or who sent a round-trip plane ticket for a two-week summer stay on the West Coast.

When Megan saw Grace standing in the doorway, she flipped her shoulder-length, shiny blonde hair and flashed a four-thousand-dollar orthodontic bill at her mother. "Mom, hi. What are you doing here?" She sounded surprised and pleased.

"Hi, sweetie," Grace said gratefully. "I'm only stopping by for a minute. I had to cover a story over at the mall. Some guy tried to kidnap a poor woman. He didn't get away with it, thank God."

Megan pushed the door open and Grace entered and hugged her. Megan shut the door but didn't lock it, setting off a charge of alarm in Grace. She gasped and secured the dead bolt and chain lock. "Honey," she chastised sternly, "how many times do I have to tell you..."

Megan joined in the oft-performed chorus, so they finish in unison, "Lock the door!"

"I know, Mom," Megan waved it off. "I always do, I promise. I'm making tea. Be right back."

She would make a good diplomat, Grace told herself, she can so readily deflect an argument. Megan disappeared into the kitchen, and Grace began to meander, looking around the room. It was furnished with reasonably new, but inexpensive, furniture. Books were stacked on the coffee table and on the two side tables beside a sofa, and Grace noticed that one was still open—meaning, she hoped, that Megan had been studying. She picked up a picture of Megan and Jeff mugging for the camera on the beach and gazed at it for several seconds, lost in a memory.

"Have you heard from your father?" she called out to Megan.

"Not for a couple of weeks," Megan responded from

the kitchen. "It's hard for him to reach me because California's two hours earlier."

"I know, Megan. It 's called Pacific time." She murmured softly to herself, "That would be his excuse."

Megan returned carrying two cups, handing one to Grace. "What?" she asked brightly.

"Nothing, Megan. Next time you're home we'll call him on video. Don't forget he has a birthday coming up."

"Forty-five. God, he'll be ancient," Megan proclaimed dramatically.

Grace laughed loudly and sipped her tea. "I can't stay," she said. "Need to get back to the station and finish some things."

"Mom, stay," Megan pleaded. "I ordered pizza. Carrie and Beth will be home from class any minute, and you haven't gotten to spend time with them."

"I know, honey. But I can't. I'll stay until the pizza gets here. I don't want you alone when some delivery guy comes."

"Oh, Mom, my roomies will be here long before it comes. Please stay for dinner?"

Grace was tempted. Trying to balance her life between the demands of the station and her desire to stay close to her sweet girl often pulled at her from different directions. But she also knew her career had been important in paying Megan's college tuition and to establishing her life here in an apartment. Jeff paid the rent and board, but he didn't cover the costs of clothing, school supplies, extra-curricular activities and other expenses that piled high in Megan's college outlay.

This time channel seven won out. "Sorry, Megan, I can't. I really do need to get back. You're sure they'll be here any minute?"

"On pizza night? They're always on time."

"Then I'd better go. Thanks, sweetie." She hugged Megan, opened the door and started out, then paused. "And don't forget..."

Megan interrupted, "I know..."

"Lock the door," they sang out in unison, laughing again. Grace hurried to her car. That zephyr she had felt when she had arrived thirty minutes ago was building into one of the famous Texas blue norther' winds. The temperature must have dropped ten degrees, she thought. She pulled out of the driveway and onto University Avenue, going to the end of the block and turning down a cross street.

Only a few seconds later, a pizza delivery car with an illuminated *Pizza Pantry* sign affixed on top shot around the corner from the other direction and pulled in beside Megan's apartment. It was a beat-up old compact that had obviously survived years of mistreatment, its quarter panel rusted out from street salt and two hub caps missing. The car slowed down, stopped, and sat idling in the driveway for a few moments.

The driver sat looking at the apartment with an unhappy, brooding stare. Finally, Udo Holthaus opened the door and got out slowly. He had lost weight since disappearing after the trial, but he had the same squinty, shifty eyes and thinning, uncombed, dishwater color hair. He looked sad and seedy, wearing faded blue jeans and beat-up running shoes. The only neat part of his clothing was his well-pressed pizza company shirt.

Holthaus walked slowly, cautiously, to the door, looking around in jerky mannerisms at the surrounding neighborhood. As he knocked, movement could be seen through the sheer curtains inside the apartment. Megan opened the door. He gave her an obsequious smile, revealing a sizeable fissure between his teeth.

"Hello, ma'am," he said in a raspy voice. "Pizza Pantry. It'll be eleven eighty-nine."

"Jeez, that was fast," Megan said, giggling in reaction to being called "ma'am" by a man so much older. "Just a minute. I have to get some money."

"Take your time," Udo said, glancing around again.

Megan disappeared through a bedroom door, leaving

the front door wide open. He peered one more time over his shoulder in both directions and then stepped into the living room. He shuffled to the kitchen door and peeked in, obviously curious to know who else was home.

"Can you make change?" Megan called from the bedroom.

Udo moved stealthily back to the front door and closed it, then started toward the bedroom door as Megan returned.

"All I have is a twent..." she continued, but stopped short and recoiled at seeing that Udo had entered and shut the front door. "All..." she stumbled on, her voice unsure and shaky, "...all I have is a twenty dollar bill."

She handed the bill to him gingerly, like a child testing the pool with her toe. Udo took the bill but made no move to retrieve the change. "I'm sure I can change it," he rasped, but still he didn't look for change. He stood frozen, holding the pizza, gaping at Megan. She took a step back.

Suddenly the front door flew open and Carrie and Beth burst into the room.

"We're home!" Carrie announced happily. She was tall and athletic-looking, with short red hair and freckles—the type of girl who probably climbed trees as a child and scared the boys at school with snakes and frogs.

"Good. Pizza. I'm famished," Beth chimed. She pulled her jacket off and tossed it onto a chair. Beth was short and subtly plump. She wore glasses and pulled her dark hair back, looking school-marmish. They had nicknamed her Marian, after the librarian in *The Music Man*. Beth was the best student of the three, and her buoyant personality turned shy and reticent when they were all around other students. But here, with her two best friends, she was confident and sociable.

Their entrance obviously unnerved Udo. Startled, he handed Megan the pizza, stepped away and dug deeply into his pocket. As he handed Megan the change, she took it carefully, as if touching him might inflict an infection. She returned a two-dollar tip in the same guarded manner.

"Thanks a lot," Udo said, now obviously in a hurry to leave. "You ladies enjoy your pizza."

Holthaus hurried to the front door, avoiding eye contact with Carrie and Beth. They had left the door open, and he rushed through it and closed it quickly behind him. Megan set the pizza down and rushed to the door, locking the dead bolt and chain. She hadn't felt this kind of fear since eighth grade when an old man in the convenience store caught her alone in back of the soft drink shelves and tried to fondle her.

"What a creepy guy." Megan gasped a sigh of relief that Udo was gone. She turned and looked at her two friends, overwhelmingly grateful that they had entered when they did. Then she stared out the window at the delivery car as it pulled rapidly out of the driveway.

"Creepy? I didn't think so," Carrie reacted matter-of-factly. "He's just shy. He's been here before."

"He has?" Megan's said with surprise. "That's the first time I've seen him. He gives me the willies."

"The whatsies?" Carrie wrinkled up her nose as she always did when she teased Megan.

"I know. I know," Megan giggled. "I get that from my mom. She says that all the time. But seriously, that guy is scare-ee."

Beth dismissed Megan's fears with a wave and a laugh. "You're being melodramatic, Megan. Come on, let's eat."

As Beth reached for the pizza box, Megan grabbed her arm in mock protest. "Not so fast," she protested. "You owe me four dollars each."

Beth and Carrie looked at each other with fake surprise. "Put it on my tab," Beth laughed, and then they all roared together as Megan opened the box.

"Shit. Hamburger," Megan exclaimed. "I ordered pepperoni. He brought us the wrong pizza. I wondered how he could possibly have gotten here so fast."

By now it was all Beth could do to resist ripping the pizza from the box and devouring it all herself. "Who cares?"

she said. "Let's eat."

Carrie bounded toward the kitchen in her long-distance runner's gait. "I'll get some plates."

Dishes rattled, cabinet doors slammed, and Carrie's voice floated from the kitchen in a sugary tone. "By the way, Megan, we saw your boyfriend on the way home."

Megan crinkled up her nose and flashed a look of mock ignorance across the room at Beth. "My boyfriend? And who might that be?"

Beth rolled her eyes. "Who do you think?"

"I don't know," Megan retorted. "Why don't you tell me who my boyfriend is?"

Beth rolled her eyes, tired of this charade. "Oh God, Megan, stop. You've had two dates with Grady Hutchinson. You drool like Pavlov's dogs every time we mention his name."

Carrie returned with a stack of plates, forks and napkins. Offering reinforcement for Beth, "See?" Carrie teased. "She's drooling right now."

Beth bristled in pretend concern. "Hey, not on the pizza. Like I said, let's eat."

"You're both too much," Megan said, laughing. "Even so, I think I lucked up when they were passing out roommates."

Finding Carrie and Beth had been a Godsend. The afternoon she agreed to attend Richardson, Megan had gone on an apartment search with her parents. By nightfall, they had signed a lease. The next morning, Megan called the university placement office and told them she needed two students to share an apartment and the rent.

After an extensive search, the office produced photos and resumes of two incoming freshmen who were looking for housing. They were Oklahoma girls, Beth from Tulsa and Carrie from Enid. They had known each other from statewide scholarship competitions and stayed in touch for several years.

When they were about to graduate from their respective high schools, the two girls encountered each other by chance at the state track meet. Carrie was running distance events for Tulsa East, and Beth was covering the Centennial Bulldogs team for her school paper.

After the meet, Beth waited for Carrie at the locker room exit.

"Hey," Carrie squealed, "I didn't know you were here."

"I write sports for the school. Great job in the fifteen hundred."

Carrie blushed, "Thanks. I should have won."

"I have to catch my bus," Beth said with urgency. "But I was wondering..." She hesitated, unsure.

"What is it?" Carrie insisted.

"I think it would be fun to go to the same college. Have you decided where you're going?"

Carrie shook her head no. "I've started looking, but that's about it. It would be awesome, though. We could room together. Let's do some research and we can text our findings."

Richardson-UT wasn't high on their list at first. As they continued to winnow down their options, Texas University in Austin became especially attractive to them. It was close to home, but not too close, and the academics appealed to their interests. Yet the main campus was larger and more intimidating than they wanted to learn to navigate, so they began to look into the suburban Dallas branch. After one visit, they learned that Richardson had much to remind them of home, and the school was first-rate. When Carrie learned she could get a partial scholarship on the track team, the deal was sealed.

Grace and Megan interviewed lots of coeds seeking housing through the placement service, but they looked no further after spending an afternoon with the two "Okies" in the school's student union, drinking cola and chatting.

As they were about to say goodbye, Megan cast a subtle glance at her mother, who nodded yes.

"Would you guys like to room with me at *University Apartments?*" Megan blurted. Carrie and Beth squealed and jumped up and down, and Megan joined in. Grace laughed harder than she had in a long time.

"There is something about Oklahoma people," Grace told Megan as they drove home, "that must be bred into them. They will give you the coat off their back in the dead of winter and then be your friend for life."

In their first weeks together, Megan had already felt camaraderie from her two new roomies in dozens of instances. Given their established friendship, it would have been easy for them to pair up and exclude her, but they don't. They included Megan in everything they did—their little jokes and their long, serious talks.

And their kidding about Grady. Megan pretended to be infuriated by their ribbing, but it was obvious from her expression of feigned exasperation that she liked it—that it made her feel included.

Udo sat in his car outside the three girls' apartment and watched them laugh through a big picture window in the living room.

CHAPTER 18: Awesome Mom

DINNER became the primary order of business. Carrie and Beth flopped down on the sofa, grabbed a slice and dug in. Megan retrieved the remote and turned on the television. She sank into a chair and started working on her piece of hamburger pizza.

Phil Sawyer, an anchorman for ten years on channel seven, was in mid-sentence as he delivered the evening news.

"Do you know him, Megan?" Carrie asked, star-struck.

"I've met him," Megan answered.

"Tell us," Beth urged.

"There's not much to tell. A couple of months ago, after my dad moved out, Mom and I were going to dinner one evening. She had to stop at the station to pick up some notes or something. When we pulled into the parking lot Mom said "Phil's car is still here. Why don't you come in with me, and you can meet him.'"

"Were you nervous?" asked Carrie, fascinated.

"Totally," Megan confessed. "But Mom said 'he's just a guy.' I had seen him a zillion times on the news—especially when my mom was covering a murder and sat next to him at the desk. But this was different—I was going to meet him in person."

"What was he like?" Carrie insisted.

"Not stuffy like he is when he's doing the news. And his voice was even more dreamy in person than it is on the air. Know what he said?"

They stared, waiting.

"'Who's this beautiful lady you're bringing in here, Grace? You're not doing an interview with Miss Texas and failed to tell me, are you?"

Carrie and Beth laughed boisterously, and Megan blushed.

"After he left, Mom said 'Careful, he's nearly thirty years older than you and married.'"

They roared hilariously again and turned back to the newscast as Phil delivered his report.

"...and the two injured in the one-car crash are reportedly in stable condition at Mercy Hospital," he said. After a brief pause, he continued with a report that captured the three girls' immediate attention.

"Earlier, our crime reporter, Grace Gleason, covered an attempted kidnapping at the Richardson Mall. Here's Grace with a recap."

Megan, Carrie and Beth grew excited, and they slid forward on the edge of their seats.

"It's your mom!" Carrie shouted as Grace's face appeared on the screen.

"Go Grace!" said Beth.

It was a ritual of their apartment each time Grace was on camera, and Megan beamed with daughterly pride. She shushed them and turned up the sound as Grace came on.

"...nineteen-year-old suspect, Johnny McPherson, is going downtown to be charged with assault and attempted kidnapping. This suspect's luck ran out thanks to the screams of his alleged victim—Maria Alvarez—and the actions of two alert young men who cell-phoned police and wrestled McPherson to the ground until the Richardson police arrived."

The video of Grace cut off and Phil returned on camera.

"McPherson is being held in county lock-up pending arraignment sometime tomorrow, according to the District Attorney's office. That's all for now from channel seven on-the-spot news. I'll see you again right here at ten o'clock. I'm Phil Sawyer."

Megan switched to MTV, but the conversation continued to focus on Grace.

"Your mom's totally awesome," Beth said.

"Yeah, I think so, too," said Megan.

"And talented," Beth chimed in.

"And beautiful," Carrie added.

Megan laughed. "And ambitious."

"But that's cool. Right?" asked Carrie.

"Sure," Megan responded.

They each grabbed another slice, emptying the box. Beth took a gigantic bite and nibbled up the long string of cheese that emerged. When she had it stuffed safely into her mouth, she burbled between swallows, "So how come she and your dad split the blankets?"

It was the first time either roommate had asked Megan about her parents' separation. She hesitated—an old wound was stinging a bit. Despite their talks during the breakup and her parents' expressed concerns that she emerge unscathed, neither Grace nor Jeff had confided in her about what had transpired behind closed doors.

"They didn't tell me. I don't really know the whole story. But I'm not stupid—there were enough innuendoes—bits and pieces from comments they'd make and some of the arguments I heard," Megan explained, squirming uncomfortably.

"Was he, you know, cheating on her or something?" Carrie continued the questioning.

"Nothing like that," Megan said, finishing the last bite of her pizza. She paused in the awkward moment, appearing to struggle for an explanation. "It's something I've never had to put into words before. I think they both felt the other one was too wrapped up in their career."

Both girls hesitated, letting Megan's thoughts settle.

"Overly ambitious or not, your mom's great," Beth said brightly. "You're lucky to have her so close."

"I know. Except when grades come out I'll probably wish she lived on Mars," Megan dismissed the subject and they all laughed uproariously.

An ancient, dented pickup zoomed down the street in

Brookwood Acres, passing the upscale homes with carefully manicured lawns and maturing trees that were beginning to provide the deep shade the subdivision developers had promised twenty years earlier. As the vehicle approached each house it slowed a bit, then sped to the next.

As it paused in front of Grace's house, a copy of the *Dallas Morning Sentinel* was flung onto her driveway with a plop. Anna Heilbronner was working in her yard next door. She had watched suspiciously as the car had approached, then relaxed when she saw it was the paper delivery. But she still frowned at the driver, as if it was her duty. She walked across Grace's driveway and picked up the newspaper.

Although she had been weeding her flowers, Anna had already brushed her hair and put on her makeup.

Grace told Jeff the first day she had met Anna—a week after they had moved in—that their neighbor didn't like the frumpy way many older women chose to look in public.

"She said it was as if society was handing them a pass because they were on the downhill side of sixty," Grace said, stirring a sauce in the kitchen before dinner. "She takes pride in appearing classy, whether she's going out for dinner in a nice dress or in the garden in a blouse and shorts. I admire that. When I complimented her, she said she would hate for someone from the church or an eligible man passing by to see her looking shabby and rundown like some of those cows you see at the malls."

"She said that?" Jeff had guffawed, repeating, "'Like some of those cows at the mall'?"

"Her words."

Inside, Grace's spacious kitchen lacked the sort of decorating attention many women give their homes. The furniture was basic, and although the windows had curtains, they were commonplace. Grace knew the place looked bland, but she had no time for interior design.

I'll get to that, she promised herself, *when life slows down.*

A TV on the counter was blaring a newscast in progress as Grace walked in pulling her jacket on. She popped a bagel into the toaster and poured a cup of coffee into a Styrofoam cup as the news continued.

"And finally," the reporter was saying, *"Nineteen-year-old Johnny McPherson continues to be held in the Dallas County jail pending his arraignment today for assault and attempted kidnapping..."*

Grace turned it off as the bagel popped out of the toaster. She spread some margarine on it and took it and the coffee cup to the door. She pressed the garage door opener and picked up a laptop computer, then entered the garage juggling the coffee, bagel and laptop. It was a routine she had perfected, with only a rare mishap from the multi-tasking. She opened the car door and put her things in, then spotted Mrs. Heilbronner making her way up the driveway toward her. She always kept an eye on the neighborhood's comings and goings.

"Morning, Mrs. Heilbronner," Grace said.

"Good morning, Grace. My, you're running late today," Anna said, handing Grace her newspaper.

"Thanks. I know. I don't have to be anywhere until they arraign that kidnapper they caught at the Richardson Mall yesterday. Did you hear about it?"

"I saw you on channel seven last night, talking about it."

"Did I look all right?" Grace asked, jokingly striking a model's pose.

"Oh, you looked marvelous. But you know, you need to be more careful."

"Do I?"

"You're always reporting those awful crime stories. I worry about you, darlin'."

"That's sweet, Mrs. Heilbronner, but really, you don't need to worry."

"There are so many dangerous people running around these days. And you talk about them on the air. They could come right up here when you're leaving for work—just like today—and do you in and not even think twice about it."

"You watch too many Agatha Christie re-runs, Mrs. Heilbronner," Grace made a gruesome face. "Don't worry. I'll be fine."

"Maybe so. But you be careful, anyway. I'll help you keep an eye out."

Mrs. Heilbronner nodded and returned to her yard work.

Grace laughed as Anna spoke, but she looked warily up and down the street before getting into her car. "I'll be careful."

CHAPTER 19: Reunion

THE DALLAS COUNTY courthouse was built in 1966, but it appeared more modern juxtaposed to the nearby former home of county justice, Old Red, a Romanesque revival style old castle that was built in 1890. Adding modernity to the surrounding courthouse plaza was an open-roofed, stark, limestone John F. Kennedy memorial constructed in the early seventies.

This complex was sitting blocks from where President Kennedy's motorcade rolled by the Texas schoolbook depository. Multitudes of visitors added to the clamor of locals who flooded in and out of the area to conduct business.

Inside the courthouse, as Grace and other members of the press looked on along with a scattering of other interested parties, Johnny McPherson stood in orange jailhouse coveralls, cuffed, facing a judge. His youthful face and timid, slumped posture belied the tough guy role he had tried to assume when he bullied Maria Alvarez in the parking lot.

Johnny's lawyer, a young public defender with rimless glasses and a stiff, upright stature, stood beside him. The lawyer seemed edgy—this could be his first assignment since passing the bar.

"My client pleads not guilty, your Honor," the lawyer said, his high-pitched voice a telling contrast to the weighty attitude he tried to exude.

The female judge looked for a brief moment over reading glasses, then turned to her docket and made a note. "All right," she said, sounding robotic and uninterested. "Trial is set for nine a.m., three weeks from this morning. Next." The judge banged her gavel and completed the entry in her book.

A deputy stepped forward, motioned to McPherson and his lawyer to follow him, and escorted them out.

Grace typed a few notes on her laptop, closed it and turned to leave. She was outside the door when she felt the presence of a man following her. She wouldn't normally think twice about it, given that the doorway was already crowded with case after case being called and dispatched quickly. But she had never quite gotten over the habit of checking her back, even in crowds, after Udo Holthaus disappeared.

As she turned to glance back, she realized the figure had come very close.

"Hello, Grace," said the voice in a thick, familiar mixture of Midwest twang and Texas drawl. At precisely the same moment, she realized it was her friend, Detective Ned Moore. They stopped outside the courtroom and moved from the doorway as the flow continued it in and out.

"Ned, it's great to see you," Grace said, sincerely pleased. "It's been way too long. How's my favorite detective?"

It had only been five months, but she marveled at how much people can change when you're not exposed to them daily. Ned's sideburns were turning gray. His husky physique and rock-solid face were gradually giving way to a slight paunch and the beginning of jowls. She wondered if the torment over not solving the Bonnie Vincent case might have taken an inordinate toll.

"Doing okay, Grace," Ned said, somewhat sadly, she thought. But he immediately brightened. "I see you on the tube all the time, so it seems like I never lose touch."

"What are you doing here?" she inquired.

"Actually, I came to see you. I figured you'd be here since I saw your coverage last night. Do you have a minute?"

"A few." She took his arm and they walked to a quiet part of the hallway next to a bench. "I have to get my story filed on this McPherson guy," she explained. "We're going to put it on the five o'clock news."

"That bastard," Ned said sharply. "At least he didn't get away with it."

He fixed a serious look directly into her eyes that made

her catch a quick breath. "I have some information I think you'll want to hear," he continued, hesitating, reluctant. "Our mutual friend has re-surfaced."

"Mutual friend?" she asked, even though she understood. She caught another breath.

"You know who I mean."

Grace's tone registered astonishment as she stepped back, processing the information. "Udo Holthaus? Why? What's happened?"

"We recently investigated a missing person case. A stripper over at the Lucky Lounge has disappeared," Ned revealed. "Suspected foul play, 'cause she has a child and hasn't been home. I talked to her mother who baby-sits the kid, and guess who was last seen with this gal?"

Grace's mouth flew open. "You're joking!"

Ned shook his head no. "Meets our old friend's description to a tee. The mother knew his name and everything. I thought I should let you know."

"I...I don't understand," Grace stammered. "What's happened? Why would he re-surface now, after getting off the hook?"

"Who knows?" the detective shrugged. "Sometimes these psychos lay low for a while, waiting for the heat to die down. Then I guess they think the coast is clear or they miss the publicity or whatever it is that turns them on, and they come out of the woodwork. Or they get tired of running and start foraging for food, like that Olympic park bomber did. Then they learn they aren't as smart as they thought. We aren't sure what pushes Udo's buttons. We're also looking at some similar unsolved cases to see if there's a pattern."

Grace sat down on the bench, obviously shaken, feeling the full weight of the bad news. She stared at the worn granite corridor floor that seemed to be swirling in front of her.

"Hey, Grace. You okay?" Ned asked.

She tried to gather herself. "I guess so. It's...a little scary, knowing he's back in the picture."

"I know. Holthaus was a lot more than pissed off at you. You had a reason to be afraid at the time."

"At the time?" she echoed. "How about right now? I thought I was over it, but I'm discovering how afraid I still am."

Ned reached out and put one of his big, catcher's-mitt hands on her shoulder. "Come on, Gracie. The guy's crazy. But he's not stupid. He would have followed through by now if he was still smoldering."

"You're right," she half-heartedly agreed.

She took a long breath to recover her poise. She stood back up and grasped Ned's arm. "Ned, it's actually good news. Obviously not for the stripper. But for Bonnie Vincent's family? Maybe another chance to nail the guy who killed Bonnie. Ned, here's what I think you should..."

Ned interrupted and chuckled to himself, "Hold on. I already know what you're going to say. You're as predictable as Christmas. If we can pin this new case on Udo, you want me to put the arm on the District Attorney's office."

"You've got to push them to re-open Bonnie's case," she said emphatically.

"That'll be tricky. You know the D.A. got sick of this case, and frankly..."

"I know," she broke in. "Sick of me, too."

The detective emitted a sharp guffaw. "I was going to say sick of hearing us both whine about it all the time. The DA's going to run for mayor. Bonnie's in the ground and no one except you and her family and me gives a rat's ass about a cold murder case that went away because those idiots lost the evidence. Getting him to stir that pot again when the campaign's about to start won't be an easy sell."

"But you'll try, right?" she asked, her tone charged and hopeful.

Ned hesitated. "Well, those dumb-asses in the DA's office were as responsible as the yahoos in the evidence room. So yes, if it turns out Holthaus had something to do with this dancer disappearing, I will."

Grace's eyes widened hopefully at this turn of events. The alarm that had registered in the pit of her stomach was gone momentarily. The old Grace Gleason drive to expose Bonnie's killer welled inside her.

"We have to expose him as the psycho you and I know he is," she persisted.

"First we have to find him," Ned cautioned. "Last we heard he was in Kentucky some-damn-where. That's when his trail went dead. Now he might be back. I promise I'm going to do my very best."

"I know you will. You always do."

CHAPTER 20: Matt Robertson

GRACE'S STATION, TXDA-TV, was the number one station in Dallas, a GBS network affiliate owned by Newsmakers Corporation. Its ratings had followed the network's lead for several seasons as GBS outscored all of its rival for several seasons, despite the runaway numbers racked up by *American Dreamers* aired on the number two network. The TXDA news operation claimed the local lead for ratings in Dallas, a fact that Grace's bosses reminded the entire news staff of repeatedly. There could be no slippage, they were told by Lloyd Hamilton and Richard Stone, or everyone at the station would feel the wrath of corporate.

The station was headquartered in a stand-alone news operations building, its roof covered by a sea of huge broadcast dishes. At any time of day, several news vans were parked outside, and station staffers, ad agency executives, sales representatives and news personnel constantly rushed in and out as though the stock market would crash if they slowed down even for a few seconds. TXDA television was a hyperactive eddy of activity.

The station's coffee shop was on the first floor, a small, utilitarian room with a food line, cash register and about a dozen laminate-topped dining tables. A half-dozen people were eating there during the noon hour as Grace, leaving the cash register, carried a tray with a salad and drink and stopped at a small table, carefully juggling her laptop.

She cautiously set down her load and heaved a sigh of relief at dropping nothing, even though she had repeated this routine successfully dozens of times. She sat down and opened her laptop between sips of her drink, and then pulled up her e-mails and started reading as she picked absently at her salad.

Grace usually ate lunch here alone, or occasionally in a nearby park on nice days. She had never been a joiner. When many of the other news staff congregated for lunch at one of the Mexican restaurants, or at Pokey Joe's for drinks after work, she rarely went with them.

Matt Robertson had asked her about it the day after they covered the attempted rape in Richardson. "Why don't you eat with the rest of us—at least sometimes?"

"It's not that I'm antisocial," she said.

"You just don't like your co-workers, is that it?" he prompted, grinning.

"Of course I do," she reached out and slapped his chest playfully. "Time for my private thoughts appeals to me. A little solitude and some privacy to catch up with e-mail or reading is more important to me than office gossip and pointless banter."

"Some of the others call you Sally Snob," Matt teased.

"I know."

She did, and it troubled her. Sometimes their insistent nagging forced her to acquiesce and agree to go with them. But the pointless conversation always felt like lost time to her, so the next time they asked she would invent an excuse and slip away to be on her own.

Everyone who knew Grace understood that this lunchroom was where she would take her breaks. Occasionally, when another staffer wanted to discuss a news matter with her, or simply had no other lunch options, Grace would find herself with company. But the atmosphere in the place was cafeteria-depressing and the menu uninviting.

That was why she was startled to see Matt Robertson approaching with a tray loaded down with food. Matt was usually in the middle of the group, opting for *Mi Casa* or *El Acapulco* with the others, leading the chorus of jokes and conversation. He had rarely eschewed the lunch crowd unless out on a story, and not once had he sought Grace out in this bleak outpost.

As he approached, his face had eagerness written

across every line and pore. "Can you use some company?" He could barely contain his enthusiasm as he stood there, politely, waiting for permission to sit with her.

Grace was paradoxically happy to see him and unsure of what her response should be. His advances after the Richardson story had put her on her guard. She liked Matt, but she didn't want to invite more complications into her complex life. *Still, she privately reasoned, it might be good for us to get better acquainted. If nothing else, we'll be more compatible when we're working on stories.*

She motioned to the chair across from her, and he sat down eagerly and began forking in a generous helping of fries.

Grace glanced at his tray and couldn't stifle a laugh. "Looks like you're fortifying yourself for a war."

"I missed breakfast," Matt lamented. "Growing lad. I need my energy to keep up with these fast-moving, hard-working news types I have to follow around." He started buttering a roll and gave her his innocent, country-boy grin.

"It's funny," Grace commented, deciding some face time and conversation would be enjoyable. "We've worked together for a while, yet we hardly know each other."

Matt's deep green eyes lit up. "I'm an open book. What do you want to know?"

"How'd you become a cameraman?"

Matt took a big bite of his roll and sat back, chewing and remembering. "I started in college up in Kansas. I loved sports and was pretty good in high school. But I tried to play basketball at the university and learned right away I wasn't good enough. So I decided the next best thing would be to get into sports journalism. I took some communications classes and one night they needed camera help at a game."

He leaned forward, the reminiscence gaining energy. "Man, that was fun. And exciting—to be right there on the floor, capturing the action, to know that if you screwed up, everyone who had tuned in would call the station and complain. I did okay, so they kept me for the whole season.

"We ended up winning our conference and going to the NCAA tournament," he continued between bites. "The Jayhawks had a great history of basketball ever since Wilt Chamberlain lit it up there. So we went to the big tournaments a lot. Anyway, the finals that year were in Denver, and I got to go out there and help the network crews run stats, move cables, take messages, odd jobs.'

"They made you a gofer," she observed.

"But I got to learn how the big boys do it. When I graduated, I worked for a station in Topeka and kept watching for opportunities in larger markets. When Dallas popped up, I said 'you betcha.'"

He shoveled in more French fries, stuffed a bite of hamburger in on top of them and sat back, chomping aggressively and grinning at the memory. "How about you?" he asked, washing his mouthful down with a swig of cola. "Did you study journalism?"

"I knew I wanted to be a news woman since middle school," she repeated the story she had told a hundred times to anyone who would listen.

He marveled, "I didn't even know how to spell 'news woman' in junior high. That's amazing. No wonder you're so driven."

The comment caught her by surprise. She had thought of her dedication to a work ethic and to the news business as an instinctive part of who she was, but driven was a word she would never have thought of to describe her behavior. "Driven?" she asked. "You think so?"

"Oh, yeah," he responded without hesitation. "You might not feel it, since you've lived with it, but every time we go out on a story I see a determination in you that I don't see in most other field reporters."

She searched for a response to the unexpected description. "I didn't realize..." she started, but he eagerly cut her off.

"Don't get me wrong," Matt said, "I like it. It gives an

edge to your reporting that people want to see. No news junkie wants to see a reporter slack off on a story."

"Maybe you're right. But it might also have something to do with being a single mom getting a daughter through college."

"Where's her dad now?" he asked, seeming sincerely interested in this personal side of her life.

"West coast. We had our differences and couldn't compromise, so he went out there to practice law and politics. Megan will see him every summer and on alternate holidays. He's too busy lobbying for the environment or energy independence or some other cause that makes lawyers a lot of money. I know it hurts her." She faded out, realizing the conversation had gotten far too deep and personal, miles beyond her comfort zone.

They sat silently for an awkward moment.

"Think you'll ever marry again?" he asked, straining to sound casual.

She reacted, growing more comfortable with their repartee, "I'm not even divorced. Right now, my career is my husband and my daughter is my passion."

"Not a bad combination," Matt nodded understanding, "but it seems a little lonely."

"I don't miss the fights or the condescension. Or the 'my career's important, yours is a hobby' attitude," she said in a strident tone.

"Not everyone is like that," he responded convincingly.

Grace caught herself and how bitter her side of the conversation had become. She changed gears. "What about you?" she sat back and smiled, trying to lower the intensity. "You've never jumped on the marital band-wagon?"

"I started to once," he said, appearing eager to share. "There was a girl in Topeka, the daughter of a big-wig politician. I met her at a charity fund-raiser I was covering. I did some shots of her bidding at the silent auction for the story, and she sort of picked me up." He laughed in an awkward and self-conscious way. "She said she was attracted to my down-home charm," he recalled. "We dated for a while and even talked about getting engaged, but I jumped right back off that marital band-wagon, as you called it."

"What pushed you off?" she asked, interested.

"We had one too many fights."

"I know that feeling," she empathized.

He sat forward in his chair, leaning toward her, deeply engrossed in telling her his story. "She was everything a lot of guys would want, this gorgeous sorority girl whose daddy had money and connections. She ran around with the A-list crowd, and I admit I felt lucky—even grateful—to be accepted into that group. I would never have been recognized as part of them on my own. But in the end I realized she was spoiled, demanding, and brought out the worst in me. At first I thought, that'll change when we get married. Then as time went along I realized it would probably get worse, not better. I'll never know for sure, but I still think I did the right thing."

"Someday you'll find someone who's the right fit. When you least expect it," she said brightly.

Matt took his last bite of hamburger and poked at the remaining fries with his fork, pensive. "Maybe. Who knows?"

They returned to stillness for a moment. Grace felt an incomprehensible attraction to this man, a compulsion to spill her past and future and hates and hopes out to him, to let him examine her flaws and frailties. Never, even with Jeff when they were young, could she remember such a curious blend inside herself of desire for, and fear of, a special friendship.

This emotion ran through her in a fleeting moment, and without any contemplation she spoke in a manner that said she had decided something important. "Matt, a few minutes ago you said I was driven."

"I didn't mean it in a bad way," he hurried his response as if not wanting to offend. "I said I like it, right? You just seem to have a—I don't know—a cause or something."

"I do. Sort of." She paused for several moments,

considering. Then, "Remember the Bonnie Vincent murder story we worked on?"

"Sure. Last winter," he recalled.

"You don't know everything I went through," Grace related. "I was really affected by the case. I know Udo Holthaus murdered his wife and got away with it."

As she told the story of Udo Holthaus, Grace felt the old familiar chill on the back of her spine and the hardness balling up in her stomach that she had tried so hard to allay, but which always seemed to follow her. Now that Udo might be back, suspected of another possible crime, the sensations were magnified.

"How can you be so sure he did it?" Matt stopped eating and sat up alertly with his attention totally focused on Grace, as if he were straining to understand the importance of Udo Holthaus to her.

"He did it," Grace assured him, mildly annoyed by the question. "I knew them both. He was as sleazy and clever as you can imagine, and she was one of the kindest, friendliest, most generous people you'd ever want to know. You saw him stalking me that day at the courthouse, remember?"

He nodded.

"It got a lot worse. He followed me around. Made hang-up calls. That day at the courthouse, he even threatened me to my face. He threatened my daughter. I've been living in fear."

Matt's thick, neat eyebrows went up in amazement and he whistled softly. "That's unbelievably scary," he said, captivated. "What happened?"

"It's a long story," she said. She wanted to share with this new friend. But her instincts guarded against divulging too many inner thoughts before it was time—before the bitterness she still harbored for the treacherous man and the evil he committed made room for a normal and pleasant existence. Grace couldn't decide if reliving those days of conflict and fright prolonged her dread or led her toward what she knew must someday be catharsis and closure. *You're a long, long way from that welcome event,* she told herself.

Matt pressed on enthusiastically. "He wasn't convicted, right? It's a cold case?"

"He was never even indicted," she gave in to Matt's obvious need for more information—and, strangely, her unexpected desire to provide it. "Two major things happened in my life as a result of the case. My husband nagged me to get off the story, but I refused."

"That's what messed up your marriage?"

"A lot of things caused us to break up. The tension over the Holthaus story was definitely part of it," she confirmed.

Matt waited to hear more, but Grace stopped, mired in retrospect.

"What was the other thing?" he asked. She looked at him inquiringly, still lost in thought. "You said two major things?" he explained.

"Oh," she said, the question jarring her back to the conversation. "I internalized such a strong sense of injustice that I seek out crime stories. I volunteer for them, sometimes even fight to get them. I want to let people know everyone doesn't get off Scot free—that the bad guys lose sometimes. Like Johnny McPherson."

"Crimes of passion are your passion. They're shaping your career," Matt deduced.

"Something like that."

"It strikes me as useless to carry out a vendetta over an old story."

Vendetta! The word jabbed at her like a shock. Sensing his lack of empathy, she bristled. "You think this is a vendetta?" she countered reflexively, loudly. A few other diners nearby stopped their conversation and stared. "I'm a single mom. I have a daughter who lived alone with me, and now she's in an apartment on her own. And I just learned Holthaus might be back."

"I didn't know," Matt grimaced, looking around uncomfortably. "Calm down."

"Don't tell me to calm down," her decibels were climbing by the second. "You sound like Lloyd Hamilton." She gathered up her laptop and tray and rose to leave.

"Come on, Grace," Matt appealed. "I didn't know. I said I was sorry, okay? Don't go away mad."

"I'm not mad," she told him, reverting to a calmer, cooler tone. "You just don't get it. I thought you would...never mind." She wanted to say more, but the right words wouldn't come. The lump in her throat felt like a softball. "See you," is all she could manage.

"See you," Matt said in resignation, slumping in his chair. His gaze followed her intently as she strode out. He pushed his tray away. "Shit."

CHAPTER 21: Heinrich Holthaus

IT IS A MYSTERY of the human family experience, how parents and siblings can share a roof, live out the same events and yet record vastly different impressions that shape them. Udo Holthaus was ten years younger than Heinrich, his only brother, and although they witnessed the same life in Fredericksburg, they did so through separate, distinctly different prisms.

When Heinrich left, disgusted and angry, he unfurled wings he didn't know he possessed and engineered a total break from all things Hans and Nelda Holthaus. A decade later, scarred and terrified, his younger brother Udo also left. But he never escaped.

Heinrich lived a nomadic life after leaving their boyhood home, abandoning his brother to survive on his own in a highly dysfunctional household. Escaping the smothering effects of their ultra-strict father who beat his wife regularly, Heinrich sneaked away at his first opportunity after high school graduation to explore.

"I'm heading out of here," he told his best friend Reinhart Schultz as they smoked a cigarette behind the school gymnasium the day after commencement.

"Where you going?" Reinhart asked.

"A place as far away from here as I can find where they don't order you around, or beat you with a belt, or knock their wives senseless."

"Bullshit, you won't do it."

"Watch me," Heinrich said. He took a drag on the cigarette, handed it to his buddy and walked across the baseball field toward the highway.

"Hey!" Reinhart shouted. Heinrich kept walking, not

looking back.

He hitchhiked west through the Southwestern states, ignoring the amusement of the drivers when he announced his target destination of California in an odd and unfamiliar German accent. It took only five days to find himself in San Diego, tired and broke but relieved and liberated.

Heinrich had picked up one useful lesson from his mother. Being the older son and having no sisters, he learned how to cook. He readily found a job flipping burgers in a small diner in the diverse urban neighborhood called Hillcrest, immediately north of downtown.

"You gay?" was the first question that Homer McMannis, the surly ex-marine who owned the place, asked him the day Heinrich applied.

"Gay?" the surprised Heinrich repeated.

"It's illegal to ask you but I don't give a shit. I ain't got nothing against homosexuals; about half our customers, maybe more, are queer. I like to know who's working for me, that's all."

Heinrich had never been exposed to gays in Fredericksburg, but he knew about homosexuality from the high school gossip of his friends and occasional exposure to the orientation in the media. He had never had a girlfriend—his father would have made short work of that. But he had felt the stirring in his genitals when one of the girls at school brushed past him in the hall with a smile. Or when a classmate in gym class found a peephole in the locker room exposing the girls' showers, each of the boys taking an excited, giggly turn to catch a glimpse of a naked female body.

Only twice had Heinrich been kissed, both times by Maragene Soltzmeier, a big-boned, busty junior.

"I think Maragene has been eyeing me," he told Reinhart as they practiced lay-ups before basketball practice in January."

"You mean the kisser?" Reinhart snickered.

"Kisser?"

"That crazy gal can't get enough lip lock," Reinhart told him. "She's probably kissed every boy in school—present company included. Except you, of course."

Heinrich stopped shooting and stared at his friend, who merely laughed, grabbed the ball from Heinrich and dribbled it toward the other end of the court.

Twice when Heinrich found himself alone with Maragene in the hallway after band practice, before graduation, she initiated the contact. "Do you want to kiss me?" Maragene queried him brassily. "Come on. You've never kissed anyone like me before."

"All right," Heinrich said timidly, and the fleshy young blonde enveloped him in her big arms and kissed away. On both occasions, he ejaculated in his overalls so quickly that he broke Maragene's death-hold and hurried down the corridor and out of the building, simultaneously embarrassed and stimulated.

During the interview in the diner, Heinrich told McMannis about the experience as if it were his duty in answer to the owner's homosexual question. "I'll never forget those kisses," he said as the older man strained to resist guffawing aloud. "I'm not gay," Heinrich confirmed seriously. "I like girls."

McMannis couldn't restrain himself any longer. The deep folds of his fleshy forehead rose to meet his burr haircut, and he let out an explosive laugh, slapping his leg. He stuck a ham-sized paw out at Heinrich, exposing a meaty bicep covered in tattoos. "All right, Heinrich Holthaus," the big man said. "You can have the job. But don't rag on any of my gay customers. Or Latinos, either."

"I think I have a lot to learn about this world away from Texas," Heinrich admitted, and McMannis hoo-hawed and slapped his leg again.

Route one-sixty-three was visible from the little eatery situated on a block of shops, restaurants and bars. As he plied his trade every day, Heinrich would glance out occasionally at the whirlwind of traffic. During down time, he would hoist himself on a bar stool and stare at the world passing.

"What the hell you watching?" McMannis asked on Heinrich's fifth day there, as they waited for the lunch crowd to stream in.

"'All those cars," Heinrich answered. "Wondering where they're all going."

"Going nowhere fast, seems to me," the boss scoffed.

"Well, I want to go there, too," Heinrich said dreamily. "This is just my first stop. After I've saved up some money, I want to see the rest of California."

McMannis frowned. "That's crazy talk. You won't find nothing better up north than you have right here. Great weather. Nice people. And a job. You need to stay put and build yourself a nest egg. Can't do that roaming around."

Heinrich nodded agreement. But as soon as he had saved three months' pay, he was gone. For the next several years, he drifted slowly north from city-to-city and job-to-job. He would look on the map and take the bus to the next populated area, get a job, stay a few months and then move on. He had little trouble finding work in truck stops, diners and burger houses, and he was willing to put in overtime, six days a week, to build up his savings.

"I've learned a lot about this state by talking to people," he told an Asian waitress named Veronica when they were on break from their work in the Fresno TravelRite Motel coffee shop. They often shared thoughts and ideas, sitting in the little staff lounge area just off the kitchen, drinking coffee. "Other workers and customers, mainly. I've read some brochures, too, and watched that travel television station. I might know as much about California as the governor."

She giggled, displaying bright white teeth contrasted by her smooth, sun-bronzed face. "You should go up to Sacramento," she told him. "It's a real nice town—bigger and prettier than Fresno."

"Maybe I will," Heinrich answered. "I've got to quit moving around, though. I've been trying to save my money, because I want to own my own restaurant. That's why I haven't bought a car yet."

"You want your own restaurant?" she said with admiration in her shiny, dark eyes. "You are ambitious."

"I don't plan to be poor all my life," he said. "I was thinking maybe a Mexican place. You could waitress for me if you want."

"No, not Mexican," she argued. "Pizza. It's the most popular here by far. I've read the statistics. More pizzas are sold than hamburgers or tacos or anything else."

I'm impressed," he said. "You really take an interest in business."

She smiled proudly. "And guess what?" she added, "Sacramento is where pizza stores started out. You could go there and learn all about the history of the business. I'll go with you, if you want. I could drive us."

"What about your job here? Don't you have a family?"

"I came up here with a guy, an American who had been working construction in my hometown. I totally thought we loved each other. He wanted to come back to the United States, so we settled right here in Fresno—it was his hometown—and got married. He started doing roofing, and I got a job in an office."

"What happened to him?" Heinrich asked with obvious eagerness.

"He ran out on me after I got my green card. He didn't even leave a note why. I had some money saved up in our joint account, and he took it. I got laid off, so I'm waitressing. I don't care about this job. I've always wanted to see Sacramento, and I could go with you and help you start your business."

They left the next week, managed to land jobs in a Shady Joe's Pizza franchise and rented a cheap apartment together. Heinrich hadn't expressed a wish that this would be anything more than a business arrangement, but as they were getting set up at work and home, Veronica told him she thought they should be a couple.

On their first night in the apartment, Heinrich was spreading a blanket on the couch, leaving the only bedroom for her to use. "I thought we would share the bed," she told him, pouting.

"Actually, I like the idea," he told her after overcoming his shock. "I think you're loyal and God knows you're pretty. But you're obviously more experienced than I am—you know, in bed—so you will have to be patient."

The first time they made love she watched him fight his shyness and ignorance, and she told him happily, "You are my lump of clay, and I will mold you,"

In four years, working double shifts and watching pennies, Heinrich and Veronica saved twenty-five thousand dollars, enough to put into a Shady Joe's pizza franchise. But as much as he loved California, Heinrich couldn't shake his Texas roots.

"My parents are getting old," he told Veronica. "I don't love them, and I have not had contact with them in years. But I feel that I should be closer to them in case they ever need help. There's no one else. My brother Udo won't ever be any use to them. Don't know where he is. The last I heard, he was in the service."

"But you've told me your father treated you like dirt," Veronica protested sadly.

"I know," Heinrich said, drawing her close, smelling the perfume of her thick, black hair and nibbling the lobe of her ear the way she had taught him. "I feel an obligation."

"All right," she told him. "We'll open a pizza place in Texas. Maybe in a college town. Students live on pizza."

CHAPTER 22: Re-emergence

IT WAS MID-AFTERNOON in Richardson, Texas. There was no one in the tiny Pizza Pantry, but soon it would probably get busy with students finishing class and stopping for a slice or ordering take-out. Walk-in trade was sporadic in the daytime; most of the business came from nighttime students trying to stretch the day or from call-in orders.

Udo Holthaus was hurriedly carrying empty pizza pouches from the delivery car to the front door. He looked up and down the street suspiciously, as he did every time since the incident with the stripper from the Lucky Lounge. He pushed quickly through the door.

Heinrich was behind the counter energetically rolling dough. He stopped his work for a moment and watched Udo come in, put the containers away and walk toward the back. "You're going to need those," Heinrich said. "I have three new orders."

Udo ignored him and picked up his pace toward the back room.

"By the way," Heinrich continued, "some guy from the police called looking for you. A detective."

Udo stopped abruptly and returned to the front, his shadowy eyes displaying unusual interest. "What did he want?" Udo sounded alarmed.

"Something about a missing girl from a dance club, I think," Henrich told him. "He didn't explain."

Udo didn't speak, but furrowed his ragged eyebrows and disappeared into the back room.

The telephone rang. "Pizza Pantry," Heinrich answered. "Sure. Your address? Phone number?" Heinrich wrote the order as he talked. "Anything to drink? About thirty minutes. Thanks."

As Heinrich hung up, Udo returned from the back. He had changed to his own shirt, much older and dingier than the uniform shirt Heinrich had provided.

"I've told you never to get mixed up with those dancing girls," Heinrich lectured as he prepared the orders. "They're bad news, like that bitch who testified against you at that rigged-up trial you had to go through. Now one of them must have done something illegal, and because you hang around them, you'll have to answer questions."

"You don't know anything," Udo responded with his head thrust back in arrogance like a delinquent schoolboy defying his teacher.

"I know enough not to hang around those places," Heinrich chirped. "You should, too."

Udo gave Heinrich an acidic look. "Now you want to be my big brother? Where were you when I needed you, Heinrich? When you left me in that shit-hole to fend for myself?"

Heinrich pulled two pizzas out of the oven and returned Udo's glare. "That again?" he barked. "I have to tell you, Udo, I'm growing tired of your constant accusations that my disappearance from our Texas home was the reason for your troubles."

Veronica had become weary of it, too. "Every time he comes over, he starts in on you," she complained to Heinrich after Udo had come for dinner the third time. "If he doesn't stop, he won't be welcome here any more."

Despite Udo's nagging, Heinrich told his wife he was loath to destroy their renewed relationship. "Let's go easy on him, he's been through so much," he pleaded with Veronica. "That must have been a horrible thing he experienced, his wife getting murdered. And then her vindictive family going after him the way they did. When we first moved here and he had disappeared, I thought I would never see him again. Now he's back, and I'm in a position to help him. We're brothers, after all."

"He's going to be trouble for you, I can feel it," Veronica

said, her voice laced with concern. Yet she agreed reluctantly not to ban Udo from their home, nor to criticize her husband for giving his brother a job. Even though she disliked Udo, she admired Heinrich for staying loyal.

Heinrich was once again defending the actions he had taken as a young man escaping from an impossible home. "Udo, I was eighteen. You were a kid—I couldn't take you with me. And I sure as hell couldn't stay with that crazy old man."

"You left me there to grow up alone in that loony bin," Udo scowled. "Don't lecture me about anything, Heinrich. You haven't earned the right."

Udo strode angrily to the door and opened it, tossing his brother a nasty look.

Heinrich shouted desperately, "I gave you a job when you showed up out of nowhere, didn't I? Where are you going? You have to deliver these orders."

"Piss off," Udo exploded and stormed out of the door, dashing to the delivery car. As he got in, Heinrich followed him outside, frantically wiping his powdery hands on his apron. Udo started the car and screeched out onto the street. Heinrich stood, helpless, with his mouth open, as the little car sped off.

The delivery car pulled off the road and sprayed dust from a rough gravel parking lot as it stopped in front of Big Tom's Roadside Bar in the outskirts of the city. The place had seen far better days. Its corrugated tin roof was rusting, and the flashing around the exhaust flues from the kitchen was so bent there was no way it could possibly prevent leaking during a downpour. The concrete block facade of the tiny building bore scars from bumpers and fenders steered there by drunken cowboys, and only about half of the neon letters in the window sign were still lit.

A screen door at the front entrance was hanging by one rusty hinge. The main door inside the screen was propped open to let whatever breeze existed inside. The twang of a steel guitar backing a country-western song piped through the sound system could be heard from fifty yards away.

Udo was still angry as he got out of the car and walked inside, looking around sourly but also warily as he always did these days whenever entering an unknown place. The bar was nearly empty. One customer sat at the bar—a leathery man whose craggy, toothless face made it impossible to guess his age.

A stripper who was probably on the wrong side of forty danced unenthusiastically on the bar in front of the old man as the country song wailed on. She had probably once worked at the better clubs on Northwest Highway—might even have been pretty—but age, bar smoke and this lifestyle had sapped her youth. This roadside bar was probably the best she could do, and she danced afternoons to a nearly empty establishment for a few dollars in her garter, and on weekends for precious little more when other dancers, younger and more attractive, showed up and stole the attention of the cowboys who partied there. The man at the bar gawked up at her as she danced, and he fished a wrinkled dollar from his pocket with a trembling hand and managed to slide it under her garter.

The bartender, a burly redneck with a buzz haircut and Confederate flag tattooed on his neck, nodded at Udo as he settled onto a stool. The barman didn't speak, instead rested his large hands on the counter and waited for the order, his yellowish eyes fixed dispassionately on Udo.

"Shot of whiskey and beer chaser," Udo snapped, hardly looking at him. The bartender nodded and went to get the drinks. When he returned with them, Udo tossed a credit card onto the bar.

"Run a tab?" the bartender asked in a hoarse, bass voice laced with boredom. Holthaus nodded absently. The bartender seemed annoyed at his customer's stoic demeanor, but shrugged and took the card toward the cash register as the dancer moved in Udo's direction. Udo refused to look at her. Instead, he picked up the shot and drained it, then sipped at the beer chaser, staring into the polished wooden bar and muttering to himself. The stripper danced in front of Udo for a few moments, but he didn't look up, so she glanced at the bartender and moved down the bar to the old customer, who appeared about to pass out.

"Another," Holthaus demanded.

The bartender brought the next round. "You oughtta tip the girl," he advised.

Udo glowered and muttered angrily to no one in particular. "...tip whoever the hell I want," Udo ranted, "...fucking hookers take your money...TV station trying to frame my ass...shoulda handled that reporter when I had the chance..."

The bartender listened for a moment, then moved away with a puzzled frown.

Udo downed the second shot and chug-a-lugged half the beer. He motioned for another, and the bartender brought them. Udo rambled louder, rapidly getting drunk and agitated. "...wouldn't give you a stinking nickel for the whole bunch of them," he raved more stridently. "Strippers, TV whores...all the same..."

"Hey, dick-for-brains. Settle down a little, huh?" the bartender tried to out-shout Udo and the music at the same time.

Holthaus looked up at the barkeep as though seeing him for the first time. He didn't respond, but quickly slung back the third shot and more of the beer. Suddenly, he yelled, "Screw you." Without warning, Udo flung his half-full glass of beer violently down the bar. It sailed in the direction of the dancer and barely missed the other customer who jumped wide-eyed off his stool and crouched behind it, shaking, confused. The stripper stopped dancing and stared at Holthaus, then opened her palms to the bartender as if seeking help.

The barman reached under the bar, and without a word of warning pulled out a baseball bat and started to climb over the bar. Udo jumped from his stool, almost falling, and speed-walked unsteadily to the door, drunk, angry and frightened.

The Pizza Pantry delivery car shot down Interstate seventy-five toward Richardson with the radio turned up high. The Eagles' Hotel California was playing, and the drunken Udo Holthaus was singing loudly, almost incoherently, with the music. "...We haven't had that spirit here since nineteen sixty-nine."

The car exited the highway and turned a corner onto University Avenue, slowing to a stop a half-block away from Megan Gleason's apartment building. As the music continued to blast away on the radio, Udo sat and stared hazily at Megan's doorway.

He looked up at the ceiling of the car, his head weaving back and forth and his eyes darting around like sparks in a fire, as if trying to track some sort of wild and psychedelic images circling above him. He strained to sing the lyrics of the song blasting out, but in a rush of confusion and drunkenness they became randomly interspersed the words with his own wild mutterings.

"...God damned naked women...but I still can't kill the beast...screaming and choking...you can check out anytime you want...miserable...despicable...trapped...can check out anytime you...but you can never leave..." he sputtered as perspiration poured freely from his sallow forehead.

He returned his gaze to the familiar apartment building, his hopeless jaw hanging half open as he tried vainly to mouth the words of the song.

CHAPTER 23: Run, Grace, Run

GRACE HAD PUSHED ASIDE her tiff with Matt in the lunchroom, but her foul mood persisted into mid-afternoon. Still, she knew she had to focus. This was the most frenetic part of the day's news-gathering operation. The newsroom was a factory-loud, inharmonious clatter of reporters, photographers, producers, managers and technicians hurrying in and out, shouting questions or answers across the low-slung cubicle dividers, working on stories, making plans. News feeds on flat-screens droned overhead.

Grace wasn't sure how, but at some point over the years she had mastered the ability to shut it all out and concentrate on the work at hand. She had a sour taste from her conversation with Matt, but she knew she could compartmentalize that as she worked. She bore down at her computer, writing some ideas for a follow-up on Johnny McPherson, when her phone rang. She turned on her cell ear piece. "News room. Gleason," she answered and continued to write, but when she heard Ned Moore's voice, she stopped typing.

"Grace, it's Ned Moore."

She was glad he had sought her out at the courthouse. Ned was the one person who had brought security and comfort to her in that dangerous time of trying to expose a murderer. His calm demeanor that had helped get her through that trying experience came through to her as they talked. Ned's voice had a reassuring effect on her, but he also made her realize how tensely she responded whenever the name "Udo Holthaus" crossed her mind.

She tried to sound composed, but she could feel her lip quiver, "Have you found him?"

"We think so."

She felt his answer enliven her. "Has he been picked up?"

"No, our guys have a line on him," Ned answered. "We found out he's helping his brother in his pizza business up in Richardson. We..."

Richardson! Her immediate reaction was to wonder if she had heard correctly. "What?" she roared the inquiry.

"We were about to bring him in for questioning, but now we can't locate him. His brother's no damned help. We'll find him."

"Ned," Grace cried, "Megan's in school in Richardson!" She couldn't control the sudden panic in her response.

"Jesus. I didn't realize," he moaned. "Keep a close eye on her until we find the son of a bitch, Grace. Don't worry. We're going to find him."

"You've got to. And fast." Urgency emphasized every word. "I'm going up there right now."

"No, you stay put," Ned advised. "I'll check my guys to see if they've drawn a bead on the guy. If they haven't, I'll personally alert the Richardson police."

"We're talking about my baby. I'm going up there." She disconnected the call and dialed her cell phone. She felt her spirits droop when she heard Megan's answering machine.

"You've reached Megan, Carrie and Beth. Leave a message."

"Megan, it's your mom," she screeched wildly. "Call me on my cell the minute you get this. It's an emergency." She slammed the phone down and stared into space.

She remembered those horrifying words from Udo that day in the courthouse, *"...I'd do everything I could to make sure little Megan stays nice and safe."* Ned's words after Holthaus disappeared careened through her mind, *"Udo Holthaus won't bother you anymore."*

Grace jumped up out of her chair, grabbed her purse and rushed to the door. She nearly plowed into Matt Robertson, who was coming in. Their earlier argument was inconsequential to her now; only one thing mattered. Without a word, she pushed past her startled cameraman and rocketed outside into the parking lot.

"Where you going in such a hurry?" the astonished photographer asked.

She shouted over her shoulder, her screeching voice the classic definition of alarm, "Richardson. Holthaus is up there. I've got to find Megan."

Grace tore across the station parking lot to her car, trying desperately to dial her cell phone and push the unlock button on her key at the same time. As she jumped into the car with her phone pressed to her ear, she heard ringing, then a switch over to Megan's voicemail response. For the second agonizing time, she heard, *You've reached Megan, Carrie and Beth. Leave a message.*

There was a beep. "Damn it, Megan," the frustrated Grace screamed. Call me back." An idea lit up her eyes. "Or look at your text messages," she blurted. Grace rapidly typed in a text message with nervous fingers and threw the phone down on the passenger seat.

As she turned the ignition key, a loud thump startled her.

Matt had arrived on the passenger side and grabbed the door. Jumping in, he shouted, "I'll navigate," to Grace's enormous relief.

Having her friend with her gave her incredible confidence.

Matt retrieved the cell phone he had nearly sat on and quickly snapped his seat belt into place as Grace's car raced out of the lot.

Megan had met Grady, a sophomore, at an orientation dance shortly after classes had begun. She was still weak and in some pain from her surgery, but she was determined not to miss this party.

Some of the upperclassmen who were in leadership positions at the school—student government officers, sports captains, newspaper editors, cheerleaders—had been tapped to attend the freshman event and greet the newcomers. They had been through the process before and could provide insights to the neophytes that even faculty members couldn't offer.

"Where you from?" Grady asked her as she and her roommates arrived at the punch bowl. He ignored Beth and Carrie who gave him exasperated looks. He was tall and slender, his light brown hair grown long enough to cover his collar. He had laughing eyes, punctuated by a deep dimple in one check when he activated them.

Grady was dressed in khakis and a pinpoint cotton shirt. He would have qualified for a "preppy" tag in the eighties. In today's collegiate world when students wore jeans and shorts and flip-flops to class, he would be described as neat and scrubbed.

Megan looked slightly embarrassed as she answered, "Dallas," to his query.

"Dallas!' Grady's eyes danced and the dimple deepened. "You're going to school in your own back yard."

"What are we, chopped bologna?" Carrie chimed in frostily.

"Sorry," laughed Grady, turning his attention to Megan's roommates. "I already knew you two were from Oklahoma. I was helping at the table when you picked up your class cards, remember?"

"Oh, yeah," Carrie responded, shrugging her shoulders and smiling guiltily. "Sorry."

"No harm, no foul," Grady made those eyes laugh again in such an easy, nonchalant manner that Megan flashed a quick, positive look in the direction of her two roommates. Beth and Carrie nodded their own approvals in return.

"I see a teacher I want to speak to," Beth said, grabbing Carrie's arm and steering her along with her across the room. Megan and Grady were alone, and they spent twenty minutes chatting, getting acquainted.

Weeks later, on the day when her mother was frantically trying to reach her, Megan was slouched on the sofa, talking to Grady on the phone. They were still "officially getting acquainted," as she had termed it to Carrie and Beth, even though she had gone on two casual dates with Grady after study hall. Grady was increasingly expressing interest in a steady relationship, but Megan protested that she couldn't let their friendship have a negative effect on her grades. They should take it slowly, she insisted.

On this call, as her mother tried frantically to reach her, Megan was emphatically reinforcing that point with the only young man she had shown interest in since the school year began.

"Grady, be reasonable," she said. "I had to study. I can't drop everything whenever you and your dorky friends want to go to Haley's Bar and party. What? Okay, maybe they're not dorky...at least not the girls. A couple of those guys you hang with definitely qualify. No, I did not have a date. I told you, I had to study. You've heard of that, haven't you? Study? I know, you can make good grades without cracking a book. But I can't. I have to work at it." She paused, sighing. "I'll make it up to you, I promise, after the mid-terms. We'll get together after that. Okay?"

Megan was startled from the conversation by a loud rapping at the front door.

"Yes, I promise," she continued, adding, "I gotta go. There's someone knocking at the door. Beth probably forgot her key again. That's about the fourth time this month. Yes, I said I promise. Okay. Bye."

Megan hung up, jumped up from the sofa and went to the door, peeking out through the peep-hole that Grace had insisted on having installed. Megan looked quizzically at what she saw—a Pizza Pantry car parked in the driveway.

"What...?" she puzzled out loud. "I didn't order pizza."

She opened the door, curious. The delivery man looked

familiar. He was the scary guy who Carrie insisted was simply shy.

"Hi," Megan said, trying her best to sound cheerful and casual. "There must have been a mistake. We didn't order anything."

Udo Holthaus stood on the apartment stoop, wobbling, his body sagging like a reed. He was gaping at Megan with a crazed and painful expression on his ashen face. He swayed, then stumbled clumsily into the room without saying a word, and Megan lurched backwards, panicky. Udo slammed the door hard behind him, took several steps forward and suddenly reeled directly at Megan. She ducked and screamed louder than she ever had in her life.

Grace's car sped crazily through the Dallas city streets, swerving around corners and dodging past slower cars as she kept the horn blaring a constant, noisy warning.

Matt's eyes were wide with apprehension as he kept watch through the windshield, pressing forward against the resistance of his seat belt. "Yellow light!" he warned.

Grace stomped the accelerator and the car shot forward, running the light as it turned red. A driver starting into the intersection from the other direction, observing her light turning green, laid on her horn. Matt swiveled his head back toward the light as they ran it and then at the driver who was mouthing angry epithets. Matt quickly turned his attention back to the windshield with even greater intensity.

"South Central looks stacked up," he shouted. "Go over to Thornton Freeway."

Grace had started to turn onto the crowded expressway, but she veered back onto the street, barely missing several cars. One of them squealed its brakes and skidded sideways into a curb. Grace's car tilted as it sped into a turn onto the Good Thornton Freeway. It gained momentum down the freeway and then ramped onto Interstate seventy-five, hurtling its way toward Richardson.

Grace's cell phone was still in Matt's hand, and it rang

the marimba tune she had programmed into it, creating a comical contrast to the hysterical nature of the moment.

"Answer it," Grace shouted.

"Yeah?" Matt answered the call, half-shouting with excitement. "Matt Robertson. I'm Grace's cameraman. Yeah, we're headed there right now. No, she can't. She's kind of busy. Yeah...yeah...yeah... yeah. Okay. I'll tell her."

"Who was it?" the urgency of the moment filled Grace's question as Matt turned off the phone.

"Detective Moore," he told her. "They found the stripper's body. She was strangled. Had a bite mark on her neck."

"Udo Holthaus," Grace cried out in terror.

"Moore said they called Holthaus's brother and told him they're on their way to pick him up," Matt related.

Grace leaned forward against her seat belt and bellowed, "Come on, car. Go faster."

They ramped off the highway and Grace maneuvered through the streets of Richardson, pushing the car well above the speed limit. She did so fearlessly; she was well known by most of Richardson's police, and being pulled over for speeding through their neighborhoods would be a plus. She could enlist their help *Besides*, her mind bent around the subject as she drove, *Ned told me he would call them. Maybe they're on their way over there, too.*

Within a few minutes, her car was streaking down University Avenue, the same route Udo Holthaus had taken in his drunken rage. Two students started across the street but jumped back to the curb as Grace's horn blasted at them and the car raced past. They stared in shock and amazement, and then in unison gave Grace and Matt the finger.

The University Apartments came into view.

"Oh, God," lamented Grace, her voice frenzied. "He's here. That's Megan's apartment!" There were no other people in sight and no other cars except a lone Pizza Pantry delivery car parked in the driveway next to Megan's building.

Matt unlatched his seat belt and pushed the passenger door open the second Grace stomped on the brake pedal. As the car screeched to a sudden stop, he was already out of the door and sprinting toward the apartment building. Grace slammed the car into park and jumped out, running as hard as she could after him. As she followed, she saw Matt barge recklessly through the front door of Megan's apartment.

Grace jumped onto the stoop and sprinted into the living room, heaving. Megan was on the floor with her eyes closed, a huge gash on her forehead bleeding bright red. Matt and Udo were in a vicious bear hug, thrashing wildly around the room, thumping against walls and furniture, overturning tables and chairs. Lamps, books and knick-knacks crashed noisily to the floor. They plunged into the sofa, and their combined four hundred pounds of weight crashing against it knocked it over backwards. Still grappling, Udo landed on top of Matt. Matt pushed him off with a grunt and lunged at Udo.

Grace ran to Megan and dropped to her knees, cradling her daughter's head and grimacing as she looked up and saw Udo lock his arms around Matt's head. In a frenzy, the two men careened through a doorway into the adjoining kitchen. Still clinging to her unconscious daughter, Grace could hear the smashing of wood and glass and metal. The grunts of the two men were almost inhuman. As her brain spun around her options, Grace felt a compelling urge to leave Megan and go to Matt's aid.

But at that moment, Megan fluttered her eyes. "Mom," she groaned.

A wave of hope and thanks swept over Grace. "Come on, honey. Don't you dare die on me," she sobbed. "Megan, wake up."

The cacophony in the next room ended with a crash, then silence. Matt reappeared through the doorway with blood oozing from his nose, and Grace's spirit soared. He was panting desperately but still standing.

"Matt," she blurted out, "Is he...?" Grace was never able

to complete the question. The despicable sight of Udo Holthaus reappearing in the doorway behind Matt gripped her with dread. She screamed as the evil man grabbed the astounded Matt from behind, pulling him around and smashing the cameraman's face with a vicious blow. The punch staggered Matt, and shaking his head in pain, he spun and staggered and then lunged back at Udo with the scream of a wounded warlord. They sparred again in a violent clinch.

Grace had never been athletic. But adrenalin was pumping through her body like a river in a downpour. *I'm not through with you, you menace!* Grace thought as she struggled to her feet and, without hesitating, dived onto Holthaus' back, flailing away at him with her fists. Matt continued to wrestle with their adversary, who was now sandwiched between them. Udo grunted loudly as he broke from Matt's grasp, grabbed the enraged Grace and flung her off of his back. She hurtled with a force she had never felt before, and she crashed into the wall and sank to the floor, breathless, a sharp pain stabbing through her entire body.

Udo returned his attention to Matt, and they continued to wrestle, once again spinning through the doorway and into the kitchen like the replay of a movie scene. Grace heard more crashing and thumping. Megan groaned again, louder.

Struggling to regain her breath and moving against the pain, Grace crawled to her daughter and gently kissed Megan's forehead. Tears ran freely down Grace's face, her body convulsing.

"Baby, come on. Wake up." Even as the jarring racket of the fight in the kitchen continued, Grace kissed Megan's cheek and lightly slapped it. Conquering the evil that had invaded this apartment was an urgent priority, but trying to revive her daughter was paramount.

"Wake up, Megan!" Grace screamed more forcefully, point blank into Megan's face. Megan's eyes opened. She moaned more loudly, and Grace cradled her daughter's head in her arms.

Suddenly, Grace stopped stone cold. Her eyes froze on the kitchen doorway as she saw Udo stagger back into the room, gasping hoarsely. Grace had been so engrossed in helping Megan that the cessation of clamor from the next room had not fazed her. Yet now she was face-to-face with the man she had grown to despise—the contemptible villain she knew had killed Bonnie Vincent. And now her heart sank at the thought that Matt Robertson may have been Udo's latest victim.

Udo slumped against the doorjamb, eyeing Grace and Megan with inhuman vitriol. A wide stream of deep crimson blood was flowing down his cheek from the corner of his eye, which was purple and nearly swollen shut. Grace stared at him, suspended in that frightening moment, scarily aware that there was no sign of Matt.

Holthaus sagged against the doorway for long seconds, a madman glaring at the woman who had dogged him, challenged him, threatened his escape from his brutal actions.

"No! No, you son of a bitch!" Grace screamed and sprang to her feet as Udo lunged headlong toward her, balling his fist and throwing a right cross at her face. She had never experienced such a violent sensation. The explosion in her head was a horrendous mixture of sound, shock and incredible pain. The blow sent her sprawling backward, and Grace slumped to the floor near Megan. Somehow she grunted in desperation and miraculously summoned the will to stagger back onto her feet.

Udo lurched toward her again, growling fiercely, an injured animal. As he stumbled closer, she rushed wildly into him and pounded violently away at the brute with her fists.

"I...hope...you...die!" Grace yelled, feeling a hatred she didn't know she was capable of. Udo reacted to each blow but stood his ground. A fury appeared to be building inside him until he emitted a loud, ruthless bellow directly into her face and pushed her back with merciless force. His gray eyes were opened wide, his teeth clenched, and as Grace tried to fight him off, screaming, Udo gripped his fingers around her neck and choked her.

His hands were strong and rough. Images of the ordeal Bonnie must have experienced ran fleetingly through Grace's mind as she tried to pry Udo's hands off, kicking and kneeing at him. But he was too strong. He kept pressing forward until Grace was backed against the wall, coughing, sputtering, fighting for breath, for life.

Grace's eyes rolled upward in her head, and as they did she caught a brief image of Udo trembling, his eyes half-closed as he strangled her. She could feel the life seeping out of her as she sputtered and wheezed. She could no longer keep her eyes open as she tried with the last of her strength to hang on.

This is how it feels for it to end, was all she could think.

Without warning, she heard the dull thud and simultaneously felt the brawny hands of her nemesis tighten for a flicker of a moment and then just as quickly, slacken. She forced her eyes open and could see Udo's pupils rolling back in his head until only the whites were visible. His death-grip slipped from Grace's neck. Instinctively she tried to scream again, but only a weak screech would come out.

Udo's hands and arms went completely limp. He sank slowly, heavily to the floor.

As he fell, Grace was looking at the most welcome sight of her life, a miracle, a happy burst of brilliant light. Ned Moore stood perfectly still, dead-serious, watching, with his Glock 17 9mm pistol held high. She knew instantly the thump she had heard was the sound of Ned's pistol cracking Udo Holthaus' skull from behind. The blow had wrested the madman's hideous hold from her throat and sent him crumpling to the floor, out cold.

Grace slumped for a moment, laboring to suck in air. Then she leaped into Ned's arms and hugged him with all of her remaining strength, quaking furiously with relief.

"Ned, Ned!" was all she could squeeze out of her aching throat.

"Thank God you're okay," Ned said, trying to catch his breath.

The detective's strong biceps wrapped around Grace.

Two Richardson police officers flew into the room, looking confused by the chaotic scene. Ned flashed his badge toward them, and Grace frantically motioned them over to Megan. As they kneeled beside Megan's stirring body, Grace gently pushed from Ned's grasp and followed the officers to her daughter as they hovered over her. One of the officers cradled Megan's head, and as her eyes continued to flutter open and she whimpered in pain and fought for consciousness, the other officer retrieved a handkerchief from his pocket and applied pressure to the gash on Megan's brow.

Ned grabbed the still-stunned and writhing Udo Holthaus and rolled him over face down on the floor, pulled the evil man's arms back and clamped handcuffs on him. As he came to, Holthaus winced from pain but said nothing.

Megan's eyes were fully open, and her moaning was sounding less like a dying dirge and more like authentic human pain. She reached up and grasped her head, trying to stand, but Grace wrapped her in a tight hug and held her still while the police officer continued to hold the makeshift compress on Megan's wound.

All of these events spanned only seconds, but the confusion of her struggle with Udo, Ned's surprising rescue and the moment of realization that Megan was alive had clouded Grace's ability to think rationally. Then, in a cogent instant, she realized what was missing. Her terrified eyes turned toward the empty doorway and searched.

"Matt? Matt?" she called frantically, fearful of hearing no response.

She felt her senses soar as Matt stumbled back into the room. His shirt was ripped to shreds, and his face was scuffed and bloody. He staggered toward Grace and Megan and kneeled beside them, sweating, groggy, spent.

Grace held Megan with one arm and wrapped the other around Matt, burying her face in his shoulder as the officers who had assisted backed away.

Adding to the chaos of the scene and the moment,

Carrie and Beth came running toward the apartment with apprehension, confused. They stopped inside the door, surveyed the tumultuous scene for an instant, then at each other and began screaming shrilly.

Detective Moore nodded toward Grace and she smiled back. Ned yanked the still-dazed Udo Holthaus to his feet and walked him past Carrie and Beth and out the front door. As Ned pulled Holthaus through the door, he read him his rights, "You have the right to remain silent. Anything you say can be used against you in a court of law. You have a right to an attorney..." His voice faded away.

The two girls watched them go, still panic-stricken, and resumed screaming.

The Richardson policemen followed Ned and Udo outside, nodding to two paramedics who were rushing in and pushing past Carrie and Beth, lugging oxygen tanks and a gurney. Grace continued to hold onto Megan and Matt, all three still panting heavily from the ordeal. Carrie and Beth hurried toward them, nearly crashing into the annoyed paramedics who motioned them out of the way and lifted Megan up, placing her on the stretcher. The paramedics applied a bandage to Megan's head wound and secured her with straps.

Matt helped Grace up and hugged her. He continued to hold her by the shoulders as they labored for breath from the struggle and chaos. "Grace, I've been wanting to apologize," he managed. "For the lunch room. I was really stupid."

She thought it was an incredibly strange subject to broach in the wake of such mayhem. *Still,* she thought, *it's sweet at the same time.*

"Are you kidding?" she tried to laugh. "You just apologized a zillion times over. You're our hero."

Megan looked curiously at Grace and Matt as the paramedics put an oxygen mask on her.

Grace realized that her daughter couldn't possibly understand any of this. "Megan, sweetie, meet Matt," she said. "He's our superman. Matt, this is my precious, very much alive, daughter Megan."

Grace and Matt could manage no more than a chuckle in relief. Megan held her face and tried to laugh, too, but flinched from the effort. The paramedics rolled her toward the door, as Carrie and Beth followed with concern.

"Mom?" Megan called out as she pulled the mask away. The EMT team, and Carrie and Beth, stopped.

"Yes, baby?" Grace answered, overwhelmingly ecstatic that her daughter's speech was coherent. She and Matt caught up, and Grace hovered over her daughter.

Megan looked up weakly at her mother. "Do you know that crazy man?"

CHAPTER 24: My Hero

NED MOORE had driven the same car for nearly seven years. It was a sedan the Dallas Police Department had souped up to help him get through tight spots. His superiors had told him recently he could get a new one, but he declined. He told his partner, Jerry Philmore, over a beer after work that he liked the comfort of familiar things that had been around for a while—his wife, his church, the law—all the natural extensions of his own life that told him who he was. And that included the sedan.

"One of the things I like most about this job," he told Jerry, "is driving that old car on pleasant errands—telling someone we've found their missing kid, or returning some loot that someone got mugged for. It's like going out there with a trusted friend."

"You've probably had enough errands of the other kind," Jerry said.

Ned glanced over at his young partner. "You're damned straight I have. Too many is right—knocking on a door to give a family some gruesome news. I hate that. I do it willingly, 'cause I'm simply offering a hand I'd want to have offered to me if the situation was reversed. But every time you have to perform that sad duty, it seems like you leave something of yourself behind."

Jerry had listened quietly and intently. He had worked with Ned for barely more than a month, and they had been assigned the horrible and vexing murder of a business woman, found nude and mutilated in the trunk of her car. Ned had told Jerry they were about to make a call on the members of Bonnie Vincent's relatives, and Jerry had expressed massive doubts.

"Shit, man, I don't ever want to have to do that," Jerry protested. "I had enough sad calls to make when I was on patrol. But this is way too much. Going to see the parents of a daughter who was killed in a car wreck was bad enough. But raped and murdered? Jesus Christ, Ned, how can you manage to do that?"

"You just gotta do it," Ned instructed. "It goes with the job. Jerry, these people don't want to hear what we have to say. But we don't want them to get it from anyone else. It's the right thing to do."

That miserable chore had taken place months ago.

Today, he was on one of the other, more positive duties, pulling into the driveway of a friend who had managed to stay alive with his help.

He stopped his trusty old sedan in Grace Gleason's driveway and breathed in the invigorating late-autumn air as he walked to the front door and rang the bell. The door opened slowly, and Anna Heilbronner looked out at him cautiously.

"Yes?" Anna summoned up her best sentinel posture.

"Detective Moore, ma'am, Dallas Police Department," Ned said. "Is Grace here?"

Anna didn't move or speak. Ned laughed and produced his badge. She surveyed it carefully and then shook her head stubbornly. "She's resting, officer. I'm her next door..."

Grace appeared behind Mrs. Heilbronner and put a hand on her shoulder. She was in a robe and slippers, and her face was badly bruised and swollen. "It's okay, Mrs. Heilbronner," she assured Anna. "I'll talk to him. He's one of the good guys. Why don't you check on Megan for me, would you please?"

Anna nodded respectfully and retreated inside the house, disappearing through a bedroom door. Ned stepped in with a smile of affection, and Grace motioned him inside to a sofa, sitting next to him.

"I wanted to see how you're doing," Ned said, surveying her bruises with alarm and making a "tch tch" sound. "That's a real shiner you've got there."

"The guy packs a wallop," Grace said, touching the purple abrasion around her eye and wincing slightly. "It looks worse than it feels. I'm good enough to go to work. I'll go in later this afternoon and write an update."

Ned frowned like a disapproving father and pulled her robe collar back slightly to examine the dark spots on her neck. "You oughtta rest for a few days. You've earned it." He glanced back toward the bedroom. "Megan's doing all right?"

"She's okay," Grace nodded reassuringly. "I can't believe she's been asleep for almost fourteen hours."

"Kids. It's how they cope, you know? Wish we could hang onto that ability when we grow up into paying rent and arresting killers. Instead, we just worry and pump our stomachs full of antacid."

Grace had conversed with Ned patiently, but she had something much weightier on her mind. She mustered some courage for the inevitable question, her heart boiling up with emotion. "What about Holthaus?" She felt something inside flutter at saying his name.

"Preliminary hearing tomorrow," Ned answered. "He's in there for assault and attempt right now, but we'll be heaping a lot more on the charges sometime today. He's got two murders to answer to. His lawyer will try to get him out on bail, but there's no way in hell."

"God, I hope not," Grace exclaimed. The mere idea that Holthaus might be out loose, running around Dallas again, had not occurred to her. Now the thought of it jolted her.

"Grace," Ned said, reaching out to put a reassuring hand on her arm. "No way in hell. The guy's done."

Later that afternoon, Grace was in her cubicle in the newsroom, typing on her laptop, feeling a sense of safety and gratitude for being in that familiar place. She stopped for a moment and fished a makeup mirror from her purse, examining her bruises for what must have been the fifth time. Her smallest injuries had begun to turn an ugly yellow hue, but the discoloration from Udo's right fist remained a hideous blackish purple. *Maybe tomorrow or the next day,* she thought, *they will all have transformed to that hideous shade of yellow. Won't that be lovely to look at?*

She replaced the mirror and resumed typing.

Lloyd Hamilton was somewhere on vacation in Mexico, but he had called her at home when the station got the news of the melee. She had not spoken to nor seen Richard Stone, but as she typed, the general manager came walking through the newsroom toward her desk like a man on an urgent mission.

Grace liked Richard. He didn't equivocate like Lloyd. You knew where he stood and what he wanted from you, and he seemed like a man with strong values. He wasn't big on small talk, but that suited Grace just fine, for neither was she.

As he approached, Richard beamed a huge welcoming smile she could see from halfway across the room. "Well, crime dog," he said, catching her off-guard with the playful moniker, since it seemed a bit out of character for the serious man. "You've had quite a time of it. How're you feeling?"

"Like a two-ton truck hit me," she tried to smile back, feeling the stabbing, pin-prick sensation tugging at her sore face as she did.

"It looks more to me like a five-ton truck caught you broadsides," he grinned broadly again. "You don't need to be here, Grace. Go home. Get better. Take a little time off. Take care of your daughter." He laughed loudly, startling her. "We can't use you on camera looking like that anyway."

"I will," she promised, feeling immediately grateful for his caring. "Let me finish up my notes so I won't forget anything."

He hooted again. She had never seen him so jovial. "Like you could forget," he teased. Then, turning serious for a moment, "Oh, that detective friend of yours—what's his name?"

"Ned Moore."

"He called before you came in," Richard told her. "You can be mighty proud, Grace. They've already charged Udo Holthaus with assault and attempted murder of Megan. Plus, the detective said it's a matter of time before they charge

Holthaus with killing that dancer."

"Yes!" Grace exhaled, pumping her fist in the air.

"And...are you ready for this?" Richard paused for effect and repeated the broad smile. "The DA has agreed to dig up the Bonnie Vincent case. Ned says they're going after the guy with—how did he put it? With all barrels smoking."

Grace beamed and started typing again, feeling a need to finish this work and get back home to Megan. Richard reached out, gently held her arm and gave her a stern and admonishing look.

She understood. "I'm out of here in just a minute," she assured him. "I'll get this final story to Phil and then go home."

"Take a week," he instructed her. "And when you come back, come and see me. I want to talk to you about your contract."

"My contract?" she asked, her curiosity enormously aroused.

"We are going to have an anchor spot coming open soon. Interested?"

An anchor spot. Like the woman in Chicago who came to Career Day, the one who had so inspired an eighth grade girl. She had told Grace's class she started as a reporter and worked her way up, and now Grace had the same opportunity. This would bring Grace full circle. Yet something nagged at her about it—the idea that there were so many more stories out there to report, so many more injustices, so many more Udo Holthauses drifting through society, robbing, assaulting, raping. Murdering.

"I don't know," she said as the prospects clashed in confusion. "I really like field reporting. And with all of the new Udo Holthaus material, I just don't know. But maybe..."

"Sleep on it," Richard said. His hand was still resting on her arm, and he gave it a small squeeze. "See me in a week." He turned to leave, but turned back. "Grace, you're a great reporter. Thanks."

A thrill ran through her. She couldn't seem to muster a response—only grinned and nodded gratefully. He smiled one more time, warmly, and left.

Matt came in from the parking lot and stopped, peeking over her shoulder at her note writing. She knew he was there, had seen him coming in her peripheral view, but she didn't acknowledge him, enjoying a unique inner joy but continuing to type. She finished finally, closed the laptop and stood up. For the first time since he had come in, she looked at him. Their eyes met in a brief second of warmth. She reached up and gently touched the scratches and bruises on his face. They were beginning to fade.

"You don't know when to quit, do you?" he said in his best lecturing tone.

"Not always. It's what I do, you know?"

"And as the old song goes, nobody does it better." He moved closer and examined her swollen eye. "You look like you're on the mend."

"So do you," Grace responded. "How do you feel?"

"The ringing in my ears is about gone," he told her, "but I still have some pretty sore ribs." He paused, looking hopeful. "So I finally get to take you out to dinner?"

"And Megan. Do you mind?" Her eyes searched his, seeking some level of commitment.

"Perfect," was all he needed to say.

They grinned at each other like old friends. Grace gathered her laptop and purse, and they walked slowly together toward the doorway. Without even thinking about it, she slipped an arm around his waist and he flinched.

"Ow!" he complained.

"Sorry, hero," she said, then, peeking playfully around his back, "Hey, where's your cape?"

Ω

About the Book

Two determined career women cross paths in the high stakes world of media and public relations. One, competing for success in business, is brutally murdered. The other, fighting for recognition in the good-old-boy news network, is stalked by the killer as she pursues the truth. Television reporter Grace Gleason covers the gruesome killing for her station, joining forces with the detective trying to unravel the thorny case. But shifty, bar-crawling suspect Udo Holthaus wriggles off the hook when a politically ambitious DA refuses to prosecute. Hell-bent on revenge, Holthaus turns the tables on Grace by targeting everything she holds dear. *Justice on Hold* is inspired by true events. Learn more at http://www.unlimitedpublishing.com/justice or at the authors' site below.

About the Authors

Donald Reichardt was a newspaper reporter and English teacher before launching a career as an award-winning editor of a corporate newspaper, then speechwriter for several CEOs and directors of communications for Fortune 50 companies. He has written numerous by-lined articles for a variety of magazines and newspapers.

Joyce Oscar spent nearly thirty years in the field covering news at multiple television stations. After beginning her career in radio, she was one of CNN's first video journalists, moving on to anchor and produce news for several television stations. Joyce has been a reporter for the top-rated television station in Atlanta, receiving broadcasting awards, including regional Emmy nominations.

Please visit http://www.justiceonhold.com for autographed copies, dates and locations of live events and more.